MW00561473

To my associate, :)

A young man who has a great future.

All the best

success to you

A.P.
5/20

"*Levi's Chalice*" is a story unlike any other. A story which begins with an outcast boy who finds himself trapped in an upper room in the ancient city of Jerusalem. The events which follow turn on this remarkable boy's personality—just as the massive door of a vault turns on a small jewel bearing.

An orphan left to his own devices, Levi goes on to learn a profound lesson and you are about to embark on this journey with him. A timeless fable which—despite all appearances—is not only a Christian story but a journey every reader will under-stand. A poignant insight which could have been taken from "The Greatest Story Ever Told." A not-to-be-missed look within the human condition. Share "*Levi's Chalice*" with your family, friends even strangers. For this easily read, but impossible-to-forget little novel, will change you as no other story could.

—CRAIG CLYDE
is an award-winning screenwriter and director of over two dozen family-based features for
    Hallmark, television and film.

"*Levi's Chalice* might appear to be merely a Christian-based story at first glance, but to peg it as only that would be a real shame and way too many people would probably miss out on its important message. You see, this is true because Levi's Chalice is a spiritual fable, a little story that gently works its own healing magic. This novel has something deep and profound to say to readers; it conveys a positive message and does so in a smooth-flowing, easy to read style. So read it. Enjoy it. Share it with your friends and loved ones."

—PROFESSOR RICHARD KREVOLIN
is an Artist, Screenwriter and author of *Screenwriting in the Land of Oz, The Hook*, and Director
    of the documentary, *Making Light In Terezin*.

"*Levi's Chalice* is a dramatic novel that will touch your soul and transform your heart! You will embark on a journey of discovery, growth and inner healing as you follow in the footsteps of Levi, a young orphan and beggar, whose feelings of abandonment and rejection direct his thoughts and choices, until the day he meets Jesus of Nazareth.

After this unexpected and blessed encounter, Levi discovers the true meaning of his own life, and surely you, like Levi, will never feel alone again. I congratulate the author for writing this story so touching and inspiring, that in many moments it gave me the feeling of being with Jesus, realizing his immense love and affection for humanity! That is why, dear reader, I invite you to read and share this book with the most significant people in your life, especially those who have not yet discovered the extraordinary power of generosity and faith!"

—ELIANA BARBOSA
is a Life coach, psychotherapist, motivational lecturer, TV host, author of 5 books in Brazil, and
    co-author of *Be the Hero of Your Story*.

Levi's Chalice

Levi's Chalice

Alfred S. Pirozzoli

RESOURCE *Publications* · Eugene, Oregon

LEVI'S CHALICE
An astonishing journey into the divine energy of the world

Copyright © 2019 Alfred S. Pirozzoli. All rights reserved. Except for brief quotations in critical publications or reviews, no part of this book may be reproduced in any manner without prior written permission from the publisher. Write: Permissions, Wipf and Stock Publishers, 199 W. 8th Ave., Suite 3, Eugene, OR 97401.

Resource Publications
An Imprint of Wipf and Stock Publishers
199 W. 8th Ave., Suite 3
Eugene, OR 97401

www.wipfandstock.com

PAPERBACK ISBN: 978-1-5326-9150-8
HARDCOVER ISBN: 978-1-5326-9151-5
EBOOK ISBN: 978-1-5326-9152-2

Manufactured in the U.S.A.   AUGUST 1, 2019

For Francine, Vincente, Gracie, Chase, Liam, Salvatore, Finnegan, and those grandchildren that may still come along: Always follow the dream God set in your heart and your life will be prosperous.

WITH APPRECIATION TO:
Joe Petricione, Rev. Ken Richard, Dr. John Huffman, Dr. James Sarfeh, Arthur F. Miller, Russ Madison, Richard Krevolin, Craig Clyde, Eliana Barbosa

WITH SINCERE THANKS TO:
Paul Pastore, my story consultant.

SPECIAL THANKS TO MY GREATEST ENCOURAGER:
Kathleen Pirozzoli

Contents

Section One—The Realization | 1

Section Two—The Journey | 69

Section Three—Home | 165

Section One

The Realization

1

"Thief! Come back!"

THE BOY COULD RUN, and he could run fast. A precious cargo held tightly in hand as he increased his pace. Hunger had pierced him before. Not like this. An emptiness in his stomach seared as fire. Hunger pangs created anxiety which overruled his normal clarity. As an orphan and beggar the boy had learned the art of surviving proficiently. In his desperation today he didn't even attempt to hide this action. If any proficient strategy compelled him at all it came down to nothing more than applying the element of surprise. The boy had bolted into a merchant's tent, grasped a loaf of bread, pulled it off the stall and sped off, not a single motion wasted.

As the boy ran out of the tent, bread in hand, the merchant yelled out, "Thief! Come back you little thief!" He immediately called to his son, "Ira, go after that little thief and bring him back."

Ira set out after him. He trailed behind seeing the boy swivel sharply on his feet and into another merchant's tent. When Ira entered he saw the merchant waving his arms and yelling out in great anger at the boy as he escaped under the back of the tent with his coveted bread. With feet pumping hectically to propel him out from under the tent he toppled over a stall of jars. Being too tall to follow the boy under the tent, Ira ran back out the front of the tent moving quickly around to the back. The merchant of jars stood there screaming at the boy with the bread who continued running ahead. Ira could not believe the speed at which the boy ran. Although Ira stood taller, he had to make even longer strides to pick up the pace. The beggar boy ran relentlessly, straining his legs to maintain speed, and drawing deeply on what little energy he had left. Hunger had at once propelled him and depleted him.

The boy turned into an alleyway passage where he ran right into a man carrying a box of fruits which sent melons, grapes and pomegranates rolling across the ground in no small explosion. The boy and the man fell to the ground along with the produce. The man cursed while totally focusing on retrieving his fruits, oblivious to anything else as he chased after his rolling melons and pomegranates to save what he could. Taking advantage of the moment the boy stood up and took off running again. In a moment Ira arrived at the chaotic scene then took chase again.

The bread still tightly clutched in hand as the beggar boy ran. Just as he came to a stack of barrels near the other end of the passage way, he fell forward under the weight of the merchant's son who had come close enough to clip his feet and send him flying. After a moment of catching a breath, the boy turned onto his back looking up at the merchant's son quickly placing his arm across his face expecting to be hit. The blow never came. Instead he felt the loaf of bread being pulled out of his hands. Too exhausted to resist; his priceless cargo gone.

"You look very sick," said Ira with distain. The toll of three days without food and unsuccessful begging of alms painted the boy's dire-looking portrait. The beggar boy said nothing. Strangely, Ira could not take his eyes away from the sad and helpless bundle of a boy on the ground with pain showing clearly on his face. Ira took the loaf of bread in both hands, looked down at the boy for a long moment as if debating something in his head.

Then he ripped a chunk off the loaf. Dropping it on the ground Ira said to the boy, "I will tell my father you got away with only a piece of the bread. He will have some satisfaction." Ira clearly observed the boy's perplexed disbelief as he stared up at him. "My father could have you in a work camp for this." Ira pointed an accusatory finger out, "Never come back to our tent, never even walk nearby." He straightened out his tunic and head cloth, turned and just as he started to walk away he turned back and added, "You have had good fortune today." Then he departed.

The boy watched the merchant's son walk back down the long alley. He sat there befuddled, completely stunned at what had just taken place. This simply could not be. He wanted to pretend it hadn't happened rather than admit that another person would ever show kindness for a beggar like him. And he would have believed it never happened except for the aroma of the freshly baked bread chunk that saturated his nostrils. Still, his mouth remained dry and unable to produce moisture. The beggar's old adage played in his head. *When you have nothing, anything is everything.*

As he tucked the bread in his tunic the man he had knocked over when he entered the alleyway now approached, yelling and cursing as he drew nearer and nearer to the boy. Under his arm he carried a limp and torn box which now held broken and damaged fruits. Juices dripped from the box and scraps of fruit covered the man's arms and hands, a threatening fist swinging in the air. His teeth tightly gritted. The boy quickly gathered himself, stood to his feet and started off running once again. The man knew he would be no match for the boy's speed so the best he could do was settle for his curse words to follow the boy.

Just another day in the life of a beggar boy. The same as every other day. But another day in which he remained alive in the streets of Jerusalem.

2

The Place of the Broken Arches

To assure he wouldn't lose the bread he placed his hand over his side holding it tightly. Walking briskly he occasionally looked back to be sure no one followed him. Still a sense of disbelief hovered as he found it hard to believe that the merchant's son let him go and with some bread as well. Being much older he could have easily dragged him back to the merchant for punishment. "You have had good fortune today," the merchant's son told him, expressed it as though he decided to offer some mercy or leniency. In thinking about it the boy realized the actual situation for what it was. The merchant's son didn't let him go because of good fortune at all. No act of mercy or kindness had been involved. The merchant's son simply saved himself a great deal of bothersome work. Had he brought him back, the merchant's son would first have to secure him so he didn't escape. Then he would have to notify the temple officials after which he would be called to testify as one of two witnesses to the crime. He would have to invest time in being questioned and making statements before the temple officials about what the boy did. The process would take too much of his time which would take him away from his other interests and his friends, all for one small loaf of bread. No, the merchant's son showed no act of mercy and there would be no good fortune. He simply didn't want to be inconvenienced. The boy wasn't foolish enough to even imagine that anyone, especially a stranger, would extend him true mercy. He remained alone in the world and no one cared about him or his situation. Like all beggars he remained invisible to others because they refused to see the reality of it.

Not far off were the broken arches; a place away from the town where piles and piles of old and unusable broken concrete arches and remnants of fallen structures and columns from old temples and buildings were dumped. The area had no visitors, only the beggars and runaways and destitute people came there to be out of the view of the town's people. Older beggars said that people who were sold into or born as slaves would stop here before they continued on a journey to escape from the Roman work camps although there were very few who succeeded. As noon had placed the sun at its peak, very few people if any would be there. The place of broken arches provided a somewhat safe haven only minutes from the marketplace where he had stolen the bread. As the boy entered he walked to a familiar section of broken interlocking concrete arches. One arch section lay across several others creating a tent-like structure. He hunched down to squeeze in. Under the cross sections were small pockets of shade which offered some relief. He took a moment to enjoy the feeling of cool concrete along his back as he sat against a broken column. Every time the boy came here he marveled at all the large broken structures. How much time and money had been required to make them. Now all the broken pieces tossed here held no value at all, just like him and the other beggars of Jerusalem.

He breathed deeply. With all that transpired he had forgotten his deep hunger. His stomach however, did not. Reaching into the tunic he removed the remaining section of bread. Biting into it he realized how famished he felt and chewed and swallowed so quickly it caused him to feel nauseous. Shifting himself to his opposite side he realized he wasn't alone. Just diagonally off to his side in partial shadow sat a young girl. Catering to the discomfort in his stomach he had to partially bend over in an effort to minimize the stomach pain. Turning his head he squinted at her feeling he'd seen her begging alms in the square on numerous occasions. In a moment he knew. Her face held a distinctive feature; a wide oval shape with the biggest round eyes black as olives. Yes, that was her. She didn't say a word nor did she look at him. When she noticed him glancing at her she moved farther back into a more shadowed area. She could sit there all she wanted, he felt. She could hope all she wanted. He had no intention of giving her even a crumb. He'd risked himself to get this bread; his reward.

Thinking it best to hide the bread from her view he twisted his front torso away from her view. Without a doubt he knew if the girl could figure a way, she would make off with his bread. He knew that to be so because if it were him, he would do the very same thing. Once again he gnawed at the loaf, head down over it in a protective stance. Again his stomach, having been empty for three days, churned more acutely. He fought off nausea. Not expecting it, and with adrenalin depleted, the exhaustion suddenly weighed down on him, beginning to cause his eyes to roll back. *No, I'm wide awake, I'm strong,* he told himself in the form of a command. His stomach churned and his body grew more and more limp. *My bread . . . she will take my bread.* Knowing he could no longer resist nodding off, he started to tuck the bread back into his tunic, but his eyes betrayed him before he could. Darkness.

When he finally awoke the sun rested at dusk. Immediately as he came to, his hands desperately searched around his body for the bread. His stomach churned again. This time not with nausea, but with a self directed anger. How could he have left the bread in the open making it easy for the girl to make off with it? Then his hand hit the chunk of bread now hardened. With caution and pacing himself he slowing ate the remainder of the bread. Its weight satisfied the hollow stomach. The moon's light now fractured apart into rays slicing though the many broken pieces of concrete. He made his way back out to the opening where he carefully glanced around.

Two older men were positioning themselves and sat down on a large concrete section not far off. They were partially visible in the moonlight. Sparsely dressed he guessed they were probably slaves escaping from the work camps. Both men bowed their heads over what looked like a small blackened piece of meat they laid on the concrete. The boy remembered being told about this gesture indicating they were praying a blessing over their food. He snickered to himself as he observed. He could see no value to such an action. In his life only that which proved practical made sense. As young as he was, he learned over time by begging alms that only three practical factors held value: knowing the rules of the street, the techniques to apply when begging, and to never trust anyone, especially adults; a practicality that had served him well. With darkness already veiled he thought it best to stay the night in the broken arches. He made his way back in, but crawled under a space barely high enough to allow him to force his body through. No one would have any idea of his presence there allowing him to sleep safely through the night. He laced his fingers behind his head using his hands as a pillow. Lying on the dirt he thought about the day. Rarely did he need to steal food outright as he had earlier. There always seemed to be a way, but these last few days had been unlike any other. Not a single opportunity panned out. Especially discouraging was the upper room over the inn, his most productive place for sustenance. The room had been closed as the landlord had his family in to celebrate one of the religious feasts. Except for that fact he could have surely gone up to the room unnoticed to likely find some leftover food scraps, and on occasion he had even found coins. An overarching thought continued to nag at him, *why did the oval faced girl not steal his bread?* She had to have walked right by him to leave. The bread sat right there in plain view. Totally perplexed, he couldn't seem to let the thought of it go.

3

He Carefully Figured
Every Step of an Escape Route

WHEN THE BOY AWOKE, heat stifled all around him. Most of the shadows were gone which told him noon had arrived. A haze of dust and noise carried all around. He squeezed out through the small opening and over to the place of entry. Across the way three wagons pulled up. Each wagon weighed down with more concrete fragments from old buildings and temples. Roman soldiers in chariots accompanied each wagon. The moment he saw the Romans he retreated back under the arched columns. Removing his head cloth he wrapped it around his nose and mouth to keep from breathing in the haze of dust or coughing and being heard. Slaves were off-loading the wagons using a lever and pulley to lift the fragments, letting them fall to the ground which sprayed up more veils of dust like moving clouds.

With no choice he sat back to wait it out. His throat now parched, he wanted to go into the town square and find an animal trough where he could drink. He looked back on the concrete where he'd sat with the bread and found several small groupings of bread crumbs remaining which he ate by licking his thumb, pushing it down into the small remaining treasure bits and lifting it to his mouth.

Unable to leave with the Romans there, he decided to plan out his afternoon. It would start with a walk to the inn where he expected to have an opportunity to go in. It had been three days, and he thought by now the inn would be back in use. So he hoped.

A man named Zohara owned the inn and served as the landlord. He rented out the upper room of the inn to various groups of people. One day in the past, the boy's clandestine visit to the upper room brought him a treasure, a Jewish shekel. But that particular day did not allow him to keep the coin. As he slyly made his way down the stairway of the upper room on that day, Zohara happened to be walking up the stairwell only to bump into him. He tried his best to quickly squeeze by the man, without success. Zohara questioned him about being in the upper room in the first place. He hadn't been asked to help clean on that day and had no business being up there. He pushed the boy back on the stairs. Deciding to search the boy, he found the coin, scolded him harshly and attempted to put him across his knee, calling him a dirty little thief. The boy's unexpected strength wrestled him away from the landlord's grip and he ran down the stairs without the coin. The incident however, did not deter the boy in the least. This simply taught him a new lesson after which he plotted an escape route out of the upper room that would not involve the stairway should he ever again be found there when he shouldn't be. Never again would he give up anything to Zohara. Methodically he had carefully figured every step of a new escape route out of the room. The service cabinet against the far wall would become his step ladder getting him up to the window next to it. From there it would be a simple matter of opening the window's hinged shutter and stepping through. Thick clinging vines covered the outside wall of the building sprawling down into an overgrown, unattended garden. The vines not only provided the perfect escape ladder, but the garden at its base would allow him to remain hidden once reaching the ground until the way out became clear. Today he hoped the timing worked out so he might have the chance to find food in the upper room.

He noticed that the sounds of the workers off loading the concrete pieces and the work wagons finally ceased. He moved to the open area to spy out the situation. The wagons were empty. The men were fastening harnesses back on the horses. In a moment the Roman soldiers hopped onto their chariots and led the wagons out. No sooner were they out of sight when the boy made haste to get to the town square where he satisfied his parched throat at a horse's water trough just outside the square. From there he walked just beyond the marketplace where the Orache shrubs grew lush. Although he didn't care for the taste the plant's younger leaves were tender and edible. He sat down, selected leaves and slowly ate them, making faces with every bite. To take his mind off the unpleasant taste of the leaves he focused his thoughts on the opportunities and the challenges he had faced in his experiences in the upper room.

Finding something of value there such as food scraps, a coin or other items that had been dropped on the floor held a high likelihood. The boy not only knew this, but to a lesser degree so did the landlord's two daughters.

Alaya, the older daughter believed that she and her sister Shira were far too important to make the effort to go look through the room in advance of cleaning so they proved to be little competition for the boy. The sisters' laziness opened a unique opportunity for him to get in the room in advance. Zohara would clean the upper room after guests departed with Alaya and Shira reluctantly following along.

The two story building had been in Zohara's family for who knows how long. He rented out the upper room for gatherings of all kinds as an important part of his livelihood, in addition to running his inn located on the first floor. A bitter and stern man, Zohara's wife died only a few years after their second daughter Shira's birth. He never achieved a personal peace with her death. At first it served as a strategy to protect him from ever being hurt again. But he continued to nurse his wounded heart rather than healing it until it became a festering wound causing him to live without any apparent joy. The boy easily recognized this trait in the landlord and on occasion had been a victim of the man's wounded heart.

The boy seemed oddly to understand the landlord's pain of loss from his own life experience. With some regularity Zohara would call the boy to help his daughters clean the upper room after meetings ended. Since Zohara didn't know where the boy would be at any given time, or how to locate him, in order to alert the boy that he needed help, the landlord draped a red cloth next to the entryway as a sign. That cloth indicated the only time the boy should be allowed in the upper room.

Zohara rarely ever paid the boy with money. Payments from the land-lord typically consisted of a meal, and that only after his work had been completed and intensely scrutinized. As young as he was, the boy stood wiry and strong, alert and diligent at his tasks; the main reason the landlord used him. He also knew that despite his daughters calling the boy stupid, he was actually quite intelligent, after all what child with the ability to live off the bitter streets could be stupid? The landlord held a second reason for hiring the boy: a reluctant and unspoken pity based on seeing how the loss of his wife had affected his own daughters. Moreover, being an orphan, to the landlord's way of thinking, signified a curse on the boy; one he could never escape or overcome. As with many orphans he assumed the boy would eventually die in the streets. And more than once when he became annoyed, the landlord would purposely remind the boy of that eventuality.

At times he found it an effort to be around the boy who held no qualms about broadcasting his disdain for adults in particular. From the boy's life experiences adults were the reason that he had been left alone as an orphan. Adults, he had come to believe, were selfish, uncaring, untrustworthy and only concerned for themselves.

Despite these issues the boy possessed a natural work ethic, a knack for being attentive to detail, and he worked in a determined way. Whenever he swept the floor or scrubbed it on hands and knees the result proved spotless, not a crumb or stain remaining. Out of necessity the boy consistently did more than his share of the cleaning because the sisters' sloppy work would be blamed on him by Zohara who would then cut his meal portion leaving him hungry. The daughters on the other hand delighted that they earned allowances to a great degree on the efforts of the boy's hard work. Still, the food in whatever amount helped fill his stomach.

Zohara gained much of the boy's labor for the paltry cost of a meal, so he coped with the boy's disposition while never looking inwardly to reflect on his own. The boy held a keen awareness of the situation and he went along because he had no choice. He felt it better to deal with the discomfort of the landlord's disposition than the pain of hunger. From time to time on opportune days immediately after groups departed the upper room the boy would sneak up before Zohara and his daughters arrived to conduct cleaning chores. In so doing he could quickly search the table for remaining food and the floor in hopes of finding a coin or other valuables that might have fallen from a guest's pocket or carry bag. Whenever he did find something it amazed him how adults could be so careless with their valuables or think nothing of leaving uneaten food behind.

"When you have nothing, anything is everything," he often repeated to himself.

4

This Remained One
of His Protected Secrets

O N ONE PAST OCCASION as the boy scrubbed the floor in the upper
room he spotted a Roman coin. A ray of sunlight filtered through the
window above the large service cabinet reflecting down between the bowls
stored under the cabinet touching the coin's finish with a shimmer that
caught his eye. Once the cleaning tasks were complete, and being the last
one out of the room he would quickly crawl under the cabinet and retrieve
the treasure.

Having so often scrubbed this floor he knew every inch of it, even
the deeper floor cracks that might capture something of value to him. The
boy alone observed how the floor under the table had become warped on
one end, and a slight incline drooped toward the service cabinet against the
wall. If anything round or smooth fell to the floor, or had inadvertently been
kicked by a foot, it would likely end up under the service cabinet. That very
thing often happened when the men who gathered for meetings drank too
much wine becoming oblivious to the realization that coins had fallen from
their bags or tunics. This remained one of his protected secrets.

Zohara's daughters paid no attention to details. They wanted only to
be done cleaning as quickly as they could, exerting the least effort possible.
They often lectured the boy on how they were above the lowly task of cleaning except for their father's unfair demand that they work to earn allowances. They persistently asked him personal questions. It wasn't long before
he realized he should no longer tell them anything, because of their relent-
less gossiping. They were no better than adults, and could not be trusted. He
could only trust himself.

He stood alone in the world from as far back as he could remember. Only one thing mattered, focusing on the situation of the moment, the present day. Nothing more. Nothing less. He knew from the hard lessons learned living on the streets that children and women were not held in much regard. With his own ears he once heard two men speaking of their families and one remarked that children and women only held value to do the work of the home, and he knew the result of such beliefs personally. It reinforced his self-belief that adults could not be trusted and that watching out for himself remained the only priority. As he witnessed the various unpleasant doings of adults he sometimes wondered if they had forgotten the fact that they too were once children. The thought made him shutter, knowing he would eventually become an adult. Yet he knew it to be unlikely he would ever live long enough to become one. Besides he couldn't rationalize which would be worst, to die or become an adult.

5

He Had to Be Fast and Efficient

ODAY WAS A NEW day. He'd eaten the stolen bread, drank his fill or water and felt stronger. That alone gave him the expectation that the upper room held a potentially new opportunity. That is exactly what led him directly from the Orache shrubs to the inn. The taste of the leaves lingered in his mouth. He continued scraping his tongue with his front teeth to no avail. As he approached the inn he stepped toward the old broken down wagon which sat diagonally across from it. When he felt that no one would notice, he slipped under the wagon.

With very little room to maneuver he forced his attention off the discomfort in his contorted legs to focus on the probable reward awaiting him. He would use that thought as a shield against the discomfort in his legs. Today he would again risk being caught in the upper room when he should not be there. Two hours had passed. Undaunted, his eyes remained trained on the inn's stairwell across the road. The boy focused as single-mindedly as any sentinel assigned by a military general. Hunched beneath the old broken wagon provided an excellent vantage point and the perfect place to hide, as he dutifully continued to observe. The old wagon had deteriorated in place over the years yet no one bothered to remove it. Over time like most things in common view the wagon became invisible to those who passed by. To the boy's way of thinking, he was no different than the wagon. No one cared about or concerned themselves with people like him. Orphans and beggars were as invisible to people as the old wagon. They walked by without the slightest regard.

Remaining steadfast, ears alert, and eyes peering forward he studied the scene watching and waiting. Details were of the utmost importance, a lesson he'd learned begging alms. Sizing people up, how to approach them, how they dressed, even the way they walked were all critical details when selecting the best possible person to approach for alms. Living in the streets had honed his survival skills well. Although a boy in age and size, the work of begging and surviving promoted an acute kind of streetwise keenness in him. While watching the inn he anticipated entering the room. Very likely there would be some food and drink left over. His mind practiced how he would run to the stairwell leading up to the room. This run to the stairs had been made many times, but he never took for granted a single detail. In his mind's eye he watched himself go through the process. He needed to be fast and efficient when the time came.

6

The Mule Brayed
and Its Muscles Rippled

FINALLY, SOUNDS OF ACTIVITY began to broadcast from the stairwell across the road. Yelling turned into laughter which echoed out as men congregated at its base. The boy leaned his head forward. They appeared to be separating some of the items they carried down. *They are merchants,* he thought. The men huddled for a few moments around the stairwell now speaking in lower tones. Pointing to a few baskets the men seemed to be appraising the distribution of items. The boy could only assume they were scheming together, after all that's what adults did best, something to which he could personally attest. The men then traded money, and gathered certain items from one another. As they separated, one of the men adjusted his tunic while others jostled their head pieces to rest squarely on their heads. Another man pointed back and forth at the baskets. They offered one another gestures of courteous affection. Two of the men worked together to load baskets onto a wagon. Another man hitched the mule to the front of the wagon and climbed onto the driver's bench. The other man, who appeared to be the leader, mounted his horse. With the cart fully loaded the driver slapped the reigns sharply. The mule brayed and its muscles rippled as it strained forward finally gaining momentum, pulling the cart, the load and the merchants. A fan of road dust arched up behind them. The clip-clop of the mule and the staccato rumble of the wagon's wooden wheels echoed. The boy could still hear their voices ricochet as they rode away. *Finally,* he thought, the room had emptied which he considered a reward for his diligent patience.

A warm breeze blew sand across his face which he barely noticed as he remained out of sight watching vigilantly, oblivious to all else. A distant sound of people talking echoed forward. He carefully scanned around the area.

Making the run became second nature and he knew exactly where to cut a turn toward the building, heading south as not to pass directly by the inn's first floor window where Alaya and Shira were sure to be looking out. They were always minding other people's business, gossiping about it and making up tales to go with it. The boy had been a target of their devious nature before and quickly became wise to them. Although the sisters were only a few years older than him they had already become as treacherous as adults. And if they caught sight of him running, they would surely call out which would bring attention to him, ending any chance of his getting into the upper room undetected to search for anything the merchants left that might be of value. He smiled as he relished the chance to get up to the upper room.

To his way of thinking, any risk taken here would hold more potential payoff and certainly less challenge than begging alms in the square or open markets. But overall, he found that surviving in Jerusalem resulted in better opportunities than the town of Heshbon where he had lived and worked since infancy in an orphanage alms house, until the night he escaped.

7

When You Have Nothing, Anything Is Everything

REMAINING VIGILANT HE CONTINUED to sit quietly beneath the old wagon in wait. He watched the dust subside as the merchant's cart finally rode out of sight. Breathing deeply he bided time. Another wagon came along, bouncing with its load of goods. *What good timing,* he thought. Running alongside the wagon would provide further cover as he crossed the road. The wagon drove across his path so he rousted himself to run swiftly alongside it then cut out toward the stairwell. Scanning the area as he sped across the road, he entered the stairwell picking up speed. The muscles of his short legs tightened as he skipped over stairs up to the top of the stairway. Scurrying into the upper room, he caught his breath. Lingering smells of leftover food and wine filled his nostrils. His mouth instantly watered, reminding him of something he ignored while waiting to make his run: hunger! On the table lay treasure for his stomach; pieces of partially eaten dried meat, some remains of fruit, and crusty bread bids left in a bowl which he quickly snatched and swallowed down. An involuntary smile broadcast his delight having found food. *Their carelessness had become his reward,* he told himself while wiping his sleeve across his mouth efficiently as a cat, not a wasted motion.

Hunting the floor while chewing the last bit of food he hoped against hope to find treasure for his pocket as well. He didn't know whether the meat tasted good or not; whatever taste it may have offered had been swallowed by hunger faster than his taste buds could discern. But that was not all he didn't know. Although he lived oblivious to anything other than his survival, today celebrated the last day of the Passover. The boy hadn't the

slightest notion that over the next few hours this day would be an experience unlike any other in his life or any day ever again. Today the events in
the upper room would begin shifting everything he knew about himself.
Nothing he believed or had experienced would ever be the same. This day
would set him off on a journey of wonder, conflict, and transformation.

8

"We Shall See Soon Enough."

WHILE THE BOY CONTINUED scouring the room, only moments from the inn two men walked briskly along the road. They looked around anxiously here and there seeking someone or something specific. Both dusty and tired, wondering if they were on a wild goose chase; one of them finally mentioned it.

"John, do you think the Lord may have been mistaken about this task? After all, it seems to me . . . what landlord is going to simply provide a room for the Passover meal because two strangers ask him?"

"I have wondered the same thing," said Peter, "And then I remember how many times he dispatched us on errands that seemed impossible, but always came to pass."

John nodded confidently. "We shall see soon enough."

The men continued walking when the one named Peter stopped his companion abruptly, placing his arm across his mid section. "Look," he said with no small amazement. "Am I seeing correctly? Can this be so?" He pointed with enthusiasm, "That man walking ahead carries a water pot!"

John's eyebrows rose as he studied the man ahead. "Indeed brother. He carries a pot of water just as the Lord foretold. Let us speak to him." When they reached the man, he glanced at them and judging by the quizzical look on their faces knew that they wanted something. He stopped to lift the water pot off his shoulder and placed it on the ground.

"Can I be of help?" the man asked.

John looked the man in the eyes and said, "Good man, the Lord inquires where is the guest chamber where he shall eat the Passover with his own disciples?"

The man didn't answer. As if on cue he lifted the pot of water back up on his shoulder gesturing they should follow him. John and Peter glanced at each other in no small amazement. They quickly arrived at an inn where they followed the man inside. He placed the water pot down and told Peter, "I am not the owner. Wait here I will bring the landlord." He walked away and informed Zohara that some men had come with a message for him. Peter and John recited the same message they expressed to the man who carried the pot. They explained to Zohara that a party of other men would be arriving within moments. The landlord desperately tried explaining that the upper room hadn't been cleaned yet, that a party of merchants had only departed moments ago. For some reason, against everything he believed, Zohara could not bring himself to discuss the price for the room, nor could he delay in agreeing to provide them immediate access to the upper room. When it came to asking for payment, Zohara never felt tongue-tied. Yet, no matter how many times he began to address payment, as well as delay in entering the room his mouth went dry and he could hardly speak. The group of other men arrived at the inn.

As they talked with the landlord, just above them, in the upper room the boy focused, continuing on his knees hunting for anything of value, his methodical search. Without a wasted move he scoured the floor under the table. Functioning in a heightened awareness he suddenly picked up faint sounds from downstairs which quickly turned into amplified sounds, and heavy footsteps. *That must be Zohara*, he immediately assumed. He didn't expect the landlord and his daughters to arrive this quickly since the merchants had just departed. He realized the footsteps and voices indicated more than a few people making their way up. Glancing around once again for any treasures left behind, he moved from the table, starting for the service cabinet which he planned to jump on, get the window shutter open, and climb down the outside wall of clinging vines. The footsteps and voices grew louder and closer and much faster than he anticipated. Having people come up to the room made no sense to the boy since it had not yet been cleaned. The landlord never allowed such a thing before. What was going on? He knew his escape strategy out through the window could no longer work. There simply wasn't time left. The men were about to arrive at the top of the stairwell landing.

9

He Enjoyed Hearing
the Landlord Squirm

THE BOY JERKED BACK and forth, startled and unsure what to do. His heart beating faster as sweat beaded his forehead. He delayed too long with indecision. The only possible place to hide now would be underneath the service cabinet. Quietly and smoothly he crab walked over to the cabinet, laid flat on his stomach and crawled under, moving some of the stored bowls to the side to get in.

Once under the cabinet he slid in and tucked in against the back wall as tightly as he could. The cabinet's depth extended well over three feet from the wall and its width some six feet. Just about everything needed to serve the table had been conveniently stored on the cabinet and in its drawers. Although familiar with being under the cabinet, he had never been under it for more than a few moments looking for or gathering up valuables. Now with people entering the room he had no idea how long he might be huddled under there. He began instructing himself on the vital need to remain still and quiet. He desperately hoped he wouldn't sneeze or cough. No sooner did he settle in, knees pulled up and lying on his side, the group of men had already paraded in, spacing themselves out around the table. Many voices spoke at one time which made it difficult for the boy to hear anything clearly. After a few moments they became quiet. Jostling floor cushions and sandals rubbing against the floor made the only sounds.

One of the men said, "The landlord did not exaggerate, Peter, this table is a mess."

More footsteps sounded up the stairs. The landlord entered, his daughters trailed behind him. "Apologies, apologies," he bowed nervously. "My previous guests remained longer than expected. We will clear off the table quickly, and be out of your way. Please forgive." The only sounds were the plates and cups being removed and muffled voices of the men slightly echoing in the air.

As the landlord walked to the wall where the service cabinet stood, he said to Alaya under his breath, "Where is that cursed boy when we need him?"

She replied in a whisper, "Oh, father you know he is lazy and we always have to do his share of the work anyway."

The boy fumed at her words, but restrained himself from yelling out.

The landlord and his daughters stood at the cabinet piling plates and utensils. Their sandaled feet were right there in striking distance. How he wished he had a rock to smash on their feet. And he would have, but even if he could he knew better than expose himself. Then in the next moment the landlord and his daughters scurried out, promising to bring the meal back up shortly. Never had the boy heard the landlord sound so nervous, attentive and submissive. These must be very important people. In either case, he enjoyed hearing the landlord squirm under such pressure. Zohara and his daughters backed their way to the door, bowing again as they departed.

The man called Peter gestured around the table and said, "I am sorry, Lord. Other than the nuisance of the table mess, I trust the room is to your satisfaction?"

"All is well, Peter," came the reply, "it is not the value of the room, but the value of what is achieved in the room."

10

"Every Word Spoken Is an Inner Thought Exposed."

A S HE CAUTIOUSLY SHIFTED himself to get more comfortable under the service cabinet, the boy listened carefully. He noticed that the words spoken by the man they referred to as Lord came across uniquely over the other voices, projecting a certain tone of authority. This tone he often heard from the Roman Generals who marched through the square with soldiers. Yet the essence of this man's voice carried something more, something deeper. Although he could not define it he sensed it clearly. With his insatiable curiosity besting him the boy slowly jostled in measured movements, edging closer to the opening under the front of the cabinet to glimpse a better look. Because he could not lift his head above the cabinet opening, the view provided little more than sandaled feet, caked with dust and dirt from the road. He estimated thirteen sets of feet. The men sat reclined on cushions against one another around the low table.

Then the sound of footsteps echoed up the staircase. Once again the landlord and his daughters entered the room and began placing bowls and items on the table while the landlord continued profusely offering apologies. Retracting to the back wall the boy again delighted in the nervousness and apologetic tone of the landlord. Yet, he knew it might still be his misfortune to be spotted under the cabinet by the landlord. The sisters were expressing something about the meal to the men around the table. Both of them spoke in pleasant and delightful tones with graceful courtesy. The boy sneered. He wanted to spit. They were so deceitful, always scheming and condemning people. They smiled at your face and harangued you behind your back. Now of course, they acted as though they were so naturally kind, attentive and considerate. He frowned, gritting his teeth. Then reminded himself to calm down and not risk being exposed. Finally the landlord and his daughters offered yet another apology making a final departure from the room. The boy didn't relax until there were no more footsteps echoing down the staircase. The men were once again talking over one another having separate conversations.

"Truly, truly I say to you, let us esteem others higher than ourselves brothers." The voice came from the one they called, Lord. No one spoke another word. The boy couldn't help but focus on the unique tone projected in the voice. Although still young he had been in the presence of many adult men in a variety of situations on the streets of Jerusalem, many not positive. He learned he could tell a great deal about a person by listening carefully to voice inflections, the words and tone used. He learned of this one day while begging alms in the square. An older man stood on portico speaking so the boy stood by to listen. The man spoke loudly, making prophetic claims to a gathered crowd. He gave warnings to them about their idle words. The boy never forgot the prophet's words because they rang so true.

The prophet emphasized that every word spoken is an inner thought exposed. The prophet's words came across as practical, after which the boy practiced being more attuned to the words men spoke out as well as the look on their faces when they were about to speak but didn't. The lesson served his begging of alms well as he became practiced in the art of listening. He also learned how a person's eyes often expressed more than their words conveyed. Through practice he could often tell by people's eyes as they walked in the square which would be more likely give him alms and which would not.

Another man in the room spoke up with a distinctly coarse and gravelly sound. The boy thought he recognized that particular voice quality. After a moment it came to him. Whenever fishermen were around they seemed to sound that same way. He supposed it to be the result of their yelling to each other loudly from boat to boat in order to be heard over the sound of the water and wind.

The man with the gravelly voice continued, "Rabbi, John and I were amazed when we came to the inn. Everything you told us came to pass. We came across the man carrying a large water pot. We spoke with him and he immediately brought us to the landlord. We shared with him the words you gave us. He asked not one question as to who we were. Everything happened exactly as you told us! We marveled, did we not, John?"

"Yes," said John, "all things happened just as we were told."

One of the other men perked up asking, "Tell us what this is you are talking about?"

The boy slowly wiggled his way back to the front edge of the cabinet cautiously as not to expose himself and wind up being punished. In his world that's all adults were good for. Still, he felt compelled to see these men, especially the one they now had given a second title, Rabbi.

The gravelly voice of the one called Peter answered the other man's query. "We asked the Lord of his plan for Passover. He instructed us to come to where we would find a man bearing a pot of water. He instructed us to talk with that man, and he led us to Zohara, the landlord of this inn."

John then interrupted and related what they were told to say about needed a room. "And brothers," John added, swinging his arms around as though presenting the room, "as you can see, here we are."

One man looked across the table gaining his knees on the cushion and asked, "Lord, is this all true? Just as Peter and John have told it?"

But another man spoke up. "Why would you question Jesus' commands this way?" A stroke of resentment rang in his voice.

11

God? The Boy Thought Harshly.

"**A**LL IS AS IT should be, brothers," the authoritative voice spoke again. The boy strained to catch a glimpse of the face behind the voice. Because the one called Rabbi sat on the opposite side of the table the viewing angle remained partially blocked by the men seated on his side of the table.

The Rabbi continued, "Brothers, I have desired to eat this Passover with you before I suffer." The boy focused his attention. "For I say unto you, I will not eat of the Passover again, until it is fulfilled in the kingdom of God to come."

"Tell us more of this, Lord Jesus," John asked.

At those words, the boy retracted again, trying to understand. What did this mean . . . suffering, and the kingdom of God? *God?* The boy thought with harshness. He had no use for God. The finely robed Pharisees touted God in the streets when all the while they spoke of punishment and laws, and they never smiled or laughed. He had never once seen them help anyone. They never so much glanced down at him. *What kind of God are they talking about who lets parents leave children? And a coming kingdom? The only kingdom power belongs to Caesar.* It amazed him, how many titles could one man have, Lord, Rabbi? Now, at least he had a name to attach to the authoritative voice: Jesus. He could not help wondering how a new kingdom would start. Despite befuddlement he felt certain that this meeting held great importance as well as secrets clearly not intended for him to hear which only added to his sense of fear that he might be caught and punished.

Jesus continued, "I called you to become fishers of men. Do you re-member when I sent you out two by two without a bag or even sandals? Brothers, did you lack for anything?"

Some men shook their heads no, and several said "No, nothing. We found no lack."

Then Jesus stood up and the boy nearly caught a cursory glimpse of him, but he then moved away from his place at the table. "Focus not on yourselves alone. Care for those in need of God. Preach the good news, serve others."

These words about serving and caring for others grew more and more frustrating to the boy. *An adult teaching caring for others?* He could not be-lieve it. There must be some scheme behind it. They could not know his world, where caring for oneself proved the only way to care. And preach something that was good news? All he heard were words of suffering, pos-sible rebellion, ushering in a new kingdom and there could be no good news in such an undertaking against Caesar. He wondered what they might actu-ally be scheming.

Suddenly there came a shuffling of sandals and a good deal of chaotic movement around the table. The men were leaning over the table in a frenzy while others stood up looking downward to the floor. Confusion seemed to reign the moment.

"Hand me the water bowl," Jesus said. More shuffling sandal squeaks and cushion noises were generated. One of the men spoke up sounding deeply incensed. His body recoiled from Jesus as though he had seen a ghost. His voice direct but strained, "Rabbi . . . no . . . what is this you are doing? You cannot do this. No Lord!"

What is happening? What is wrong? The boy grew unsettled yet still struggling to see. In a moment many of the other men were also questioning Jesus, incensed at his actions. They pointed out that he should in no way be doing such a thing. The protests continued. "We should be the ones doing this for you, and not you for us. You must stop this. This is not right, Lord," protested one of the men."

The boy had all he could do not to crawl out from under the cabinet and walk over to see. With that he inched forward ever so slightly, watch-ing and waiting. He could now see cushions upon which the men sat being shuffled as they stood up frantically. He caught glimpses of Jesus who had kneeled, holding a section of his tunic out and appeared to be washing the feet of each man. The boy gasped at observing the strangest thing he had ever seen. Yes. He was washing feet! The boy's mouth dropped open. To his knowledge, washing dirty feet remained the task of the servant in a noble's house. When visitors arrived the servant would go out to the front of the house with a bowl and wash the visitor's feet before they entered the house. This man however, held titles; Lord and Rabbi. The boy believed the men were right; he should not be washing their feet while holding such titles of importance.

Regardless of the men's protests Jesus continued moving to each man, bowing down, washing feet. He moved around to the side of the table facing the service cabinet. The boy now held an open, unobstructed view of Jesus as he washed the men's feet.

12

The Room Stood in Total Silence

J ESUS MOVED TOWARD THE last man at the table, closest to the service
cabinet and as he approached, the man immediately stood, recoiling.

"Master," he protested with hands extended, "You *will not* wash my
feet. This cannot be."

"Peter, you . . . each of you . . . cannot understand what I do now, but
you shall understand later," said Jesus.

Peter stood, taking another step back from Jesus. With a trembling
voice he said, "No Lord, may it never be."

Jesus moved the water bowl closer. He looked up into Peter's face and
said to him, "Let it be so at this time. For if I do not wash your feet you will
have no part in me, and cannot be my disciple."

At those words all the men were leaned over one another watching
and waiting for what would take place next. For a moment no one moved.
Not a sound. No one spoke. It seemed as though no one was even breathing. Without a word, Peter lowered himself back down to the cushion and
removed his sandals. Jesus washed his feet while Peter looked the other
way. As Jesus bathed Peter's feet he deliberately turned his head slightly, just
enough of an angle to look directly at the boy. Due to his stooped posture
Jesus could easily see under the cabinet, without attracting anyone's attention. He looked right into the boy's eyes. The gesture direct in intent.

I've been caught, the boy froze with apprehension. In the next moment something overshadowed his fear. Thoughts flooded that he could not
figure, but somehow he understood that Jesus already knew that he had
been under the service cabinet. He knew this to be true as he glanced at
Jesus then quickly turned away. Jesus showed no sign of surprise. The boy's

heart squeezed, and his chest compressed, anticipating being called out and made an example as he had experienced in other situations. Jesus however, continued performing his task. The boy remained frozen in place, almost forgetting to breathe as though he had become part of the wall behind him. Jesus looked over at the boy again, lifting his forefinger to his pursed lips to convey, *not a word!* The boy could no longer turn his eyes away from Jesus.

His face was not a handsome face, but it radiated certain strength. His complexion dark with ruddy skin that had been burnished by the sun to a leather-like texture. His body lean and solid. The boy felt Jesus' eyes piercing into him, but not ominously. The distinctive sense came over the boy that behind those intense eyes both power and softness shown through. Still, part of him wanted very much to run out of the room, but Jesus' eyes were magnetic as though holding the boy in place. He looked out with uncertainty.

Jesus began drying Peter's feet, glancing back under the service cabinet again. He smiled at the boy. Strangely, with that the boy's uncertainty lifted as smoke from a pipe. The washing of feet came to an end. As Jesus gathered the bowl and adjusted his partially wet tunic, Peter continued looking away. Then Jesus reached his hand inside, grasping for something. Slowly he removed a coin, holding it between his forefinger and thumb. He gestured the coin toward the boy then placed it under the cushion where Peter was about to sit back down. Again, Jesus looked at him, a smile shown through his eyes. The boy's anxious countenance eased. A definitive physical warmth of a kind he had never known before engulfed him. The sensation so uniquely soothing he didn't want it to end. In the next moment Jesus stood up, and walked back to the opposite side of the table. The room stood in silence. The boy remained bathed in the tingling warmth.

"Rabbi," said Peter as he sat in his place, "We do not understand what you have done."

"Yes, Teacher, this is difficult," another man added.

The boy thought Jesus looked too young to be a Rabbi. Those he encountered in the square and by the temple were always older men who looked stern and unapproachable. They made him feel like a dog inconveniently under foot. Although the boy no longer held fear of being exposed, he remained confused about the situation taking place. One surprising and strange feeling overwhelmed him; he wanted to know more about this man they now referred to as *Teacher*. Such a desire came as totally foreign to the boy. All he ever needed to know, and all he ever thought about came down to survival. Nonetheless, he felt distinctively compelled to learn what Jesus and the men were planning to do, where they were going and what he meant by all the words he had spoken? What did the washing of feet signify? After all, he stood among them as the leader, the important one in the group. The men had acknowledged this by the many honoring titles they applied to him. The boy knew of no grown up that would do such a demeaning thing as washing the feet of his underlings. To his experience, grownups were all just users of one another. His storehouse of wounded thoughts began to rise up along with questions and uncertainty about what he had observed.

13

"Do You Know What I Have Done to You Today?"

WHEN JESUS RETURNED TO his place at the table, he sat down. All the men reclined on their cushions as well. A long silence passed.

"He who has bathed is already clean, and needs only to wash his feet. But not all of you are clean."

"What do these words mean, Master?" one of the men asked.

"Do you know what I have done to you today? You call me Teacher and Lord, and such I am. So if I have washed your feet, so you should wash one another's feet. For I gave you an example that you should care for others as I have done while with you."

The boy noted another title. Now they called him Master! The words Jesus spoke to the men were somber. But to the boy they seemed to be some kind of a code with some deeper hidden meaning. *A code . . . he is speaking a secret code to them. Maybe he will explain.* That particular point held great interest to the boy. Everything about his life dealt with watching out for himself. Jesus spoke the very opposite, watch out for others. Why would an adult place such great emphasis on others? How would they benefit by such an action?

"Teacher, tell us, what you began to say . . . that one of us is not clean," John asked.

Jesus stood. "I do not say all of you, but one of you . . . will betray me."

The room broke out in instant frenzy of panic. Fingers pointing. Heads turning, all talking over each other asking, "It can't be me, Lord!" The questions moved around the table. "Teacher, is it me?" They looked back and forth at each other, some with accusatory expressions. "Surely not I, Lord?"

"Please, say it isn't me, Lord." These responses didn't surprise the boy. What adult would ever admit to anything bad about himself? They were always pointing fingers away from themselves.

"I have told you brothers, the prophecies must be fulfilled," Jesus said. "Yet the one who betrays me is the one who dips his bread with me at the table."

What a strange thing to say, the boy thought. What sense did that make when all the men were there to eat the meal together? Jesus said one man would betray him, the one who ate with him, yet they were all going to eat with him. His young mind processed troubling thoughts. Why would anyone share his meal with a person who would betray him? To the boy's way of thinking, nothing could be worse than betrayal. And if anyone held personal familiarity with betrayal he surely did. His parents . . . he never knew. Whether they abandoned him or died he didn't know. They betrayed him by leaving him alone in the world. And his brief residence at the alms house where other boys like him were kept turned out to be nothing more than a place where they all worked like slaves, and were given barely enough food to sustain them. Yes, they were all the same. Every grown up; every one of them, betrayers who cared only about their own well being. That reality had confirmed his decision to plot running away from the alms house. He would escape and run away from there at the first chance, and he did so very late one night. Another boy escaped with him, but they became separated in the darkness. He determined he would be better on his own and so he learned the ways of survival on the street. With that recollection in mind he reconsidered, growing uncomfortable about Jesus looking him in the eye and placing a coin for him under the cushion. What did he expect in return? Why do something like that for a boy he didn't even know unless he held some intention to exploit him somehow. After all, in his world, nothing came free. Not even receiving alms came free. It carried a cost. The looks of distain, the scoffing, at times being abused, the sense of dependency; no he would not be fooled, nothing came free. Still, it sat like a pebble in his scandal as to why Jesus didn't expose him and hand him over to the landlord? Mistrust began to fester. Remembering his intention of coming into the upper room early in hopes of finding something valuable, he scoffed at the wasted time he had been forced to spend under this cabinet. He longed for the day that would make him tall enough and strong enough. Then no one would take advantage of him ever again.

He sighed. Time for a decision. His thoughts shifted to consider the odds of making his way out from under the cabinet, running over to snatch the coin from under the cushion and hit the stairs at full speed. Practiced at running down those stairs, he could easily skip several at a time. If the boy had anything it was speed. *I'll be even faster jumping up on the service cabinet and going out the window.* Then he reconsidered that strategy to be far too risky. They could send someone out to the garden and catch him at the bottom. If they caught him the landlord would know his escape route. He contemplated the risk and almost decided to go by way of the stairs. Yet another thought vied for him to remain, to ask his questions of this Teacher, to understand why he left him the coin, why he did not turn him in? Why he would eat with a betrayer? Why he had so many titles? And then there was that powerful look on his face when he glanced over, seeing him hiding beneath the cabinet, the way his eyes felt. They were different, radically different than the expressions of other adults. The boy hovered in conflict; stay and risk having his expectations trampled or take his chance at running out?

14

"He Is Too Secretive . . ."

THE BOY THOUGHT HE would take his chances with the stairs and began poising himself to break out and run when his intentions were interrupted as Jesus again spoke.

"Peter, pass the bowl of bread to me."

Grasping the bowl Peter handed it over. Jesus reached in and lifted up a small loaf. Looking up to heaven he gave thanks to God and broke the bread. Then he passed the broken bread bits to the men, saying, "This is my body given for you. Eat it. Do this in remembrance of me."

Following a silent moment he reached for the wine pitcher, pouring it into a chalice. He lifted it giving another blessing saying, "Take this among you and drink. This cup is the new covenant in my blood, which is poured out for you." The room drew silent as the chalice passed to each man, Jesus spoke again, his voice now somber. "The hand to betray me is at the table as prophesied."

As these very words were being spoken, one of the men abruptly rose from his cushion. The boy had found a better view by shifting to the left side of the service cabinet. The man stood up, turned and walked toward the door, his long thick beard bounced on his chest with each stride. His eyes were what the boy noticed above all, dull gray, vacant. A piercing chill braced the boy's skin running up his back as the man passed by the cabinet mumbling something about having had enough as he walked out of the room making his way down the stairs. His muffled words conveyed deep seated anger. Two men seated nearest the cabinet, discussed what had just taken place. They assumed that the man left to go collect alms for the poor or thought Jesus had dispatched him to purchase more items for the gathering since he was the one who carried the money bag.

One man commented, "Judas sometimes seems to think about gathering alms for the poor more than anything else."

Another said, "He is too secretive . . . we have no idea who he distributes the alms to," raising both arms in frustration.

The boy's ability to read eyes with an inner confidence about certain matters rarely proved wrong. In fact these occurrences had saved him from harm many times so he learned to give them credence. He held no doubt the man they called Judas must be the one. How obvious could it be? How could they not know Judas would carry out a betrayal?

Why would he get up and leave after Jesus spoke the words about betrayal? He clearly separated himself from the others by walking out. Why didn't the Teacher do something? Why don't the men stop him? The boy became troubled by this to the degree that he himself wanted to do something about it. But what could he do, crawl out and suddenly announce that he knew Judas to be the betrayer? That would never work. Begging for alms taught him the most effective method of gaining any money wasn't to ask while walking toward a person and surprising him, but rather to walk along with the person. Some portion of people became uncomfortable with that and gave him something to get rid of him. It also got him knocked to the ground more often than once. No, he had no credibility to do anything. Then he caught himself. None of this could do anything to aid his goal of survival. The unfamiliarity with this thinking out of nowhere felt disorienting, holding him in place. He sorely wished he had not been stuck here. Why did he pick this day to be in the upper room? He chided himself.

15

Knowledge of Secrets
Often Got Men Killed

I NSTEAD OF ANSWERING THE men's questions about betrayal, Jesus simply said, "My brothers, do what I have done here and as often as you eat and drink this supper do so in remembrance of me. The greatest among you should be like the lowest, and the one who rules like the one who serves. For I ask, who is the greater, the one who is at the table or the one who serves the table? Is it not the one who is at the table? And yet, I am among you as one who serves. Serve as you have observed me in the villages we traveled. I confer upon you a kingdom, just as my Father conferred on me. I will come back for you. I will surely not leave you as orphans, so that you may eat and drink at my table in my kingdom and judge the tribes of Israel."

By this the boy could only conclude the meeting to be some kind of pending revolution as Jesus spoke of a coming kingdom and how his disciples would judge the tribes of Israel. This suddenly frightened him. What he heard had to be secret information, much like the Roman soldiers planned secret strategies. Knowledge of secrets often got men killed. Even beggars understood that. Then it struck him above all he had heard, Jesus mentioned not leaving them as orphans. This astonished him completely. The thoughts he had just considered now vanished as he became drawn to the last words of the Teacher.

All these men could not be orphans like me, could they? They must be, the Teacher called them orphans. The boy wondered if he should come out and tell them that he too was an orphan. The excitement of the thought quickly flickered out as it would be as foolish as standing to proclaim he knew Judas would betray the Teacher. Nonetheless, it became apparent these men were orphans and that's all that mattered to him now. And although the men didn't know it, they had that in common with him.

"Remember always brothers . . . my Father loves you because you have loved me and believed that I came forth from the Father," Jesus proclaimed.

This now became too much for his tossing young mind. He covered his ears with both hands. Care? Love? Father? The words vibrated in his head despite his covered ears. What was all this talk? And who was Jesus' father that he would care for all of these men? Was he some rich nobleman or some great general from another place planning to overthrow the Roman leadership and establish his own kingdom? Strangely some inner voice assured him through all the questions and confusion, that the Teacher's words were truth. The boy faced difficulty with such thoughts. He struggled with the memories of being beaten, left hungry and more than once had what few coins he begged for in the street taken from him. As to love? No one loved orphans. And that, to his way of thinking, remained the very reason why they were orphans.

In fact, adults used love as a tool to get what they wanted. And care? His life revolved around survival, fighting for every scrap he could manage. Why even the landlord would occasionally claim arbitrarily that he did a poor cleaning job, and gave him a meal in less portion. The boy understood why the landlord did this; to show him that he held all the power and he could help or deny anytime he desired. He knew what it felt like to be treated as a dog.

Again, Jesus' voice lifted him out of his darkening thoughts. He simply stated, "It is time." The words were spoken as a commander sending soldiers out to battle. The men shuffled about, rising from the cushions and moving toward the stairwell. His thoughts persisted. *These men are orphans like me. Why would the Teacher say he would not leave them as orphans if they were not orphans? Wherever Jesus determined to go, he said he would return for them and bring a kingdom as well.* The boy had been around other young beggars and orphans, in fact they covered all ages, but they were all separate from one another. The men in this room were orphans yet they seemed to be together almost as family. Nothing like this had ever been experienced in his life before. *Maybe I can join them.* He sensed somehow being transferred to a place out of Jerusalem to the new place where the new kingdom the Teacher spoke of would be found. It took a moment before the boy again restrained himself from announcing his presence, but he had come close.

For now waiting would be his best action. He determined that he might follow the men, and find some way to join them in the new place. On the other hand if they were plotting some revolution, the thought crossed his mind that he might gain some payment, some reward by turning them in to the Roman Guard. He quickly discarded that notion realizing he would be placing himself in direct danger. Who would even believe a beggar, an orphan? What proof would he give the Romans? Such an act would surely get him sent to a work camp. No, he shook his head trying to remove this kind of thinking from his mind. Forget all of these strange thoughts and simply get back to his work of surviving. Yet in the conflict he felt drawn to go and follow these men. The decision came from a thought he would never have imagined considering. A thought so foreign he swallowed hard and squeezed his eyes tightly closed. And yet as unsettling as it became, it clung to his mind as if someone or something placed such a notion in his head. *What if I do follow them?* The question itself held out far beyond his own capacity to deliberate . . . he could not believe his thinking. Then he rationalized that if he followed them to find the new place, wherever it might lead, wherever the Teacher and his men were going, could not be worse than how he lived every day? Never had such a radical thought intrigued and frightened him in the same moment.

16

How Could He Know His Name?

T HE GROUP OF MEN stood and gathered their things. They announced that they planned to head east and then emptied out of the upper room, some still murmuring among themselves. Finally, the boy let out a long sigh, with satisfied relief. He could finally get out from under the service cabinet, and just in time as minor cramping throbbed across his thighs. Waiting a bit longer to be certain they were all gone, he became startled hearing his name called out. At first he wasn't certain he actually heard it since the room had emptied out. But indeed, his name had been called. And again . . .

"Levi!" He readily knew that voice by now. The Teacher called out his name. How could he know his name? This frightened him, and could not bode well. Could this be the time for his punishment? He tensed. In the next moment he made a decision; *I've been punished for being here before, this will just be one more time . . . I don't care*, he stiffened up.

"Levi, come out."

Strangely, the call came not as a demand, but a warm invitation. He made another long exhale and his heart beat loudly as if a bell tolling in the square. Surely the whole town could hear it. With mounting trepidation, the boy moved on his stomach wiggling himself forward until his entire head shown out of the opening below the cabinet. Standing on the opposite side of the table, Jesus looked at him. "Come," he said holding in his hand the chalice that had been passed around to the men during the meal. Jesus offered that unique smile again. The one that had made the boy feel distinctively bathed in wondrous warmth.

Jesus' eyes captured him with what appeared to be a glow. Jesus then leaned his body forward stretching across the table, placing the chalice close to the table's edge nearest the boy.

"Levi, come. Fear not!" The voice, like a small explosion and authoritative in tone so intense, it seemed to vibrate the room. The boy turned his head back and jostled his body out from under the cabinet finally standing up looking cautiously at Jesus. His presence so compelling it seemed as though everything in the room, even the air, had given its full attention to him. Something in the room's atmosphere had shifted.

"Levi . . . hear my words well . . . you are no longer alone!" said Jesus.

The words had almost come from some far off place. Before realizing it, the boy bowed his head with an overwhelming awe mingled with a warm attraction. Never had he been in anyone's presence under this kind of sensation. The words spoken caused him to hold his head down for a moment. Upon lifting his head and opening his eyes, Jesus' clothing seemed to reflect a glow. The experience did not feel frightening, but wonderful and above all he sensed something new, something totally foreign to his entire existence; safety!

"Listen carefully," Jesus said, "many will abandon me. I will be alone, but this is only for a moment as I must fulfill the prophecy. Then I will no longer be alone. And such will be the same for you. This you shall come to know in time, Levi. You are no longer alone!" he emphasized. Tilting his head and raising his finger he said, "You must however, set your mind on the messages yet to come."

The boy closed his eyes tightly, determined not to weep. The experience transfixed him and he didn't know how to respond to it. At length he opened his eyes. Jesus no longer stood at the table. The boy quickly perused the room, walking over to the other side of the table. He heard no foot falls, no sound of feet moving. He darted to the stairwell to see if Jesus might be there. The stairs were empty. Hadn't the Teacher just said that he was no longer alone? Yet, there he stood, alone. He walked back to the table, his pondering interrupted by the small chalice Jesus left on the table's edge. He glanced at it then suddenly remembered the coin, and his eyes quickly glanced down to the cushion where Jesus left it. His first instinct urged him to bend down and retrieve the coin under the cushion and run out, while a stronger impulse held him at the table. Reaching to the chalice, he gripped it with both hands bringing it to his face. Looking inside he found the shallowest amount of wine pooled in the bottom; barely a mouthful. He lifted the chalice to his mouth then stopped abruptly. He recalled Jesus telling the men that the chalice held his blood as a covenant. His pulse rate quickened. Could this be blood? Should he drink it? He had tasted blood more than once, when slapped across the face simply because he didn't move out of the way of a passerby quickly enough. The cut on his lip had filtered blood into his mouth. He recalled its irony taste. Should he trust and drink? Why would Jesus have left this chalice for him anyway? What value did it have? It was a common drinking cup. What could he do with it? Becoming weary of his questions he reflexively tipped it up. The wine's dryness tingled as it moved across his tongue. He swallowed nothing more than wine and placed the chalice back on the table. Quickly bending over he began lifting the cushion when he felt warmth all over him, just as when he stood before Jesus. He stepped back, being bathed in the warmth. This time it took place inside his body not only outwardly.

From the corner of his eye, he thought Jesus stood in the room again. He turned quickly to look. He called out, but he remained alone. Yet he felt assured beyond any question that Jesus had again been present when he felt the warmth. In fact he had enjoyed the feeling of being in Jesus' presence. He couldn't explain the embrace of warmth that felt wonderful and uniquely different from what the streets offered.

17

Live or Die.
That's How Survival Worked.

NOTHING THAT OCCURRED IN his twelve years of life ever overly impacted him because he had learned to live only for the moment. Hunger
required food. Thirst required water. Pain required soothing. Cold required
warmth. And loneliness required something he could never find. It all came
down to solving the immediate issue at hand. He didn't dwell on things he
simply dealt with them. Live or die. That's how survival worked. The experience in which he currently found himself seemed somehow to be shifting
that experience.

In a few moments the physical sensation of warmth dissipated, seeing
again that despite what the Teacher said, he remained alone. "Are you here?
You said I was . . ." his voice trailed off. The boy now stood unsure if the
Teacher meant he was no longer alone because the men would be returning,
or the Teacher himself would return? Thinking this he sensed that somehow there was more to what the Teacher spoke about his not being alone
anymore. He remembered the Teacher saying he would be abandoned and
alone, but only for a time, and then he would not be alone. *'And such it will
be for you,'* the Teacher had emphasized. What puzzled the boy came in the
last statement when the Teacher told him that he must set his mind on the
messages yet to come. What messages? How would he receive these messages? Who would provide them, and how would he even recognize them as
messages? The only certainty came in the fact of the coin that had been left.

Stepping back to the cushion he lifted it and there rested the coin. Now
that coin would provide him with abundant provisions. As he beheld the
coin it occurred to him how strange that this coin turned out to be the exact

same coin he had once found in this very upper room. The one the landlord had taken from him with a scolding and nearly the rod. Something he could not figure out, something very strange was taking place. Now at least he had something to show for all his waiting under the wagon and waiting under the service cabinet. Starting for the stairs he heard the landlord talking to his daughters echoing up from the base of the stairwell as they made their way up. Zohara's angry tone reverberated loud and distinctive. The boy made haste to exit by his new escape route. *The landlord will never take this coin from me*, he thought with a confident smile. He jumped up onto the service cabinet, swung the window open and reached his arm out grasping the outer wall's clinging vine to make his getaway when all at once he froze. Turning his head back he looked directly at the chalice sitting on the edge of the table. He stayed in place. He couldn't leave. He felt overwhelmingly that he couldn't leave it. The chalice must not be left. That is all he knew. It must not be left.

Footsteps grew louder and closer up the stairwell. The boy wanted desperately to climb out. He looked out the window then back at the chalice. Footsteps growing closer by the moment. He glanced out the window then back at the chalice. He could not believe he took the risk as he swung back inside onto the service cabinet, jumped down, and stepped over to the table to lift the chalice. As he moved back toward the cabinet he opened a portion of his tunic and jammed the chalice into the large inner pocket he had fashioned to carry items found out in the streets. Quickly mounting the cabinet again, no sooner did he swing his body through the window grasping a vine, when the landlord and his daughters entered the room, complaining loudly that they had another mess to clean and he ranted on furiously about it. Fearful that he would make too much noise climbing down the vine, the boy secured his footing as best he could, then wrapped his arm around a thick vine and held tight, breathing shallow, pressing himself against the vines.

"They left the window open, Father," said one of the sisters.

Levi froze. He would easily be seen if they came to the window.

"Don't worry about the window now. We have too much to handle in here. I'll close it afterward," said Zohara.

Each time the landlord shouted out his anger at the situation, the boy would drop a few feet down. The loud complaining yells covered the noise he made climbing down from the vines. Finally making his way down to the bottom of the wall the boy ran across the garden into the road heading for the open marketplace. He couldn't help thinking about all that had happened.

Why would he be told he was no longer alone and then leave him alone? Why leave him a coin? Why leave the chalice? And above all why did he risk himself going back in to retrieve the chalice? None of it made sense, and he didn't like it.

Glancing back at the landlord's building an idea occurred to him. One of such surprise that he stopped, and then dropped under a wagon tied to a post. Nestling up behind the thick spokes of the wheel the boy continued looking over at the inn. That very moment he knew. He knew for sure this would be the last time he would ever view the inn. Tonight would be the last time he would ever be concerned about the landlord or his daughters. His mind racing, he desperately wanted to believe what he heard about the new place, the new kingdom. The boy wanted to be part of it when this new kingdom arrived. Clearly he realized it would not be here in Jerusalem. No, he would not stay here any longer. He would have to find this new place where the Teacher and his men were going to launch the new kingdom. He could sense inner change which caused him both excitement and uncertainty. But then again he knew Jerusalem. He knew the ways of people here. He knew the best places to beg. It held familiarity. Leaving to go find this new place would take him somewhere he had no familiarity with at all. He pondered this while looking across at the inn. Making this decision posed strain against his thoughts of familiarity. He deliberated this as he looked across at the inn.

18

"And What If You Find Nothing When You Go?"

As he considered what to do, at that very moment he recalled walking behind two men in the marketplace from whom he planned to ask alms. One man tried to talk the other man out of leaving Jerusalem. As many obstacles as the one man mentioned in trying to convince his friend not to leave, the other man finally stopped walking.

He placed his hand on the shorter man's shoulder and said to him, "You know Jerusalem. I know Jerusalem! I also know everything that I can find in Jerusalem because I have already found it all. There is nothing else. Out there may be many things I have not seen. There may be a place where I belong. I will never find if it I remain here. In Jerusalem I can only find what I already know."

"And what if you find nothing when you go?" the shorter man asked.

"Then I would have lost nothing more than I have already lost. If on the other hand, I stay here, I will never know, my friend . . . I will never know."

Listening to the two men the boy realized by their dispositions, it would not be an opportune moment to ask them for alms, and moved on.

Still looking at the inn he replayed in his mind the words of the man who said that if he stayed he would have already lost. *I have no friends here,* the boy thought. *I have no one here in Jerusalem.* He felt that man had been right to leave and now he would be right in doing the same. Yes, he allowed the bold thought to capture him; he would leave Jerusalem. He would certainly not be any more lost going to seek out the new place than he was already lost to the begging streets here. After a time he made his way out from under the wagon and into an alley he knew well. There he gathered his thoughts for a moment in peace. The boy played over all the titles the men had used when referencing Jesus. He knew the meaning of each one. But when the men used the title, Teacher, it felt like the most appropriate title for him. The entire time in the room he had been the teaching the men. Whether they were secret codes being taught or not he didn't know, but they were some kind of lessons.

The entire gathering focused on teaching and preparing. Until now no experience in his life had ever given him even a tiniest ember of hope. Still, along with his new found expectation the uncertainty about a rebellion, and a new kingdom were difficult to fend off. Anger overcame him as he thought about the many disappointments, dangers and mistreatments he had endured, and for a moment it nearly stamped out the newly stoked tiny ember of hope he gained from being in the upper room.

His mind echoed the words of the Teacher about no longer being alone. To his amazement what began as his great disappointment turned just the opposite, the thought began building his vigor. Finding the new place would now truly be his intention. "Yes, I will leave Jerusalem and find this new place. I will go," he spoke to himself softly. He needed to hear his own words of commitment. The new place is where the Teacher would teach him of great things and secrets and codes and he would finally be with the men who were orphans like him.

19

"The Doves Will Only Come to You When You Are Calm."

T HE BOY SCURRIED OUT from the alley into the bazaar where some of the merchants were closing stalls while others swept out their tents and others still crafted goods to sell for the following day. He turned to have one last look at the particular booth where he would often go to be fascinated by the candle maker who molded and shaped the wax to his will. The boy sighed, often wishing he could shape his own life as the man did with candle wax. He then glanced uncomfortably at the stall across the way which held dozens of doves in cages which were sold to be used in sacrifices.

The boy recalled a day when the dove seller negotiated with a buyer. Once agreeing on a price the buyer thrust his hand into the large cage causing the doves to jostle violently. The merchant quickly acted. "Stop, look what you are doing," he called out to the buyer. "My doves can be injured by this action." The buyer apologized. The merchant waited until the doves settled down. Then he gently opened the cage and slowly placed his hand at the opening, palm up. "The doves will only come to you when you are calm," the buyer said.

The boy had always viewed the cage of doves with distain. That cage represented the opposite of the candle maker who formed each candle with care and uniqueness. The only form the doves could take was looking out of their cages to a freedom they would never obtain. Tonight he understood that he had something in common with the doves. He too remained in a cage of sorts. *Enough!* He told himself as he moved briskly between the merchant tents. Stepping quickly around a barrel he toppled over, barely breaking his fall with his hands outstretched.

Rising to his feet, he glanced up and lost his breath. The man called Judas stood over him. There was no mistaking the vacant eyes he observed when Judas stormed out of the upper room. Whatever the boy did not know about this man, he knew enough that he could not be trusted. There are times when the heart speaks out a deep need that circumvents practical logic to not speak. And this in fact came to such a moment as he peered up. Judas looked deeply into the boy's face and started to turn away when to his astonishment the boy yelled up to him, pointing an accusatory finger. "Why are you going to betray Jesus?"

Judas immediately glanced side to side to determine if other people were close enough to hear. He didn't have a notion how this boy could be privy to his secret undertaking. The key was to move quickly and keep the boy quiet.

"You dare speak this way to your elder?" Leaning over to grab the boy by his clothes he spoke quietly in an ominous tone, his lips had become one thin line, "I don't know who sent you, but one call for a Roman Guard, and I can turn you in for this accusation." Judas grasped the boy by the arm and shook him. "Now, who sent you to spy on me and why?"

"No one sent me. I was in the upper room." Levi spoke it loudly and boldly as if to sound as though he were an adult.

"The upper room? How is that?"

"I was hiding under the service cabinet. I clean for the landlord sometimes."

"You haven't come here of your own accord, boy . . . now I ask once more only." Judas clamped his grip on the boy's shoulder. "Who sent you and why?" The man's intense eyes frightened the boy as his fingers dug into his shoulder.

"I will . . . tell everyone." But the boy's words no longer sounded adult-like, but just what they were, the words of a boy trying to mask his fear.

Judas gritted his teeth, "Have you any idea what they do to people in the Roman work camp, boy? They are always looking for young, strong workers."

That flashed a heightened spark of fright through the boy because he knew of the camps. Everyone did. The threat of the camps provided an effective way to keep the citizens in check minimize uprisings, and obtain free labor. No one who went into the camps ever came out again. Caesar essentially owned everything and everyone. The Romans used the work camp of slaves for breaking stone and digging dirt for the production of concrete to build their towers, temples and aqueducts. Many a lost orphan had been scurried away to the camps never to be seen again. If Judas did summon the guards the boy knew full well they would not take his word over that of an adult. Any attempt to defend against Judas's accusation would be futile.

"Let me go!" and with that, in a split second the boy took advantage of knowing Judas would not expect what he was about to do. He forcibly dropped his body straight down and out of the grip, then darting like a cat between Judas' legs, moving as fast as he knew how, but Judas managed to reach between his legs and grab onto the boy's ankle.

"Thief! Thief!" Judas yelled loudly, "Stop that little thief!" People began to look over. Some of them echoed Judas' call getting the attention of a Roman Guard. The advantage of a strong young body is the ability to contort, which is exactly what he did. Turning back over on his stomach he reached the hand clamping him in place. He drove his teeth into the back of Judas' hand, biting deeply. Judas yelled, instinctively releasing the ankle. His eyes became slits, his nostrils flared, and his teeth gnashing like a wild horse rearing up to stomp a snake. And then, the boy found himself running. The Roman Guard ran past Judas to pursue the boy while calling for him to halt. The Roman turned out to be faster than the boy expected. A few people in the marketplace tried to stop the boy, but his wiry quick moves deflected them.

Picking up his pace he turned to the east heading out of the marketplace. As he rounded the corner directly ahead stood a nomad experiencing difficulty controlling his camels. These dromedaries were large, over six feet tall at the hump, 1,300 pounds and dark black. The boy had no way of knowing it, but mating season caused the camels to be agitated and they bellowed loudly. The handler struggled with them. The camels appeared to have large bag-like tongues hanging out of their mouths, but they were actually pink glandular sacs inflated during mating season to attract females. Moving far too fast to even think of stopping in time the boy had no choice but dive under the large camel and through its legs. Being too tall and muscular to be that limber plus the fact that he ran at speed unable to stop, the Roman Guard helplessly crashed directly into the camel and the handler at which point the agitated camel's inflated sac burst open shooting a waterfall of the vilest smelling cud and fluid all over them. The two men were too busy yelling at one another and dealing with their wet, noxious smelling bath to even think about following after the boy.

20

He Had Forgotten about the Chalice

THE DISTANCE BETWEEN THE boy and the Roman Guard had grown far too wide to ever close now. When he felt far enough away he finally stopped running and sat next to a small building panting, spitting and coughing. A good while passed until he became calm once again. Along the side of the building he found a water trough for horses and donkeys. The desperate need to quench his thirst drew him to it. He knew standing water would not taste very good, but he also knew that drinking a few mouthfuls would not hurt him since he had done so when no other water source could be found. As he stood up he heard a clink and felt the chalice knock against the wall of the trough. So small and light weight he had totally forgotten about the chalice. Reaching down he felt it to see if it had been damaged. It felt intact. Readjusting himself he bent down to the water trough and drank again, placing his entire head into the water to refresh himself. As he used his hands to wring the excess water out of his hair, he noticed the uniquely designed fence by the farm across the way.

Although he had entered the area from another geographic approach and not paying attention to location, he now recognized this place. His long desperate run placed him only several miles away from the abandoned barn under which he lived in a crawl space. Again he took to running in order to reach the barn where he would gather what few belongings he owned and set out to find the new place and the Teacher and the orphaned men. How much time remained before Judas would act out his betrayal, he could not know. Realistically he hadn't the slightest notion of what to do about Judas, but the boy hoped he could to do something, at least inform the Teacher and his men. This unexpected desire continued bewildering him. Why did he feel so driven to involve himself in affairs that did not concern him, especially dealing with adults? His thoughts flowed with a notion that he could stop at least one adult from getting away with betrayal, somehow it would be a small way to experience some justice in his own abandonment which he considered a betrayal as well.

21

Loyalty or self-preservation?

J UDAS CLEANED THE BITE marks on his hand using a wet cloth. The boy's
bite made a deep wound and a good deal of blood flowed. "Cursed boy,"
Judas said. He wrapped a cloth around the hand tightly. All the commotion calmed down as the Roman Guard returned where he spent a moment
to talk with Judas gathering details of the event, The Roman Guard asked
if Judas knew the boy. All he could tell the guard is that the boy worked
at cleaning Zohara's inn. The Roman then quickly departed to clean himself of the stench from the camel's cud. Judas felt somewhat light-headed
concerned about who might have dispatched the boy to follow him. His
mind raced through scenarios about the boy; a very strange occurrence he
couldn't figure out. He felt unsure at the moment. Who could be looking
into his plans for Jesus? As to betrayal he believed no choice remained for
him other than self-preservation; after all it had become clear that Jesus
planned to launch some kind of revolt to usher in some new kingdom. He
continued his incessant talks about his coming kingdom. The other disciples could die with Jesus for a cause they did not understand, but he held no
intention of joining them in some rebellious suicide mission. The friendship
he'd had with Jesus could not endure against the potential of dying for some
undefined new kingdom. Besides, he was only being realistic since Jesus
held no official position. At best an unauthorized rabbi with unrealistic
plans and a few untrained, uneducated followers. Caesar would crush such
a revolt in mere moments. His well trained and battle-hardened soldiers
would end the attempt by Jesus' men as though swiping away a child's toys
across the floor. No man could win against Rome. Judas had invested nearly
three years of wandering the country side with these men and what did he

have to show for it? An occasional benefit from the treasury purse, which could never compensate him for the effort he had given to the cause.

The whole plan of Jesus was going to crash in on them. It's all going to end anyway. It's only logical for me to make some final gain. But Judas struggled with an inner dichotomy. If his decision had been so logical, then why was he still rationalizing it to himself?

While in the upper room he endured great discomfort just moments after Jesus spoke of a betraying hand. Friendship or betrayal? Faithfulness or desertion? Loyalty or self preservation? He felt at war with himself. Then Jesus actually mentioned betrayal at the table . . . the look of disappointment and sadness in Jesus' eyes overwhelmed Judas and he could no longer stand to be in the presence of his friend. The self pressure of his guilt and betrayal of his friend bore down on him with such intensity he could no longer remain still; he could no longer look Jesus in the face.

The hand of him who is going to betray me is with me on the table. Judas kept hearing the words repeated over and over and he could no longer tolerate it. His chest tightened and that moment drove him out of the upper room. And now the boy's appearance and accusations added more weight to it all. He would need to be much more cautious than he realized, especially in covering up his meeting with the Chief Priest where he made final arrangements to collect his silver payment for the betrayal. He played it over in his mind again.

"It is done!" he said out loud as he stormed off into the night carrying more darkness in him than the shadowed sky had painted.

22

And now that too
might be taken from him

WITH DARKENED SKIES AS cover the boy approached the abandoned barn from the hillside as it provided a more tree and bush lined path to help keep him well hidden. He would take no chances nor take his safety for granted. He didn't own but a few items. A knife and a few small cowhides. But the shepherd's staff; that was his prize possession, the one thing he owned that displayed the only caring act given to him by one single adult. He often wondered why he didn't stay there with that shepherd and his son. They had pleaded with him to stay. Gaining his thoughts the boy peered over the hill top. His eyes bulged as wide as a canyon when he observed a group of people holding torches standing around the barn where he lived. He recognized one of the two Roman Guards by his uniform color as the one who had chased after him. He gasped when he saw Judas standing next to a Pharisee. And in the middle of the group which completely caught him dumbfounded, he saw Zohara and his two daughters pointing here and there. The boy quickly retreated back into the bushes sizing up his predicament. He became furious with himself. He shook his head in disgust. Why, he now wondered, would he ever have told the two sisters where he stayed . . . he knew they could not be trusted, and right there in front of the barn; living proof. Plus, it became evident that it didn't take long for Judas' animated performance in the marketplace to turn him into a fugitive and necessarily, a recruit for the work camp. Fear brings on sweat which is intended to cool the body as its temperature rises. He sweated profusely as he watched the activity below, but it failed to cool him. The sweat carried more than fear for the boy. It brought a depth of sorrowful, mental pain because

57

his most valuable possession, the staff, could now be at stake. The Romans might take it. The boy shook his head back and forth to gain some alertness. He wondered if they would leave his shepherd's staff or take it. Never had he left his staff before. Not once since the man carved it and presented it to him had he ever let it out of his sight. *Why did I leave it? What was I thinking? What is wrong with me?* His stomach tightened and soured as though he were about to vomit. He gritted with anger at himself, fists clenched. He desperately needed to get his staff. And now that too might be taken from him. But he had no choice other than wait it out.

After another few minutes, Zohara and his daughters walked behind the Pharisee and Judas departing along the road. The two Romans were laughing about something. They went through the few items left on the ground that belonged to the boy. His anger stewed as he observed. Once again, grownups were throwing their weight around as though they were kings making judgments. One of the Romans lifted the cowhides and after examining them, threw them over his shoulder. The other man picked up a knife in a sheath and tucked it under his breastplate. The taller Roman then reached down to pick up the staff and examined it. The boy held his breath. After sizing it up several ways he realized the staff would be far too short to be of value to him so he grasped it by its end, swung it around, and heaved it into the air where it arched into the darkness toward the tall grasses alongside the barn. Both Roman guards walked away still laughing. The boy's face hardened. "One day . . . I'll wipe those smirks off their faces . . . one day!" Now however, a chance remained that the staff didn't break having been thrown, and he focused solely on that expectation.

23

"You are the only thing
I can always depend on."

S O MANY THINGS SEEMED to be working against him. No parents, no one to trust, no knife or cowhides to trade and now no place to live. The boy owned practically nothing and now less than that. Unless he could find his staff, he would have nothing at all. The boy had learned to disregard things including any kind of emotional attachments to anything. That he learned while listening to several older beggars talking by a fire years ago. Seeing him they emphasized what they had said as a way of instruction to the boy. He never forgot the lesson and held to the ability to remain detached.

Yet the staff had invaded that rule offering the only experience of care and appreciation he had ever known. Feeling assured the men were gone he walked down the hill to search for the staff. The partial moon cast its light which helped him search. His squinting eyes roamed back and forth across the ground, his heart racing as he swung his foot in a semi circular motion in the grass hoping to hit the staff. Occasionally he would glance back at the road for any signs of anyone coming. Methodically he foraged for quite some time through the grass until his shin finally hit the staff sticking out of the ground on an angle as though a spear tossed in battle. It remained intact. The boy embraced it as though a long lost friend. The staff had become a symbol of survival for him. After all, that's exactly what a shepherd's staff meant to the sheep; to guide them and fend off wolves to protect them. The staff held his high esteem as the only gift he'd ever been given and he prized it. "You are the only thing I can always depend on . . . always there," he said as he brushed some of the dirt off the end of the staff with his hand. Then he moved the staff into the tall grass using it as a cloth to wipe it clean.

59

The time had come to seek out the new place and find the Teacher, and the men. His mind played back something the Teacher said in the upper room. He recalled it distinctly now. 'I called you to become fishers of men. Do you remember when I sent you out two by two without a bag or even sandals? Did you lack for anything?'

The positive responses of the men answering questions impressed upon him. It didn't occur to him until now, but those men clearly trusted and respected the Teacher. They had to. How else could they agree to be sent out with no provisions? Although he held no idea what the men did when they were sent out, whatever it involved, they traveled out into the world with nothing! The realization did not puzzle him because he lived that way every day. The fact that they were given provisions along the way is what caught his attention. As to the words about making fishers of men, he thought it might be some type of riddle. It made no sense—men fishing for men. This had to hold some hidden meaning. The words of the Teacher soothed the boy in the notion that if the men were sent out with nothing, and they like him were orphans, and were taken care of along the journey, then he too being an orphan might have the same result. Oh he knew this as foolish to think, and yet he found the idea appealing. So he embraced it without any real belief or expectation.

As the boy made the first step forward with staff in hand, it occurred to him that in the course of one day how so much had changed. The thought that he could leave Jerusalem and find another world out there, the new place—a kingdom—he could hardly believe he would take the first steps. Maybe the new place did exist, where people cared for each other; where women and children were not treated as dogs, and parents stayed with their children. Then he caught himself, stopped smiling by brushing the back of his hand across his mouth, and pushed that nonsensical feeling away; time to grasp onto reality not foolish fantasies. He started back up the hill above the barn to the old massive sycamore tree. With its thick spider-like multiple twisted trunk roots the sycamore provided several open gaps just wide enough to allow him to lean back into it and rest his head back. The exhaustion of the last few hours commandeered him. In a moment sleep brought him to rest, ending his intention to depart right away.

As he awoke the following day, his head clunked against the tree root. After a few minutes he refocused as he squeezed himself out of the tree. He determined it would be best to go into the town square one more time to beg alms that would help support his traveling needs in addition to the coin Jesus had left him. When he noticed the position of the sun he realized that he'd slept through to late morning. He hurried to make his way to the town square. Upon arriving the people and activity were already hectic.

Cautiously on guard he made his way through the merchants and crowds. His ability to concentrate on asking for alms became hampered as he worried about the off chance he would run into Judas or the Roman Guard again. Looking at the oncoming individuals he scanned their faces evaluating their eyes seeking the best potential people to approach. He also paid attention to what they were saying and how they said it. This he learned one day when overhearing an old blind beggar, explaining it to another beggar. He listened as the man instructed that people who were deeply engaged in conversation were good targets because they didn't want to be interrupted, and by walking alongside them asking alms would often result in getting at least something from them just to rid themselves of the nuisance. Begging did not come easy, not only due to the attitudes of people, but the growing competition for alms.

Some of the poor and street beggars were allowed to glean in the fields to gather whatever the land produced, but that permission could only be granted on years in which it was not tilled. Others became so desperate that they pledged themselves as bond servants to rich families and nobles. Still others had managed somehow to secure a specified place at the corners of the streets to beg. Beggars were found along the side of the main byways. Some sat at the gate called Beautiful. Still, other beggars were positioned in small booths. The boy had only seen professional beggars a few times in the square. They wore distinctive cloaks which identified them as such. Faced with growing competition the boy learned well to experiment with various techniques to win people over.

24

He ducked behind a stack of barrels

A S HE CONTINUED WALKING the perimeter of the square he observed two men of small stature walking together in an apparent argument complete with hands waving. He cut into the crowd to make his way over to them and once he did, he walked right up alongside the men and maintained their pace. But something gnawed at him. The feeling grew distinct so he glanced around where he spotted a taller, older boy wearing a sash and who appeared to be following him along. His senses were rarely wrong. He had spotted him earlier when he arrived in the square and they caught each other's eyes briefly, so he knew full well he recognized him. He knew it wasn't uncommon for beggars to steal from one another and at times it involved violence.

Levi began begging. "Alms for a poor boy! Alms to help!" He repeated the phrase keeping pace with the two arguing men. It wasn't long before one of the men dropped a coin on the ground while picking up their pace to distance themselves. He picked up the coin and immediately pivoted to the right briskly walking to the opposite side of the square hoping to avoid the tall boy he knew had been following him. This coin now added to the one he already had from the upper room which would provide good provisions for the journey. The far end of the square had thinned out making him more visible than he cared to be so he turned into a small merchant's tent. The seller could tell the boy state as a dirty beggar with no wherewithal to make a purchase and ushered him out. He ducked behind a stack of barrels. After a time he peeked out looking for the other boy. Knowing he was being followed he tried not to place himself in an obvious position as best he could. Growing impatient to leave the city and begin his journey he slipped himself along the front of several merchant tents stopping briefly behind stacked baskets and barrels. That's when he caught a brief glimpse of the other boy. At that point he held uncertainty as to whether he had evaded him or not so he continued forward until he came to an alleyway. Peering down its length he saw several stacks of crates and a few barrels. Nothing seemed unusual. Standing up he slapped the dirt off his palms and began walking. That's when he heard it, the moaning sound of someone injured. Walking cautiously forward the sound grew louder to the left side of the alley where the barrels were stacked. The boy stopped to identify where the sound might be. Not that he intended to offer help, but perhaps he could find some valuables, take them and run off as quickly as he could. As he stepped forward his foot caught against a loose barrel strap, and as he fell forward his staff tipped out of his hand falling sideways in between two barrels on his left. Just ahead on his left a small person lay on the ground moaning. As he picked himself up a sharp pain behind his head knocked him back down. Throwing his hands forward to soften his landing, everything turned black.

25

The girl that had been under the broken arches

A S HE CAME TO he asked groggily, "What happened?" as he looked up to see an oval face with large black olive eyes. He squinted to be sure. It was her, the girl that had been under the broken arches.

"I don't know what happened," she said. But she did know. She had witnessed the two boys trick him and take his coins. She looked down into his face as she had cradled his head in her lap, "I found you here. I think the cool cloth on the bump behind your head will help."

Finally coming to himself he recalled what had taken place. The older boy and someone else had somehow managed to trick him, and he didn't like being made a fool when he knew better than to let his guard down. *Did he take my*— His hands moved quickly to check in his tunic. As he expected the coins were gone. Still dizzy he laid his head back down on the girl's lap. The throbbing behind his head pulsed. The girl continued to dab water on the back of his head with the rag.

No sooner had he focused on her face when he realized it. "It was you . . . you were under the broken arches with me. You could have stolen my bread when I fainted. Why didn't you steal my bread after I fainted?" he demanded as he managed to prop himself up to a seated position despite the throbbing pain. "Why didn't you take my bread?"

The girl shrugged her shoulders.

"I've seen you begging alms in the square before . . . who are you?" asked the boy.

"My name is Metha."

"Why are you helping me?" he snapped.

64

The girl shrugged her shoulders again, "I don't know. I just am."

"What do you want," he emphasized.

"Nothing," she said.

"Nothing? No one helps anyone unless they want something." He rose to his knees. "I have nothing and now that they stole my money, I have even less. Why are you doing this?"

"Does it matter?" she stated.

The boy's eyes grew wide and he forced himself to stand. Frantically he padded himself. *The chalice, they took the chalice too?* And that thought surprised him. The coins were important, but he seemed more distraught about the possible loss of chalice.

Metha swiveled her body and pointed to the ground behind him. "There's a cup over there, is that what you are looking for?"

There on the dirt lay the chalice. He slowly stood, somewhat shaky, walked over to pick it up holding one hand behind his head carefully caressing the throbbing bump. He lifted it up, the chalice showed a slight crack. Becoming light-headed he had to focus for a moment not to fall.

"Maybe the people that tricked you didn't think they could sell it so they left it," Metha said without emotion. "It's just a cup."

The boy nearly stumbled passing by her, hoping they hadn't taken his staff. Relief removed the tension when he found his staff lying on the ground between the barrels where it fell from his hand. As he bent over to retrieve it his dizziness toppled him over.

Metha scurried to him, "Are you all right? You should rest a while longer. I have more water in my flask."

Levi slowly got to his knees and then stood up carefully.

Metha reached over to grasp his staff. As she held it up to him she noticed the carved images. "These are beautiful carvings," she said while examining the artwork.

Levi reached over and took the staff from her. "It's just a staff, that's all."

26

Her eyes perked up. "A secret?"

THE BOY REMAINED PUZZLED. He insisted in his tone. "Why would you care about me? And why did you leave without taking my bread . . . what are you up to?" he demanded.

She tipped her head sideways almost blushing. "I think you are kind."

Throwing his head back and breaking out into a cynical laugh, "Kind? We are beggars. We are only kind to ourselves." The back of his head throbbed again from jerking his head back when he laughed. His face soured as he quickly reached up to massage it.

"Maybe you shouldn't have laughed at that," she poked at him.

He rolled his eyes as he moved to his knees.

"I saw you that day. You helped a small dog in the marketplace. You asked a man for alms and he pushed you down. You fell on a small dog. It yelped in pain. Instead of leaving it you held the dog, and you gave the dog something to eat. I saw you take it from your pocket, and you petted him until he stopped yelping," she recounted.

The boy grizzled his face as though denying it.

"Yes, I saw you. It was kind," she said.

He growled throwing his hands up as he slowly came to his feet. "You must have confused me with someone else. I don't care about a stupid dog." Then he tucked the chalice into his tunic, grasped the staff, turned and walked away. As he departed an unexpected, unfamiliar but heavy weight of guilt clouded over him. Metha's dirty oval face appeared in his mind's eye. He stopped abruptly. *I should tell her, but I don't have the time.* He started off again. The thoughts became an active self debate. *I don't have time. I don't need to do anything for her. I don't owe her anything.* But in fact he did.

And that is what gnawed at him. And he didn't like it one bit. Such feelings hadn't struck him before, but Metha's presence weighed in his thoughts. He stopped walking. Frustrated, he finally lost the debate. Turning around he reluctantly started back. *What if she isn't there? I'll be wasting more time*, he tried convincing himself. He stopped, then started again. He felt as though someone had tied a rope around him and he pulled back in a tug of war. Once he arrived he found her scavenging around the alley for things she might be able to use. The boy felt perplexed that he would actually do this, but felt strongly compelled.

"I thought you left?" she said looking up at him.

"I must go find someone. It's important."

"Why don't I go with you?" she suggested.

"I have to go alone."

"Will you come back?"

Shaking his head he said, "I will never come back to Jerusalem. Why do *you* come back? I have noticed that you are gone from the square for a time, and then you come back," he said.

Metha bowed her head guilty of the charge, saying nothing.

Knowing she would not answer he came to the point. "I want to give you something."

Metha looked up with surprise, "Give *me* something?" She smiled.

"Yes. A secret that will help you." There, he said it, to his own disbelief.

Her eyes perked up. "A secret?"

"Yes," the boy said. Then he explained in detail about the inn and the upper room and what to expect. He told Metha about the coins and other provisions he'd found there. He offered details about the landlord and the two sisters so she would know the best way to act around them. In great detail he explained how to get in, the best times to do so, and about the escape route from the window. He drew a sketch in the dirt to show the room's layout as well. "You can do well there if you are careful. Can you run fast?"

"Why did you come back to tell me this?" she asked, ignoring his question.

After a moment's hesitation he said, "Just as you said . . . does it matter?"

"What is your name?"

"Levi."

The girl retained a look of surprise that he shared the secret with her, but she said nothing.

"Goodbye Metha," he said then grasped his staff and walked away.

Just as he turned to depart Metha called to him, "If you come back to Jerusalem, come to where I stay." and she described in detail the two places where she held up. He did not respond to her as he continued walking. Her voice carried on the breeze behind him, "Thank you for remembering me, Levi."

Her sentiment caught him by total surprise. When he turned his head to glance back she exited the opposite end of alley melding out into the crowd. The boy turned back to start his journey. He felt an unintended smile on his face, immediately halting it. Much time had already been wasted.

With his first step he suddenly perceived distinct and significant throbbing warmth in his tunic pocket where the chalice rested. Startled by it he jumped back as though a scorpion appeared on his tunic. He lifted the tunic way from his side, stepped back, reached in and when his hand touched the chalice the warmth lightly pulsated. Upon touching it he came to calmness. Comfort overtook him. Within a few moments it subsided. He continued walking telling himself he was imagining things. Several times as he walked along he reached into the tunic to check the chalice. Once he stepped back into the square he begged alms hoping to replenish what had been stolen from him. With no small effort he succeeded in obtaining two coins. Now feeling somewhat better prepared he walked on.

Section Two

The Journey

27

The chalice did not feel warm now

B<small>Y THE TIME HE</small> walked to the road he intended to take afternoon set in. Although night travel did hold potential dangers the boy could no longer delay. He feared that giving too much thought to leaving Jerusalem might sway him into uncertainty and decide to stay. He determined not to allow that to happen so he started off, planning to find a place to sleep before the darkness fell.

Remembering that one of the men in the upper room said they were going to head east, he set his course to do the same. He walked on through the late afternoon without encountering anyone. After tiring he stepped off the road to inspect the area where he spotted a large growth of bushes. Using his staff he separated the branches of the bush apart which allowed him to step as far in as he could. He laid the staff across his lap and rested his back against the thick trunk. Over and over the boy replayed the hardships he had endured, and how the decision to leave Jerusalem so quickly took place. Reaching his hand to the chalice inside his tunic he could not figure out where the warmth came from, still unsure it had even happened. The chalice did not feel warm now. His mind raced with questions, especially the encounter with Metha. He would never have given up such information about the inn. Something in him seemed to be shifting. That concerned him. Beggars had no luxury of caring for anyone but themselves. Leaning his head back he closed his eyes and went off.

Then came a tightening around his throat—increasing—finally making him aware of the discomfort. He struggled as the pain tightened around his neck. Then he heard Judas' voice, "Who sent you, boy?" Shifting side to side his fear clamored as he swung his arms to fend off the attack. His breathing labored. In the struggle the back of his hand hit something and the pain snapped his eyes open. Grasping at his neck he realized his leather necklace had caught on a branch which tightened around his neck while he slept. Reflections of the nightmare continued to send shivers across the back of his neck as he heaved, struggling to catch his breath. His spine tingled, the hairs on his neck stood. Although relieved to know it was a nightmare, his chest continued pounding for a few minutes until he settled once again. Judas had not found him. At least for the moment he remained safe. Only having dozed off a short while he noticed how labored the sky appeared, seemly to be holding off the coming of night. The aftermath of his nightmare left him uneasy so he determined not to sleep. However, his eyes pulled night's blanket over, drawing him asleep.

28

"We could do nothing more."

THE BOY'S DEPARTURE DID not halt Jerusalem as a city at work. The day had been more work intensive for the man than usual, working as a laborer on the Roman aqueduct designed to carry water to the cattle market. The main architect had been on site this day and the workers were instructed to leave the site early as he figured out a problematic structural revision, one that would not allow any further work to proceed. An early release from work for a Roman laborer was unheard of and a laborer named Simon looked forward to returning to his family. He had been away nearly two weeks on this project.

Anxious to return home he decided to cut through the center of Jerusalem which would save him many miles. As he moved through the city he came upon a gathering mob, some people were calling out, "Crucify him!" Others were trying to shout those men down. Many other people were weeping and screaming at the Roman soldiers. Both hatred and a wailing sorrow filled the air; the scene chaotic. He noticed many Roman soldiers pushing people back to make room as a small group of men were passing. The mob moved forward like a school of fish along the road toward Mount Calvary. A Roman soldier scanned across the crowd and spotted him. The laborer watched nervously as the soldier walked up to him and asked, "What is your name?"

"I am Simon of Cyrene, making my way home from work."

The soldier grasped Simon by the shoulder pulling him into the street. The soldier then commanded him, "You are strong and firm of body, carry the cross of this man." The soldiers did this because they were falling behind in time due to Jesus falling and the interruptions of the crowd.

The soldier turned Simon around. There he saw a man on his knees holding a large wooden beam. The man's face and hair mated in blood and his body appeared to be contorted in laboring pain. The soldier pushed Simon forward and commanded him to take the wooden beam from the man and carry it. Filled with fear at what he observed he followed the command. Made of poplar wood, soaked through with the rains of winter, the beam weighed heavily and Simon held no small astonishment that the man could have carried the beam in his condition. Splinters of wood from the roughed out wooden beam pierced his shoulder and upper back, but he dared not stop with the Roman Guard alongside him yelling to keep moving. He followed behind the bloodied man who continued to move one agonizing step over another. *Who was this man*, he wondered? Somehow he did not sense him to be a criminal or thief. He had seen other crucifixions and the condemned men always lashed out swearing at Roman soldiers, and claiming their innocence. This man spoke not a word. The street narrowed which thinned the crowd to accommodate the space. Two women, one named Adina and the other, Veronica were being pushed along with the crowd as they observed while stretching their necks in order to see.

"Here are the soldiers," Adina said.

Just then Veronica stepped out of the crowd and dashed into the passageway. Adina called after her to come back. A Roman soldier moved toward Veronica waving his arms and shouting her back. The crowd rose in uproar again as the bloodied man fell once more. With that the soldier disregarded the woman which allowed her to slip by him and over to the bloodied man. She lifted a small towel from her belt and placed it on his face to wipe it clean of sweat and blood. Simon heard her weeping and calling out, "Jesus!"

Veronica turned her head toward the Roman soldier nearby and screamed out, "Why are you doing this? He has hurt no one . . . he has healed many people."

At her words a deeper fear gripped Simon, thinking this man might be a holy man from some religious sect or perhaps a prophet.

A soldier grasped her from behind, lifted and dragged her away, tossing her back into the crowd. A second soldier pushed Simon again, "Keep moving!" and slapped his back with the blunt end of his sword.

The crowd knocked Veronica to the ground and nearly trampled her. She finally managed to stand up. Adina finally located Veronica and held her as they walked out of the flow of the crowd. Veronica couldn't see clearly, her eyes were completely flooded. Her clothes stained in blood. She held the small blanket close to her. She started back down the road with Adina to return to the house where she had been staying with Peter and his family. She walked dazed and confused tripping several times.

"Oh how I wish I could have done more to help Jesus," Veronica wailed.

"We could do nothing more," Adina tried to comfort her.

Overcome with grief, Veronica spoke in short gasps, "My name . . . it means . . . bearer of victory. But I brought him no victory." Weeping bitterly until not a drop of moisture remained to be enlivened, Adina helped her stand up. Veronica continued carrying her despair under its heavy weight. The sky darkened casting an eerie stillness as though the entire earth had stopped to take notice. Rumbles echoed from the sky. The screams and yelling ceased. All the people departed. The spectacle had ended. Three crosses stood on the Mount of Golgotha.

29

No one wants to be too close to the Praetorian Guard

F AR FROM THE EVENTS of the previous night morning broke, and Levi
stirred awake still somewhat groggy. He quickly felt for the broken
leather necklace. He found it on the ground. After the nightmare he had
snapped it off. He rolled up the leather and placed it in his pocket. The clip
clop of horses focused his attention.

The sound of neighing and snorting brought the boy to a wakened
state as he rubbed his hands briskly across his face. Remaining very still,
he listened intently. The sound conveyed that many horses were approaching along the road just beyond the scrub brushes. Slowly he twisted his
body enough to allow his head to peak through the tall branches around
him. Through the branches and flickering rays of sunlight the unmistak-
able horsehair plume that crowned metal helmets appeared. The Praetorian
Guard! Once the horses passed, the marching front row lined with important officials marched by.

Cuirass with imprinted muscles were strapped across their chests; the
armor gleaming as the sun reflected off them. Marching behind the front
line, the common soldiers in white togas bearing tall shields at their sides
stepped in unison, each man facing straight ahead. Although he realized
they were not there to pursue him, the boy pulled his head back. No one
wanted to be too close to the Praetorian Guard. At any moment they could,
by law, force a person to carry their loads for a minimum of one mile although they routinely disregarded that detail of the law. When the sounds
of the horses' hoofs died down, he pushed himself out from the brush, and
rose up. He pulled a few remaining berries from a bush and knelt beside a

large bolder to drink the cool water puddle at its base. Gripping his staff he cautiously walked out of the grove until he reached the edge of the roadway. Tilting his head he glanced up the road and down the road. The guard had moved a distance away giving him enough of a gap to start walking while remaining close to the edge of the road out of direct view. Just ahead a small group of men, women and children were walking in the same direction as the Praetorian Guard, but a good distance behind. He picked up his pace and walked near them to avoid being conspicuous. The men were discussing Caesar's latest crucifixions having taken place last night to make an example of the latest band of thieves and zealots. He had never witnessed a crucifixion. However, having overheard enough details, he would never want to witness such an event. The conversations he'd overheard were frightening enough. At first he couldn't help wondering if this had something to do with the Teacher and his men, considering the claims about a new kingdom and that he said he would have to suffer. Had Judas already betrayed him? In either case the fact remained that people died last night at Caesar's decree. Anyone and everyone alive understood with no uncertainty that Caesar commanded with a heavy iron hand, strong enough to hold anything but mercy. He shuttered as he continued walking well behind the soldiers.

He couldn't shake off the possibility that the crucifixion had something to do with the Teacher. If Judas had gone to the temple to tell of the Teacher's coming kingdom, well, even a boy like him knew that such a thing would never be tolerated by the Romans. He held an unexplainable discomfort about it. If the Teacher had been involved then all was lost. There would be no new place, no new kingdom. All the men would remain orphans, lost and alone just as he would be. *If only the Teacher and his men had been . . .* he stopped himself, shook his head and breathed deeply, picking up his pace.

30

"Watch out boy!"

O VER THE NEXT FEW miles, more groups of people had gathered, walking toward the region of the far side of Jerusalem. Ahead lay a small marketplace with merchants showing their wares. Not only his eyes, but his hunger and thirst attended him to their presence. The berries he enjoyed in the grove and the few sips of clear water from the puddle at the base of the rocks had worn off. Rather than walk directly into the marketplace he made his way along a hill on the outside perimeter affording him a wider view of the merchants and the people below. Scanning around carefully, he didn't want to be surprised by Judas or anyone else who might recognize him. This vantage point offered a way to review the situation below. With his eyes focused and scanning the market he walked right into something. As he tumbled over he heard the warning called out too late, "Watch out boy!"

With his body falling forward he rolled over onto his side, staff still clutched in his hand. As he stood up he turned his head back only to find a scruffy-haired old man seated on a small wooden pallet. A beggar! The man lifted his eyes not responding. The boy dusted himself off, quickly checking to be sure the coins and chalice remained in his tunic. All in place. The beggar intently looked at him still saying nothing. The boy's first thought focused on how the old man could stand to be wearing sackcloth. There were three openings in the extremely course black goat's hair, one for his head and one for each arm. It appeared to be an oversized, poorly fitting bag. The pallet immediately conveyed the man's crippled state. How the man could have made his way up here the boy could not even imagine, since no other person stood nearby. They were alone. The whole encounter came across odd. Why would he be up here on the hill above the marketplace when all the activity took place down there? He should be sitting as close to the merchant sellers as he could. The more people the greater the take. The old man couldn't possibly receive any alms being up here alone.

"I didn't see you there," the boy said.

The old man did not respond. The boy studied his face. Dirty, pale with deep lines forged in it. His hair matted and un-kept, a mix of gray and white with the dried out consistency of hay, which he realized was caked in dirt. He sat with his legs crossed in front of him; an unfurled turban lay between his legs. No coins sat on it.

"Why didn't you see me?" The man asked.

He shrugged his shoulders, "I was watching the merchants. Why are you up here away from all the people? You cannot receive any alms if there are no people."

"I would if I could, but I have other tasks today."

"Oh?" was all the boy could say.

"Are you in need, boy?"

This came across as a strange question to the boy. *I am standing, and have money. He is crippled and can't move without help, and he asks if I am in need?* The boy moved a step closer to the old man. "No. I have begged alms many times."

The old man let out a muffled reply, "And that is who you believe you are."

Just like every other grown up who passed judgment and acted superior, thought the boy as he straightened out his tunic and adjusted his head piece. As he walked away, a loud droning filled the air, almost unworldly in its tone, "Alms! Alms for a poor man!"

He continued walking away from the beggar.

"Alms! Alms! If your heart can hear!"

The boy stopped. A conflict of thoughts rushed through his mind. Reaching into his tunic, he felt the two coins, gripping them tightly. Why in the world would he ever even entertain such a foolish thought of giving these away and to an old beggar yet? He didn't like this strange thinking at all. First it was Metha, now these strange thoughts. It made no sense. Besides, his hunger complained in his stomach. *If I give him the coins then I'll be left with nothing. I need to watch out for myself.* A feeling of intensity overcame him, almost a compelling. It felt the same as when he jumped back down from the window to retrieve the chalice off the table, and giving his secret to Metha in the alley. In both cases he did something totally contrary to self survival which concerned him. Without another thought he turned back, walking toward him. He didn't like this one bit. He stopped abruptly. *I am not giving him my coins.* He turned away from the beggar and walked away again.

"Alms for the poor!" called the old beggar.

Stopping again, the boy swiveled himself around, starting toward the old beggar, yet again in a conflicting argument with himself.

Give the coins.

(But I need the coins.)

Give the coins.

(Do not give them.)

The coins will not last.

(They remain in my hands now.)

He is in need.

(I am in need.)

He struggled greatly with such unfamiliar thoughts and feelings. He shook his head as though he might regain himself.

31

He didn't want to unclasp
his hand to release the coins

BACK AND FORTH HE battled determined to win. *'Care not only for your-self but others.'* The words of the Teacher appeared in his mind. Shaking his head he hoped to jostle off the words. Again he halted his footsteps, turned and walked away. Suddenly he squeezed his hand, tightly clasping the coins almost to a cramp then walked back toward the old beggar. Upon reaching him, he hesitated. He didn't want to unclasp his hand to release the coins. His hand continued to cramp from the pressure.

Release it.

(No hold it.)

Again the words of the Teacher spoken in the upper room echoed. He looked the old man in the eyes. Deep within him he felt he must give up the coins. The boy didn't toss the coins onto the unfurled turban on the ground; instead he leaned over holding the coins between his thumb and forefinger. He held his hand hovering over the beggar who then lifted his hand, opened his fingers exposing his palm. The boy gently placed the coins into the beg-gar's open hand. He had no way to rationalize giving away his only funds to the beggar. Never before had he experienced giving away something he so badly needed for his own well being; for that matter never giving anything away for any reason. He thought he might be losing his senses altogether. He wanted to retrieve the coins and run when the old beggar lifted his head, and slowly searched to meet the boy's gaze. Being so close to the beggar's face, the man's eyes shown amazingly. How strange the boy thought, every-thing about the man appeared old and worn and dirty except his eyes. They were new, young and vibrant and completely out of place in that body. The boy almost became light headed looking into them.

"Why didn't you just throw the coins down, boy?"

He straightened up looking directly at the beggar. "When I . . . begged in the street, people threw coins at me as they passed by, like I was worthless and deserved no respect . . . they didn't bother to even look at me or come near me. To them I didn't have the worth of a stray dog." Then the boy caught himself aggressively saying. "But I don't care anyway. I think all of them were beggars too, in some way."

"Does a beggar have worth, boy?"

"Food and a place to live, that has worth," he replied.

"Is that what you believe?"

"I believe in myself," The boy said sternly. Then throwing his shoulders back and standing as straight and tall as he could, "I believe in surviving . . . there is nothing else."

The beggar glanced down, removing the coins from his palm and placing them on the unfurled turban. Looking up at him with his eyes almost glowing he asked with a low, soft tone, "If this is what you truly believe, then why did you give me what is so valuable to you?"

He couldn't find an answer. The beggar's question pierced his heart. In a moment he realized what at first appeared to be a shimmering forming in the beggar's eyes were actually a quiet moistening of tears. The boy's face flushed, he gave an awkward cough as though needing more time to respond. His thoughts rapidly revisited his anger and experiences. At the same moment imagery of the Teacher giving him the coin caught his thoughts. He could not reconcile his actions with the concrete belief that he fought to hold fast; his own well being first above all. Two opposing thoughts in conflict. Without intention he suddenly spoke out, "I didn't want to give you my coins." He stood blank-faced. There, he said it.

"Then why did you? The coins are yours to keep. How you use them is yours alone to decide."

Again, the boy could offer no answer, as the beggar's reply was unexpected.

The beggar lifted his finger as if to accent a point. "*He* spoke to you, didn't he?" The beggar clearly posed the question as a statement of fact.

"Who, spoke to me?"

"The Teacher!"

At this statement the boy leaped back from the beggar, almost falling over, taken back at these words. How could this man know the Teacher had spoken to him? How could the beggar know he had been in the upper room? A foreboding uncertainty overcame him. Now he held no doubts that since his experience in the upper room, strange events were occurring.

"Who are you?" The boy insisted. "How can you know who spoke to me?"

"Levi, I am a messenger, nothing more."

The boy's heart raced at the thought that the man knew his name. This completely stunned him. *A messenger? What kind of messenger could a crippled beggar be?* Something strange was taking place here, but he couldn't figure it out so he did the next best thing he could think of, "I have to go now," the boy stated with concern in his face and a trembling voice.

32

"Things are not always as they seem, Levi."

T HE OLD BEGGAR REVEALED the slightest smile and said, "Fear not, Levi. Just as the coins are yours to do with as you wish, your journey will be the same. But consider . . . what has been happening to you?"

The question sat unclear. The boy simply nodded his head while stepping away from the old beggar. Then he exploded in frustration, speaking out in rapid succession. "What happened to me? I know what happened to me. I could have been given over to the work camps. I've been abandoned. I've been beaten. I lost my things. I've been a fool giving Metha and you what I needed for myself. That's what happened to me." The boy stopped backing up and lost his breath. The thought came to him as he looked at the old beggar again with a notion that he expressed. "I think we are the same, both beggars. Only, my legs can walk away and yours cannot."

"Things are not always as they seem, Levi. *You* are as paralyzed as I am. No . . . perhaps not in your physical legs, but your mind is paralyzed. You are unable to walk away from who you believe you are, and who you believe other people are."

The boy turned slowly then began walking off.

The beggar called out, "Levi, look at me. Hear this well. An event has taken place. A prophesy long ago foretold. When you learn of this event you will become bewildered and deeply discouraged. Listen very carefully now. You will immediately believe what was spoken over you in the upper room will not occur. At that moment you must determine to continue your journey. What I have said must remain above all things to you; important!"

At that, Levi began to ask, but the beggar vanished. He ran to the place where the beggar had been sitting but nothing remained other than the imprint of the wooden pallet in the dirt. He found no drag marks making it obvious that the man hadn't been pulled away and even if someone did pull him away, the beggar could not have disappeared from sight in the seconds it took him to spin around. His face furrowed, his eyes squinting. Dropping down on one knee he touched the imprints in the dirt, and the moment he did the chalice heated against the side of his torso. The warmth intensified with a comforting heat as though he had been near a campfire. Reaching into his tunic he placed his hand around the chalice to feel the warmth emanating just as he had the first time it occurred.

One thing after another continued turning into stranger and stranger occurrences. Discomfort lingered in thinking how the beggar could possibly know his name and his talk with the Teacher. He sensed a foreboding about some unclarified event he needed to prepare for. This did not sound like a good thing to come. Why didn't the old beggar just tell him instead of using his riddles? He dropped his head sensing frustration when warmth from the chalice calmed him, causing him to hold his hand against it for a long while. The same saturating warmth overcame him when he spoke with the Teacher in the upper room, a warmth accepted and welcoming to the boy. Not merely due to the physical feeling, but the fact that he felt a calmness encompass him when he should have felt otherwise. At certain times when he encountered some unpleasantness or difficulty while begging, he would go to the candle maker's tent. The flames of the candles, and their aroma provided some sense of soothing, but nothing like what he felt with the warmth of the chalice.

After waiting a time to see if the old beggar would return, the boy made his way down into the marketplace. Walking down the embankment he glanced back again to see if the beggar might be there. He didn't know whether that entire event scared him or confused him, or if it had been real. The pallet's imprint in the dirt coupled with the missing coins confirmed the event. During his encounter with the beggar, he forgot his hunger; nevertheless his grumbling stomach reminded him with no gentleness. Now he would have to deal with the difficulty of some way to access food and water.

33

"Halt. What is your business here?"

THE CROWDS WERE GONE from Mount Calvary. Only the Roman guards remained. Two men approached the guards who stood before the bodies hanging on three crosses. One of the two men, named Nicodemus, carried a large bolt of fine linen cloth under his arm. The other man with him, Joseph of Arimathea carried spices and a sealed letter. As they cautiously approached, one of the Roman guards lowered his spear.

"Halt. What is your business here?"

Both men stopped advancing. "I am Joseph of Arimathea, a member of the Council. Pontius Pilate has granted me permission to take the body of that man." He pointed to the middle cross bearing the body of Jesus. "Here is a sealed letter from Pilate which he instructed me to provide to you."

At the mention of Pilate's name the Roman guard lowered his spear, broke the seal on the letter and read the decree.

"Go forward and do what you wish. Do so quickly," commanded the Roman.

Joseph and Nicodemus removed the body, bound it in the linens, adding spices to it as they wrapped. Joseph waved to a number of other men who had waited farther off to come forward. The men lifted the linen bound body and carried it to a man-made tomb hewn from rock, owned by Joseph. Together all the men rolled a large and heavy stone into a furrowed out gully just deep enough and angled enough to allow the stone to roll closed, sealing the tomb. They had worked at speed as the Sabbath was closing in.

Afterward Nicodemus made his way back to the garden where Jesus had prayed with his disciples and passed between the twisted boughs of the olive trees. Life now cast ugly and barren, he fell to his knees weeping.

The Roman guard immediately came to the tomb. They set the seal of Rome across the stone. It was common knowledge that anyone breaking the seal would be put to death. The sixteen men that made up the guard then took positions, each man responsible to guard six square feet of space with his very life.

After hearing what the men did, Mary Magdalene, Joanna, and Mary along with some other women came to the tomb with the intention of anointing the body of Jesus with spices and oils. When they arrived the stone had been rolled away and the seal of Rome broken. They entered the tomb and found nothing but the empty linens that had wrapped Jesus' body. They told the disciples of this, but the women were not believed at first. Later that day Jesus appeared to Mary Magdalene, then to some other women, and finally to the disciples. Then they realized that Jesus fulfilled his promise to be raised from the dead in three days. Then others reported appearances of Jesus. Word of these events traveled quickly, giving credence to all that Jesus taught and promised.

34

The man wore a tallit

LEVI CONTINUED WALKING THROUGH the market. Now hunger registered more realistically as he smelled varied aromas of food around him. His mouth watered as he passed numerous food sellers. The coins he gave away would have purchased more than one decent meal. He thought again about how foolishly he had given them away. That played in his head with confusion; why in the world would he have felt so compelled to give the coins? He didn't want to entertain a deep, distant feeling warming in his heart that made him feel good about giving away the coins.

How could such a foolish decision hold any sense of good? He disallowed the silly notion so he focused on chiding himself under his breath until the feeling dissipated. Slowing his pace, he observed the area carefully as he weaved through groups of people. Musicians were playing music and singing. The atmosphere played festive, at least for those with meals, but he had little to be festive about. Perhaps as on other occasions his natural attention to detail might just find him an opportunity for a meal.

He stopped abruptly as a wooden toy rolled out from a seller's stall and across his feet.

"Don't try to steal that," the seller yelled out as he chased after the toy. The boy did not respond. He had encountered this before. Nothing he could say would convince the man that he didn't intent to steal the toy. His ragged clothing and dirty face projected him as a beggar, and as far as adults were concerned, begging and stealing were the same thing. The first few times this happened to the boy it bothered him to be judged so quickly, but now it had become common place to him. He continued walking on.

Passing by a large tent filled with vibrantly colored stacks of jars he observed the shopkeeper who stood up straight while slightly rocking back and forth in place. At first he thought the man might be in some kind of trance. All the movement, people yelling over prices, bartering, animals sounding off, and music bellowing, didn't seem to distract the man at all. This caught his interest so he observed with astonishment at how the man could seemingly block it all out.

The rocking man stood amidst jars of many sizes and shapes with an array of brilliant colors and designs. He had seen pots before in the Jerusalem marketplace, but never as beautiful as these. The colors and designs seemed to play with his eyes. Slowly he stepped a bit closer into the tent, totally fascinated. The man wore a tallit. The long, rectangular cloth draped down over his body with four corners at the bottom. Each of the four corners held hanging tassels. He noticed the man not only rocked back and forth, but he would at intervals; read aloud an inscription embroidered into his shawl. Then the man placed his lips exactly over what looked like a symbol or writing on the shawl kissing it with great reverence. He did this a second time then followed suit until all four corners of the shawl received a reverent kiss. Once he did so he lifted the shawl from his shoulders over his head, closing his eyes again. As he did so, a very tall man wearing a black turban walked under the tent looking over all the jars. The man appeared impressed as he viewed the jars. All at once the tall man's eyes lit up as he reached out to lift a beautiful jar off the stand. He turned it with inspection and a smile of satisfied discovery. With the large jar in his arms he walked over to the shop owner who continued rocking, eyes closed, with the shawl over his head and shoulders. The tall man began speaking to him. For some reason the tall man didn't seem to take into account that the shop owner stood rocking with eyes closed.

The boy shook his head and shrugged his shoulders. He could not believe the shop owner would risk losing a sale by not responding. The boy's exaggerated expression conveyed his bewilderment which caught the notice of a short, stout man who had been standing behind him. The stout man slightly leaned over and said, "Your eyes are wide . . . it is plain to see you are observing something you do not comprehend."

The boy quickly turned at hearing the unexpected voice while backing away a bit.

The stout man continued, "I did not mean to startle you, boy. Can it be you have never observed a man in prayer?"

"Not in this way," he replied. "That shop owner may lose a sale because he is not giving attention to a buyer."

"I shall explain then . . . but only if you wish to learn," the stout man said, looking and waiting for a response.

"Yes, I do." Of course he wanted to learn, he wanted to learn of many things. After all, in searching for the new place, the more he knew the more likely he would make better decisions. *But why would a stranger care to teach me anything?* Curiosity overruled his caution.

The stout man gestured pointing his finger. "As you see, the seller wears a prayer shawl. He kisses the sacred words with reverence. As you see, there are four tassels, each formed from strands of thread." He pointed again, "Only one tassel is blue and longer than the others."

The boy stretched his neck for a better view.

"Each tassel is tied by five knots. They represent the Torah."

"What is that word you said?"

"The Torah!" The stout man spoke with great reverence when pronouncing it, his hands lifted in exasperation. What have your parents taught you? The Torah . . . the five books given to us by Moses . . . the books of the Law. It is the book of eternity," he emphasized."

With embarrassment the boy looked at the stout man. "I . . . I do not know of this."

The stout man looked up, pondering something. "Then I shall tell you more, for these are the matters of God."

Levi had already become predisposed about God to the degree that he had experienced life. However, rather than dismissing it, seeing the stout man's sincerity, he decided to listen.

"Each letter of our Hebrew alphabet carries a numerical value," the man went on. "The first three windings of the knots are seven plus eight plus eleven, making a total of twenty-six. This number is equal to our Hebrew value for the name of God. The tassels are a constant reminder of each man's relationship to God and to God's Law."

"Do the tassels do anything?"

"Of course! Why would there be such detail and careful threading if there were no practical purpose? Do you have ears which serve no purpose! Everything must have a purpose, boy. Consider this, there are four tassels, therefore no matter what direction a man turns in whatever he does, he is reminded of God's Law being everywhere, and his responsibility to it."

At this, the boy's eyes widened, eyebrows raised.

The stout man took note of his intense amazement.

The boy continued in his curiosity as the tall man carrying the brightly covered jar spoke to the shop owner in the prayer shawl, who did not respond, but continued rocking and praying, eyes closed. The stout man stepped closer. The boy followed.

"Seller!" the tall man said, "I offer you more than the price you have marked on the jar," but the seller being in prayer did not respond.

Then the tall man spoke with a louder voice, "I have made a generous offer! This jar will be a suitable gift for a wedding I am attending." The tall man shifted the heavy jar in his arms, then placed it back on the shelf. Talking with his hands in motion, he offered yet another increase in price to the seller. Still no response.

"I cannot for the life of me understand why you are driving such an unreasonable bargain with me, seller."

The stout man leaned over to the boy and said, "You see, how the man concludes that the seller is negotiating for more money using his non-responsiveness as a ploy? That man is a foreigner; he knows nothing of respect for our customs."

35

"I would have charged even more."

THE SELLER FINALLY STOPPED rocking, lifted the prayer shawl off his shoulders, kissed it and folded it. He then addressed the man. "I am happy to sell the jar."

"I have made several offers," insisted the tall man.

The seller asked the man to look under the jar where he had written the price which showed three times lower than the offered price.

"Seller, I have already viewed the marked price. But you could have tripled your money with my offer. Do you wish to negotiate an even higher price?" asked the buyer in frustration.

"I have already agreed to a selling price as marked on the jar, and on my heart. I agreed to a selling price and that is what the price shall be." The tall man conveyed amazement, shaking his head at this then paid the seller and departed with the colorful jar.

The boy snickered. The stout man asked, "You disagree with what you observed?"

"The seller should have charged the highest price he could for the jar. The buyer offered much more money. I would have charged even more. The buyer truly wanted that jar . . . the seller is foolish."

"We must not take such liberties, boy."

"Why? This is a marketplace to sell goods."

"The Law instructs us not to cheat others. Not to seek gain improperly. This is the Law given by Moses. We must not gain on the loss of another."

The boy couldn't get the seller of jars out of his mind. He could have gotten three times the asking price but declined. And all this talk about God and Torah Laws seemed totally impractical. Conflict in the boy's demeanor telegraphed clearly.

"You do not understand?" the stout man asked.

"Why would the seller not want to triple his money? This seems foolish to me."

"What is right in the heart is right in the purse," said the stout man.

"Well he would have had a larger purse . . . I think now that one low sale price may not concern that seller . . . anyone can see he has many jars to sell. I have only this staff." He said it feeling upset with himself for expressing it.

The stout man could only conclude that the boy had either run away or had somehow been separated from his family. The boy adjusted his headpiece exposing his ear and the stout man glimpsed the small triangular wedge shape that had been cut out of the ear lobe identifying him as an orphan. On closer inspection it became obvious by the boy's ashen face and dull eyes that he hadn't eaten in some time.

"As you see, there is much to know of these matters, boy. I will explain further if you wish to learn." After hesitating for a moment he added, "Let us go to my tent and talk and eat."

All the boy heard at that moment was the word, *eat*. Against his better judgment his stomach persuaded him to follow behind the stout man. After a few steps he stopped and said, "I have no money for food."

"I invited you to talk and eat. I did not invite you to purchase merchandise. This way."

36

"Your eyes have filled with the beauty of my hookahs."

STEPPING INTO THE STOUT man's tent a strong, vibrant tobacco aroma greeted them. To the right side of the tent the boy noticed a wooden stall nearly as tall as the tent and nearly as wide. Its shelves stacked with the most ornate hookahs he had ever seen. The beautiful array of colors, textures, shapes and designs engaged his eyes. The stout man pointed to the cushions around the table where they sat down. In a moment a bowl of bread, dried meat and legumes were placed on the table. The stout man sat down holding a small pitcher of juice. The boy wanted to ask about the hookahs, but the aroma of the food enticed his nostrils causing him to reach in and begin eating voraciously.

"Slow down, boy, you'll choke, and what your stomach craves now, it will eject. And my carpets are exquisitely expensive," the man laughingly joked. "Besides, we must first give thanks for what we have." The man posed a short blessing. The boy never closed his eyes; they were too focused on the free meal. How wonderful to have food and be welcomed, although a new experience to him, he nursed a lingering distrust. Upon entering the tent he deliberately sat on the cushion closest to the tent's opening should he need to escape for any reason. His staff strategically positioned across his lap. He chewed while glancing around the room, eyes darting back and forth from the bowl of food and back to the stall of hookahs. The designs and colors fascinated him.

Following the boy's glances the stout man gazed at the stall, "Your eyes have filled with the beauty of my hookahs," he said proudly while swirling his upturned hand toward the stall.

"I have seen them in my city, where men meet and smoke and drink and talk. But never have I seen any like these. They look too beautiful to smoke with."

The stout man appreciated the comment, and he smiled with no small pride. Waving toward the stall he announced, "This is my business. Each hookah is handmade. Each one designed distinctively. They are most expensive." With that he stood up, walked to the stall, lifted a hookah off the shelf then placed it on the table gingerly as though a delicate infant. The bowl at the base that held the water glimmered with etched designs. A tall, ornate stem rose out of the water bowl with small vines of gold and highly polished metal. The hose from which to draw out the smoke carried bands of gold and silver strands. Truly a work of art.

The boy finished the last of the fruits and bread. As he looked the hookah over he turned to the stout man and asked, "Why have you been kind to me?"

"The Law."

His face flushed with amazement, "Caesar gives a law that you must feed strangers?" His head cocked waiting for an answer.

The stout man laughed out loud. "Roman law? Caesar? May it never be! Not Rome, boy. Have you not heard a word I've said? Heaven's law!"

The boy's face telegraphed doubt, as though he believed the man spoke nonsense.

"This is doubtful to you? Yet you saw heaven in the marketplace today did you not?"

The boy shrugged his shoulders. "Heaven? How did I see heaven?"

"You intently observed the seller with the prayer shawl. You could not understand why he accepted the original price for the jar, and not a penny more."

"I did."

"The Law expects exemplary behavior, can you not see this? Here, look at it in this way. I must assume you have seen a candle burning?"

"I have seen many candles," Levi said with a look conveying how obvious it was that he knew what a candle was.

"You have observed a lighted candle . . . surely! But I ask, have you really? You see, the candle does not give its own light. The flame must be given. Now give attention to this." He gestured as though lighting a candle. "Once the flame touches the wick, the candle burns. It gives light to all in the room." He waited for the boy to respond, which he did with a nod. "In so doing, the candle consumes itself until the wick, and the wax is no more. It has served its purpose well."

Levi listened attentively. Thoughts accelerated. At length, he looked at the stout man. "You are making a story about sacrifice."

"Precisely," the stout man smiled widely, "you are a perceptive young man."

"So that is what the seller did . . . and now you do the same with me?"

"Yes," the stout man said. "You see, in truth, giving is receiving. The seller sacrificed a higher price for his integrity."

This made the boy chuckle. He wondered if the coins he had given to the old beggar could be considered a sacrifice. "Thank you, sir. The food is good . . . you are very kind." He surprised himself speaking words that had never before come out of his mouth. He slightly reached for the hookah and turned it, hoping to move past the feeling.

"I wonder, then, since you have an eye for the beauty of hookahs, have you interest in learning the art of making hookahs? I seek an apprentice, and you have what is most required, an eye for beauty." The stout man moved his hands caressingly over the hookah at the table's center. After a moment he lifted his head to look at the boy and continued. "Many people see beauty with their eyes, but those who are drawn to it also view beauty through the heart. The designs and the colors . . . there are not many who experience having their eyes washed with it. Yes, I believe you have an eye for beauty."

The boy liked the compliment. *An eye for beauty?* Even more, someone actually wanted him for something other than mere labor. He momentarily imagined staying with the stout man, working as an apprentice making even more beautiful hookahs than these. And for the first time it crossed his mind that if he did stay it would not be due to his need for food and shelter, but he would stay because someone wanted him. Crowding this notion a conflict arose. Should he become the man's apprentice? That would end his need for begging and perhaps even sooth his sense of being alone. Certainly, selling expensive hookahs would also provide prosperity.

The greater question arose, this place or the new place? An immediate self lesson became clear that the stout man's offer did not hold the strength over what he knew he must do. He thought of the man who tried to convince his friend not to leave Jerusalem, and how the other man spoke of losing what might wait out there ahead of him if he stayed. The boy glanced around at all the hookahs. The idea of making beautifully artistic smoking pipes appealed to him as most of his life had been filled with ugliness.

The stout man tented his fingers in front of his face and paced back and forth.

37

"You did not merely
see the beauty you felt it."

W HEN HE STOPPED PACING he turned to the boy and in a low voice said, "I am alone, I have no son or family to continue my business," the man added.

Levi said, "You told me I have an eye for beauty?" He knew compliments were often tools adults used to get what they wanted.

The stout man replied, "But of course."

"How can you know that so quickly? You do not know me."

The stout man gently ran his fingers over various parts of the hookah. "Because art creates beauty, and those who perceive such beauty are unique, just as I said. You immediately were attracted to and studied my hookahs and your smile grew wide and your eyes smiled. I noticed that you caught a breath as their beauty called to you. These responses were natural, expressing your appreciation. You did not merely see the beauty you felt it. I need no further proof than what I have already observed," he instructed with his tone focused and serious.

The chalice warmed. He glanced down. No one had ever attached value to him. How strange, exciting and cautious all at the same time. Everything around him seemed to be unveiling things and people in unexpected ways. A very brief thought crossed his mind, how the Teacher had told him about being mindful of messages. He could not determine if this could be a message, but something told him to be cautious with his decision. After a long silence, he found it surprisingly difficult to say, realizing the stout man's sincerity and the fact that he too had no one. The realization seemed to strike the boy deeply. He was a beggar always looking for something to take to sustain himself. This, man on the other hand, sought to give something away. They were both alone in the world. He wanted to find a way not to respond, but the stout man waited patiently. Hoping he had made the right decision the boy finally spoke, "First I must find someone. It is important," he replied.

"Perhaps I can help. Who are you seeking?"

"The Teacher."

"Ah, I see. Then you will have to go to the synagogue. For that is where you will find the teachers. They teach the Law. This will be good for you and perhaps you can remain here and learn of these things as well as design hookahs," the stout man stated. "I will be right here waiting while you go to the teachers."

"They are not the teachers I seek."

"Who then?" quizzed the stout man.

Levi felt uneasy to answer because of the words the Teacher spoke about a new kingdom. Unsure what to say, he did not respond.

"Do you not know what teacher you are seeking? That will be like a donkey pulling a grinding stone . . . round and round in one big circle to nowhere," the stout man emphasized.

Following a long pause, the boy said, "I know who he is. I have seen him."

"What is this teacher's name?"

At first the boy debated telling him. "They called him Master and Rabbi, but I heard his name . . . Jesus!"

The stout man abruptly heaved back. His face conveyed concern. "Jesus? The one from Nazareth? He and some followers passed through here not long ago. In fact, as he passed through the gate of our city, a widow walked along in a funeral procession to bury her son, with mourners following behind. The people say that this Jesus stepped up to the coffin, touched it and her son revived to life. Nothing like this has ever occurred in our city. Ever!"

Incredulous, the boy nearly slurred out his words as he responded so fast, "He made a dead person live again?"

"The people claim a great prophet has risen among us. Our religious leaders have forbid us to accept such a thing. You must be careful of this man, my boy. There are things taking place that are not yet understood."

The boy could agree with things taking place that were not understood, but following the man's response he regretted sharing his intention. Standing, he adjusted himself, then with staff in hand said, "I must go. I will think about what you have offered."

"This is a large tent, colorful and easy to find. Why you can simply follow the aroma to my tobaccos to return," he said lightheartedly. "I will be here. And what may I ask is your name, boy?"

"I am Levi."

"Levi, I am Hyfa. I trust this journey holds your pearl," said the stout man.

"Pearl? What do you mean?"

"Something in your journey . . . it must hold great value . . . a pearl, you see?"

"I have seen pearls in the marketplace. The merchants guard them in their stalls."

"Yes because they hold great value. Do you know that pearls are the only gems that are formed within a living creature?"

Levi looked blank.

"True. Oysters produce pearls. This is perhaps what gives it such distinctive value."

"I will never have a pearl."

"Of course you will and *you do*," the stout man emphasized.

"How do I have a pearl when I do not?" Levi asked.

"The pearl is the value that leads you on your journey. Something compels you. It must hold great value for you since you have turned down my good offer. You see, there is something of greater value to you than my apprenticeship. Therein rests your pearl of great price."

On the spur of that moment, Levi remembered the Teacher's words over him in the upper room. He wanted those words to become his reality, that he would no longer be alone. Perhaps the man had opened a new window in his thinking. *A pearl of great price*, he pondered it.

After a few moments, the stout man walked out of the tent behind the boy. Once outside he told him of another bazaar in the City of Beit Shemesh, not far off. The boy bid the stout man goodbye, offering thanks and started off. He hadn't walked but a few feet away when the stout man called out to him.

"Levi, wait! Come back!"

Levi turned to see the man waving him back to the tent. Arriving at the tent the man told him to come back in. He moved about, gathering items. While he did so he said, "If you like, the apprentice position remains open should you return." He handed over several pieces of dried meat and a small flask of water. At that moment the chalice in his tunic warmed. No longer believing this to be coincidence he began to contemplate as he moved his hand into his tunic to touch the warmth. He walked out into the crowd of people, stopping once to look back at the stout man who continued watching, wondering what would become of the boy. As he walked away, Levi wondered what would become of the man's business. The words about the pearl rang in his thoughts. Could the new place be such a pearl?

He also wondered if he had made the right decision by leaving something that would take him off the street. Maybe it would be good to work with the man. In the same moment he sensed something bigger, an insight that told him his path could not lie behind him, but ahead. The new place above all things had to be new, and behind him lay nothing new. He continued walking through the crowd. Despite the stout man's kindness, he remained troubled about what he had said about the Teacher. The thought crossed his mind that what the old beggar said about an event that had taken place might have something to do with what the stout man said about the Teacher. The oddest thing confusing the boy surrounded on why people would be against the Teacher after he had helped them. A mother's son taken from death to life by the Teacher and the people turned away from his kindness. For a moment he once again held his belief that adults were not only self serving, but just like Zohara's daughters they would turn on you.

38

The old feeling of
being alone revisited him

LEVI WALKED ALONG WITH his thoughts rumbling over the stout man's offer to be his apprentice. The man's comment about his ability to see beauty at once felt foreign and welcoming. Realizing how much embracing consideration he'd given this notion, he thought it better and safer to reject the compliment as just another game of words. Concerned he would soften his feelings he told himself that the man needed an apprentice and he happened to come along. He assured himself that if it had been another boy he would have offered the same thing. Considering that the Teacher healed a dead boy, he wondered who the Teacher really was to accomplish such a thing. After continuing on he came to a large boulder with a smoothly accommodating natural groove running its length, so he sat against it to relax for a few moments. As he laid his head back against the stone, the old feeling of being alone revisited him. He couldn't help thinking exactly what he didn't want to think; that perhaps there were some good people in the world after all. Still, he feared believing it. Lifting his flask he sipped. Although thirsty, he knew enough to conserve since he had no idea where he would find provisions again and if he did, how to pay for them. The thought crossed his mind again, how the Teacher had sent his men out with no provisions yet they lacked nothing. Seemingly farfetched, yet now that he consciously thought about the fact, so far he too lacked nothing. Food, drink and a kindness had come to him without his effort. He would have to ask the Teacher about this and all the other happenings taking place. He again considered the stout man's report about the Teacher bringing a woman's son back to life.

Hearing that the religious leaders defamed the Teacher for doing such a great miracle annoyed him. He breathed out a long breath and dropped his hands on his lap which shifted the chalice in his tunic. Then it struck him . . . he had intended to make a closer examination of the chalice ever since his departure from Jerusalem. As his hand groped around inside the pocket to grasp it a droning call came, "Alms! A bit of kindness. Alms!"

Levi jolted in place, stood up and walked around to the opposite side of the bolder. There once again sat the old dirty beggar.

"You! I cannot give you any more money. Why are you bothering me?"

"What bothers you is not the issue," the old beggar stated.

"You are bothering me, nothing else."

"The hookahs bother you, boy. You turned down the man's apprenticeship not because you had to seek the Teacher as you told him."

"You are some kind of a magician, and have already tricked me out of my coins. What else are you here to take from me?"

"Nothing has been taken from you that you have not given away."

"You make more riddles. I have to go," the boy said as he straightened himself up.

"You have given your future to the landlord of the inn. Zohara has become the landlord of your beliefs."

Levi froze at this. Stunned, that this beggar also knew of Zohara and the inn.

"The man with the hookahs showed you have value and yet you chose to remain in the landlord's proclamation over you," the old beggar said. "Only days before you left Jerusalem Zohara became frustrated and upset with his daughters and he took it out on you; did he not? You allowed his words to become your words."

Levi sat back down, overwhelmed and confused. "How . . . can . . . you know these things?"

"I know he told you that as an orphan you were cursed and would likely die in the streets begging like most of the other child beggars. You now walk in the shadow of his words as you have accepted them into your belief. You believe you must live in that curse. This is why you departed the man's apprenticeship. You are not good enough for it that is what you believe."

Sitting there with his chin down against his chest, Levi did not respond.

The old beggar continued, "I tell you this; men die of abandoned hope more often than of starvation in the streets. If a man's hope is but a tiny ember he can recover, but if those embers are allowed to be snuffed out he will die spiritually and nothing remains. You believe you are alone and therefore nothing good can accompany you."

Levi could hardly see the old beggar for the tears blotting his eyes. "I do not know what to do. I have always been alone, and I fear what you told me . . . that an event has taken place that will—"

"Listen. Give heed to the chalice—you must continue your journey. There is only one thing to fear . . . not completing the journey to where you belong."

"It is a riddle," Levi said.

"No this is about determination. As I have spoken, when you learn of the event you must not lose confidence in what the Teacher spoke over you. You must become like a man in prayer."

"What does this mean, like a man in prayer?" Levi asked.

The old beggar looked to the sky then lowered his eyes to the boy. "When a man is in prayer he is no longer there when he stands. He is lifted to a new reality. He is present there while he is here. It is an intensity of focus."

Levi listened with great attention and trepidation. The old beggar's tone held deep sincerity. "When I come to learn of this event you are saying I must pray?"

"As in prayer you must focus with intensity on what the Teacher spoke over you. That will be the essence of you finding what is necessary to your life. Heed my words well."

Levi began to repeat in his head, *I must not lose confidence in what the Teacher spoke to me.* The boy disregarded that he did not fully understand it. He simply spoke the words in his mind. When he did so the chalice warmed.

As before, when the boy looked up to ask another question the old beggar had vanished. He sat back against the boulder and over the next few moments pondered as much as he could understand. The old beggar had been correct about Zohara's proclamation of the orphan's curse over him. He was also correct about him not accepting the stout man's words that valued him. Oh, he did mean what he said about needing to find the Teacher, but he also believed that the streets of begging tightly grasped his destiny. He wanted to be certain that he made the right decision with the stout man's offer. *'Give heed to the chalice as you go on.'* The old beggar's words sounded in his head as though muffling over the ideas about the apprenticeship. But the echoing words did not ease his growing trepidation regarding the event that he would learn about. He wished the beggar had just told him then and there. Then he wished the old beggar had never told him. He remained seated composing himself and sorting through all that was spoken.

39

"And it is not safe to be out here at night."

THE SOUND OF FOOTSTEPS accompanied voices echoed just beyond the boulder bringing the boy back to attention. He reached for the staff. The footsteps and voices grew louder and closer. He stood up silently behind the boulder with his back against it. In a moment a man, a woman and little girl passed nearby along the roadway. The woman carried an infant in her arms, wrapped in a small blanket with blue tassels dangling off. He wondered how much farther the City of Beit Shemesh might be so he stood up, walked at a quick pace and caught up to them. Courteously he asked if they knew how much farther the city might be?

Without stopping, the man called back, "At this pace just before nightfall. And it is not safe to be out here at night."

It's not safe to be anywhere, day or night, the boy thought. Then he noticed that the woman whispered something into the man's ear. They stopped walking and the man turned back saying, "You are welcome to walk along with us. Beit Shemesh is our home."

Surprised at the invitation he stepped forward. It happened again, the chalice warmed. He rested his hand on it from the outside and walked along quietly. As they walked, the little girl kept twisting her head back to look at him. Finally, she asked, "Where are his sheep, father?"

"Perhaps he's on the way to find some sheep in Beit Shemesh, besides this is not our concern."

Levi responded, "This staff was given to me as a gift." That was all he would say about it and he regretted responding at all. Proceeding further down the roadway, the little girl continued to glance back, curiously. He didn't want her to open up more questions about him. Slowly he stepped over to the side where the father walked, making it more difficult for the girl to see him.

After walking several miles they came up to the top of a steep incline, the man stopped and spoke again, "There!" he said, extending his arm forward, pointing down into the valley far below. Levi took in the view. This was no little town. Torch lamps were already sparkling across the view below as the vault of night closed in. The shimmering effect of the many light points over the city magnified the sense of space making the area look larger than it actually might be. The father gathered his wife and daughter to him and began to guide them toward the slope down when he realized the boy no longer followed along.

The father turned and called out, "This is the only direct path down into the city. The rest of the area is all cliffs."

"I need to do something first," said Levi, "thank you."

"As you wish. Be cautious, night is upon us." Then he turned back to his family, stretched his arm out carefully guiding their steps forward watching protectively over their every move. In a moment they were out of view. Levi had watched as the father carefully guided his family down the steep slope. He thought about the little girl and the infant, how they were not alone and they were cared for. The boy could not fathom how such a life could feel. The chalice warmed. He placed his hand on it, and sat down to overlook the glimmer of lights from torches and fire pits that lit the streets. Darkness made it difficult to make anyone out. Only the moving lights gave them away.

Although he fended off dwelling on the caring he'd just witnessed, the act did impact him. He turned his thinking over to consider his situation. And at that moment it did not look very promising. *I'm not sure why I'm here anymore, or what to do next.* He concluded at this point that he hadn't the slightest idea where to look for the Teacher or where he would find the new place, something he forced himself not to admit until now. So many things happened to him in such a short time. For some reason he wasn't ready to walk down into the city. The array of lights and the dark and the uncertainty held him in place. This journey walked him farther and farther away from Jerusalem, a place he knew well. Looking over the city below the reality struck him, too far to turn back and too far away from the Teacher and the new place not too continue. In his heart he knew going back could not be his future.

Recalling the man's warning about this area being dangerous at night, he began searching for a place to stay as the sky had darkened to black. Not far off appeared to be a somewhat sharp upward incline. In the darkness he couldn't tell if it was the side of a hill or some kind of a structure. It seemed to be moving and carried the sound of rustling. Cautiously he moved up the incline toward it.

As he approached his eyes adjusted to the darkness. Ahead of him appeared to be an entire wall of wild grapes; thick vines overgrown as though someone once abandoned them. They rustled as they moved with the gusts of wind. He reached out to touch the vines. Poking his hand in hoping to find an open section where he might be able to crawl in behind the vines. His hand hit a wall. As he moved along the vines poking his hand in at random his arm moved farther into the vines up to his shoulder. His hand searched what turned out to an inset section in the wall behind the vines. The boy used his strong arms with the staff to wrangle aside the vine branches. Then, with considerable effort, he wrestled his body through the opening where he found a perfect sized open area.

With the moon's glow he noticed several holes carved into the wall behind him. It appeared to have once been part of fixture of some type. Perhaps an irrigation system. The boy swept away the small branches and debris from the ground with his hands, leaving a fairly smooth place to sit. Nestled in fairly comfortably the vines provided a curtain to hide his presence and it blocked the wind that had kicked up. Methodically he shifted some of the vine branches back in place rearranging them to close up the gap. Leaning back against the wall he let out a long breath and sat. Lifting the water flask he finished the remaining water that the stout man gave him. One piece of bread remained which he decided to leave for morning breakfast. He thought again about what he was doing here and why. Since he had never traveled out of Jerusalem, he no longer had any idea of his geographic location. As he laid his staff across his legs he thought about the stout man's comments regarding his talent for seeing beauty. With that he rotated his staff until the carved markings showed. Due to the darkness he could not see much so he ran his fingers over the carved images realizing he had never really appreciated or studied the beauty of the carvings cut into the staff. Nor had he truly appreciated the gift of the staff given by the shepherd that fateful day. The staff had become a companion of sorts. His eyes drifted as his last thoughts reflected back to the day he had been in the pasture to help the shepherd's son; the event that resulted in his receiving the staff. He thought kindly of the shepherd and the boy and how he could have remained with them following the incident. As he pondered that day he now could not recall a single reason why he did not remain with them. Strange, he thought, about the way he had made many decisions and now wondered how many were poor ones. Then as abruptly as an extinguished candle he fell asleep before his thoughts could continue.

40

The vines had come alive with birds

THE BOY AWOKE WITH a start, not remembering where he was for a moment. Birds chirped loudly above his head. The vines had come alive with birds. As he rubbed his face to awaken, he heard what he thought to be trickling water. Shifting his body left he suddenly felt wetness under him. Quickly shifting over he looked to find water dripping from the holes in the wall behind him. His eyes followed the trail of water down a slight inclined gully under him, none of which he could see last night. Birds were now poking their beaks in under the vines, pecking at the water. He dipped his finger into the hole and touched the water to his tongue. Extremely cold and fresh. He washed his face, caught some in his cupped hands and drank deeply. Then he lifted his flask letting the water drip into it. Once he closed the flask he felt the chalice warm again. As always, he held his hand on the warmth until it dissipated. Now with bright morning light he decided to look at this mystery for himself. Reaching into his tunic he twisted and turned the chalice until he finally worked it out of the lined pocket in his tunic. Rays of light beamed in through the vine openings giving him a clear view and making for a beautiful presentation. The chalice had been fashioned in a simple clay design. He found nothing unique about it. No gold filling or trim. No precious gems. He'd seen many like it, just another ordinary cup, but he knew it to be far from ordinary. How it warmed at certain times remained puzzling. He had observed many magicians in the marketplace. They could make things disappear before your eyes. He always knew magic to be trickery, making it untrustworthy. With that notion he dismissed magic as having anything to do with the chalice.

He turned it over in his hands. Felt all around it, looked under it and even smelled it. He thought back to the times he felt its warmth. As he reconsidered the events, a pattern seemed to solidify. Each time he did something kind or something helpful came to him, the chalice warmed. He recalled the first occurrence when he helped Metha by sharing his secret about the inn. Having observed the washing of feet perked his attention to the idea that doing for others in some mysterious way translated to doing for oneself as well. He couldn't be absolutely certain about that and he wasn't even sure if it only played in his imagination. He worried that he might not ever understand why the Teacher gave him the chalice and miss something important to do with the messages he should heed. He recalled his first look into it when he removed it from the table in the upper room, feeling uneasy that there might be blood in it. It seemed to him that the Teacher told the men his blood held some covenant something got placed in the cup when he passed it to them. But there was no blood when he swallowed barely a mouthful. The small amount of wine hardly filled his mouth. Holding the chalice the boy recalled Jesus' hands holding it as he placed it on the table before him and noticed the roughness of his skin. The hands appeared very strong. Feeling an unexpected but welcoming confidence he assured himself that he would keep on going. *Somehow I will learn about these things that are happening. I have traveled all this way.*

Life had been difficult every single step of the way, and he knew better than expect too much from anything, as it always led to disappointments. To him the world remained a place of hard reality yet deep inside he heard another logic: *I will find the Teacher and his men. Then I will no longer be alone in the new place.* He encouraged himself with this thought. What other choice did he have? Jerusalem remained back there somewhere.

41

He had much to reconsider

A S THE MORNING LIFTED the sun up, Levi cautiously peered out from the vines checking to see if anyone might be out there. Other than a cacophony of birds everything appeared at peace until a hawk flew over the vines causing many of the smaller birds to take flight. Wrestling his way out between the thick vines presented as much of a challenge as when he had entered. No easy task. Back on the outside he adjusted his tunic, pushed the chalice back down into the interior pocket and tied on his water flask. He brushed the vine leaves off his clothing and his hair.

Grasping the staff, he walked and reached into the small pouch removing the last piece of bread the stout man provided. As he took a small bite his foot stepped into a small depression which knocked him off balance, but he caught himself. The remainder of the bread shot out of his hand. No sooner did it hit the ground when several small birds zoomed down and ripped it apart, all flying away with small bits. Staring at this for a moment it occurred how the bread that had been given to him to fill his stomach had become sustenance for the birds. He could almost hear the Teacher reminding the men how he had sent them out with no provisions and yet they were cared for. Now this caught the boy's amazement in no small way. Reluctantly he pondered the notion that the Teacher and his men actually might be part of something much larger than he originally imagined. He started down the hill along the same path the man and his family followed the night before.

Entering Beit Shemesh, the city brimmed with people and animals. He focused himself on staying alert in hopes of learning if the Teacher could be in the city or if someone knew of his location. He hoped that his good fortune in finding the wall of vines, the fresh water, and the stout man would continue. Normally he wouldn't allow himself to count on something like that.

He arrived at a place in his thoughts where he could see things affecting him that were not physical. The men in the upper room had been sent out on journeys with no provisions and were cared for. He had much to reconsider.

Already many traders and merchants were setting up their booths and wares in open-air locations. Some of the sellers constructed overhanging fabrics to provide protection from the sun. The wide assortment of products, rugs, vegetables, olive oils, and meats amazed him. He walked by artisans selling wood carvings, rugs, and jewelry. There were polishers of metal at work, a man selling hides and another in a corral with camels for sale. The area bordered by workshops, with what appeared to be residences scattered in between. This marketplace mirrored the first one where he encountered the stout man, only much larger in scope. Walking slowly he studied the transactions taking place between buyers and sellers. Occasionally he would stop and step in close enough to hear and observe the negotiations. In one booth filled with large carpets, the seller invited the buyer to sit down. The seller offered tea to the buyer while they bantered about the price of the carpet. He knew this interaction to be important because he often heard shopkeepers in Jerusalem say that making the very first sale of the day for the right price set the tone of good luck for the remainder of their day.

As he continued on he observed the wide variety of merchant tents, and noticed a group of men just ahead. Even from a distance he heard them speaking with great excitement, hands gesturing in the air as they spoke. This drew his attention. Following that notion he walked up to the group just close enough to be able to hear their conversation

Two men stood in front of a group of four men and a woman as they spoke. The taller of the two men wore a purple sash that ran across his shoulder and down around his waist. He was the one speaking. Levi listened.

"Yes I say again, it is true. Jesus walked along the road with us just as I have recounted for you. It is true," said the man in the purple sash. His voice determined.

Levi heard the name, Jesus spoken as clearly as a bell ringing which caused him to step closer. In a moment the man ended his talk and the group agreed to follow the man's instructions and then departed. The man in the purple sash and his companion walked off. Levi followed. After a short distance he could wait no longer. He caught up to the men and asked. "I heard you speak of the Teacher." Then he corrected by saying, "I heard you speak about Jesus."

"You did indeed, boy," said the man in the purple sash. "Why do you ask?"

"I have been traveling trying to find him and his men. Can you tell me where he is?"

The man in the purple sash looked at his companion regretfully. Then he looked down at Levi. He stared at the boy for a long moment as though gathering his thoughts. "Do you live here in Beit Shemesh?"

"No, I am here to find Jesus, the Teacher."

The man could see how the boy responded with great earnest and sincerity. He rubbed his forehead with both hands. "Let us move to the side over there so we can talk in less activity."

Levi followed behind the two men, remaining cautious.

"I see you have no knowledge of what has happened over the past days in Jerusalem. I am Cleopas, and this is Asher. We are disciples of Jesus."

"I did not see you in the upper room during the supper," Levi said.

Cleopas asked, "What do you mean?"

"I was in the upper room of the inn. I saw twelve men, but I did not see either of you."

Asher asked, "What do you mean, you were in the room? You were at the Lord's Passover supper?"

"I help clean that room for the landlord and I . . . I was not supposed to be there when the supper took place so I hid under a cabinet. After they finished eating the Teacher spoke with me. I need to find him."

"Who is the teacher you speak of?" Cleopas asked for clarification.

"Jesus. I have called him Teacher because everything he spoke to them held a teaching lesson."

"I see," said Cleopas, "You say he spoke with you in the upper room?"

"Yes, he was kind and told me something important about my life. I want to follow him but I have not found him yet or his men. Will you tell me where he is?"

42

"When you learn of the event you must not lose confidence."

A LTHOUGH HE KNEW THE news would affect the boy, he had to tell him the truth. Cleopas inhaled deeply and said it. "Jesus and two others were crucified on Mt. Calvary."

Levi's eyes glossed over. His mouth fell open. His knees buckled, dropping him to the ground. He could not believe what he heard. *But how can that be? He said he would not leave us as orphans . . . he said he would start a new kingdom.*

The boy broke down and wept in severity. For the first time in his life he found himself weeping for someone else. *How could it be? What did it mean? What will I do now?* There was a deep ache in his chest. His eyes dimmed with utter loss.

The two men allowed him time to release his sadness and deal with the obvious shocking news.

Levi clearly heard the words of the old beggar echo. '*When you learn of the event you must not lose confidence in what the Teacher spoke over you.*' He tried hard to compose himself and focus on what the old beggar warned him about. This, the boy knew was that event. Otherwise what would he have left? What value would his journey now hold? Stirring himself, he stood up.

"What happened? He asked."

"They held a trial and they condemned him to death on a cross along with a criminal and a zealot."

"What is a zealot?"

"A fanatic who believes in something so deeply that he militantly opposes Rome," Asher said.

"However," Cleopas added quickly, "there is also good news, boy."

Levi's head hung down. "What can be good if he is gone from us?"

"He is alive. Jesus is alive," Cleopas said with overflowing joy.

Levi looked at Cleopas, "You said he was crucified; how can he be alive?"

"Yes. But he told us, his disciples, that he would be raised from the dead. And he has done so!"

The first thoughts that ran through Levi's head were, *more riddles.*

Cleopas continued, "I have seen him myself and so have others."

"I do not understand."

"What is your name?" Cleopas asked.

"I am Levi."

"Levi, I only know this certainty, Jesus is alive."

"When did you see the Teacher?" Levi asked.

"After his death I was walking the road with my wife Mary going to Emmaus. We were talking about all the things which had taken place. A man approached and walked along with us. He overheard us speaking about Jesus, and asked what we were talking about. His question caused us to stop walking. After all, who could not have heard of this shocking event? How the chief priests and rulers delivered him to the sentence of death."

"Yes," added Asher, "and we were all dismayed at this. But, as Cleopas has said, he is appearing to many people. Some women among us were at the tomb, and did not find his body. They told us that they had also seen a vision of angels who said that he was alive."

Levi looked puzzled. "You saw him yourself?"

"I did. I shall finish the story because it is important, which is why we are here in Beit Shemesh to tell others about these events so they may believe and rejoice along with us. Now back to the man who walked with us. He startled us as he taught. Beginning with Moses and the prophets he spoke of events from the scriptures showing us of his coming foretold. Mary and I were amazed at his teachings. Our hearts burned within us as we listened. When we came to Emmaus, he decided to take his leave, but we urged him to stay with us as the day was nearly over. Once at the table in our home he took bread and broke it. As he passed it to us our eyes were suddenly opened, and we recognized him, and how we rejoiced. Jesus had been with us all along!" Cleopas proclaimed this with great joy and animated movement.

With renewed excitement Levi expectantly said, "Then I can go to him?"

Cleopas quickly confirmed, "I cannot give you a location. As I have said, he is appearing to people in various places."

A graying tone of discouragement fell over the boy's face.

With that Cleopas dropped onto one knee to look at the boy. "Do not be troubled Levi. Hold this in your heart. Jesus is very likely to find *you* instead of you finding him. Since he spoke with you in the upper room, he may well appear to you. I am certain that the best way to expect to find him . . . is believe he will find you."

"How will he know how to find me?"

"There are many happenings we do not yet understand. Not everything real is in physical form. There is another realm and Jesus now functions in that mystery. I assure you, he will have no trouble finding you . . . after all, he found us," Cleopas stated with a firm confidence.

43

Something much bigger had been taking place than he could know

DESPITE HIS TRYING TO process the news, Levi accepted the counsel from Cleopas. *The Teacher held enough power to bring a dead boy to life, surely he holds enough power to find me.* He also thought again about the warning of the old beggar about what would happen to him upon learning of the event. Cleopas confirmed that message. It was becoming clearer to the boy that something much bigger had been taking place than he could know.

"Can you believe in what I've told you?" Cleopas asked Levi.

Levi nodded.

"Asher and I will be traveling to another city tomorrow to share the good news. You are welcome to accompany us. Think about it, and if you want to come along, we will meet you right back here in the morning," Cleopas said. "Are you going to be all right?" Cleopas asked the boy.

"Maybe I should go back to Jerusalem." He could hardly believe he'd said that.

"If you do, you will find Peter and the other disciples there. They can tell you more. Remain firm Levi, great things are taking place. Again, we will be here in the morning should you decide to join us." said Cleopas. The two men departed. As they walked away they looked back several times to see Levi.

With elbows on his knees gazing at the ground the boy worked at clearing his mind. The old beggar's warning rang true. In learning of this event, he did feel an urge to give up. The greatest shadow overcoming him formed as despair. Could everything he sought after be lost now that these things had taken place? Would there still be a new place to find? Would he still be alone? Were the Teacher's disciples going to separate? Who would lead them without the Teacher? His confusion above all, rested up a conflicting thought, the Teacher had died; the Teacher had not died. Could both be true? Recalling how Jesus stood in the upper room with him and in a moment disappeared completely. Yes he did both. Whatever his power it could do both, he thought. The chalice warmed at the same moment. In some unexplainable way, he suddenly considered that the Teacher might be controlling the chalice. He had no way to know that, but decided to believe it. The Teacher held some other form of power. If he could bring himself back to life, he could control the chalice and do things beyond the physical. Although he found this decision to be difficult against what he could see and feel, he knew his thinking had to shift. How could he ever accept what the Teacher spoke over him in the upper room if he didn't? Standing up he began his walk into the town square.

44

"You have cheated this man's barley weight."

THE BOY WALKED ON. His sense of finding the Teacher became different. He gained some tentative confidence in what Cleopas said about the Teacher finding him. This carried some practicality. Not that he intended to stop looking; it made sense that he would now be looking in a different way. The Teacher's men were also important for him to find.

Just ahead of him walked an older man with a leashed dog. His beard long and pointed, his head bald. The bald man moved with more of a tight shuffle than walking in normal gated steps, and he did so methodically, slowly and carefully.

The man did not wear a shawl indicating he was blind, but it seemed obvious that the man could not see very well. The man appeared to be talking to his dog. Levi became intrigued by this so he stopped and observed as the man and his dog finally moved into a seller's booth. Stepping in closer, behind the bald man he pretended to be looking at the bags of barley and other grains for sale. The bald man asked the seller for a bag of barley at a certain weight. The seller reached back for a small woven bag. He placed the bag on his scales, as he spoke to the man. The boy quickly observed that the seller watched the bald man's eyes, realizing his vision to be impaired. Then the seller scooped up some barley and poured it into the bag on the scale. After a quick glance around, he lifted off the weight already positioned on the scale and placed it behind him, pulling out another weight. He placed the new weight on the scale and announced a fabricated weight and correlating price. The seller changed the metal weight in order to charge the man for greater value than the barley actually weighed. Anyone with good eyes would have quickly noticed the injustice, but the bald man could not.

Without a second thought and at great surprise to himself, Levi spoke to the seller, "You have cheated this man's barley weight." With that outburst he immediately shrunk back, stunned that he would say any such thing.

The seller's eyes bulged and he said sternly, "Leave my shop, are you trying to discredit me and perhaps steal from me, boy?"

"Just one moment, shopkeeper," said the bald man, "what have you done?" The tenseness of the bald man's voice caused his dog to begin barking, and people were beginning to look over to see the commotion taking place.

The seller could not afford to invite trouble so he took immediate action. "There has been some mistake here. I do not wish to do business with you and your boy. Please leave my shop."

"He is not my boy, but I am grateful for his courage. You would have taken advantage of me because of my poor sight. I should report you to the officials, and perhaps I will, but in either case your own sin will find you out." The man tugged the dog's leash and started out of the booth. "Are you behind me, boy?"

"I'm over here."

"Walk with me then."

As he walked with the man the dog pushed his nose against Levi.

"My dog likes you. This is a good sign to me. Tell me, I must know . . . why did you speak up about the false weights?"

He wasn't really sure why. "I saw him change the weights and I just said it. Only a few days ago a man accused me of being a thief in another marketplace. He falsely accused me. I didn't like how that made me feel."

"What happened?"

"I ran away from the Roman Guard he called and lied to about me. I didn't want to be punished for something I didn't do."

They walked a little farther and the man said, "You do not come from Beit Shemesh."

"No. But this is a large city. I saw it from the top of the hill last night."

"Why have you come here and why are you alone?" The man stopped walking and his dog sat at attention still nosing the boy.

"I am seeking . . ." For the first time since he started his journey, he was not sure what the answer should be, "the new place."

"What is this new place? How will you know when you have found it?"

Levi replied, "I will know when I find the Teacher who is there."

"Who is this teacher?"

"You will not know who he is."

"Hmmm," the man said, "perhaps you are right. Beit Shemesh is large city with many people." The man gestured with his hand, "My house is just ahead, I would like you to come and visit. We shall have something to eat." Once again the boy felt amazement at another kind offer.

When they arrived at the house, the bald man stepped up the few stairs carefully. He removed his sandals, placing them to one side, and washed his feet. The dog sat quietly next to them. Levi removed his sandals and did the same, then followed the man into the house. In his mind's eye he immediately recalled Jesus washing his men's feet. The man's home was small and neat, orderly piles of different items were positioned all around the room. A short woman busied herself doing chores. The man told his wife what had taken place. She turned to smile at the boy then went about doing her work.

45

"Can you not see that God used you as my eyes today?"

"WHY DID YOU NOT turn in the shop keeper?" Levi asked.

"Mercy."

"But he had no mercy on you. He took advantage of you because of your poor sight."

"God sees for me."

"God sees for you?" Levi repeated with a cynical tone.

The man laughed. "Can you not see that he used you as my eyes today?"

As he scuffled around, the man asked his wife to bring some food. She gathered a basket of bread and fruits, and a small jar of wine, then placed them down on the small table. Once she turned and moved back across the room, Levi asked, exuding a certain cynicism, "God used *my* eyes?"

The man slid the bowl of food in front of the boy, then he rubbed his chin in thought and said, "It is written, that one must have accurate and honest weights and measures in business, so that one may live long in the land. You observed the change in his weights." The man glanced up then down, "From heaven to your eyes, to the shop keeper. So you see then, God is present everywhere my boy. He called on you today to use your young eyes to see in place of my old eyes," the man said smiling widely.

Levi bit into the fruit enjoying the sweet flavor of the juice flooding his mouth. Using the back of his hand he wiped the cool juices from his chin. No one had ever told him God would use him. And if he did, he somehow entered into the physical world, specifically in him. But at the same time, it occurred to him that this was an old, lonely man with dimming eyes and a dog. He concluded it to be an old man's tale. "What happened to your eyes?" he asked the man.

"I am uncertain except that it happened over time. Still, I am grateful I see well enough to carefully walk about. I have also come to know that there are many people whose eyes are wide open, yet they cannot see. They are blind."

"How are they blind?" the boy wondered.

"Take the shopkeeper . . . he is blind to what is just. What he sees is greed which is a wall in his life that he is unable to see beyond. But worse, he believes no one sees his dishonesty, but God sees it."

"I have seen many people who are hurt, and treated like dogs. Why doesn't God see them?"

"He does see them, boy. What you really wish to ask is why God allows these things?"

"Yes," he replied, boldly. "Why would God let bad things happen?"

"But that is the wrong question," the man stated as a matter of fact. "The right question is always more valuable than the answer."

Levi wrinkled his face wondering what that meant.

"Here is the right question . . . why should God do what men are charged to do? We have tradition, we have examples, we have scriptures of the forefathers, and we have laws, and we have and we have and we have, and yet men allow evil to persist and often participate in it. One must stand as a barrier against evil. Do you know that Beth Shemesh was placed here as a barrier between Israel and the Philistines? We had to protect ourselves against the Philistines who threatened our people. Our fathers built up the city giving it the means to withstand attack, and we have survived. Great men such as Samson were here."

"Samson? I have heard men mention him in the marketplace . . . the strongest of all men."

"Strong? Samson had been given supernatural strength by God in or-der to combat his enemies and perform heroic feats. He destroyed an entire army with only the jawbone of an ass. He stood against evil as a barrier."

"But why does God let evil and pain come?"

"Ah, here again consider the right question to ask. God is not the one allowing these things to happen . . . people are."

Levi's face formed incredulous. Never had a proclamation filled his ears with such a great impact. The man's dog began barking. The man asked Levi to open the door, and bring his dog into the house. The sun had grown hotter outside. The dog entered, immediately snuggled right up to Levi, placing his head on his lap. Levi petted its head vigorously.

The old man smiled. "He has always been a good judge of character."

At that, another compliment, the boy felt a pang of guilt. He had been called many names in his short life, but never one associated with good character. He lowered his head, "I am just an orphan and a beggar . . . I have always been alone." The words spilled out as though confessing to a crime.

The old man pursed his lips. "Well, consider this. If someone is watching you, you are not alone."

"Someone is watching me?" said the boy incredulous.

"Of course," the old man stated emphatically.

"Who is watching me?"

"Why, heaven, of course." He threw his hands in the air.

The boy didn't have to say he was confused, his face confirmed it.

"You were used today in the barley seller's tent. For that to happen, someone had to be watching you. If someone is watching you, then you cannot be alone."

Levi thought a moment. "Something I cannot see is not practical."

"Of course it is practical, boy. You saved me and others from being cheated today. That is practical . . . very practical."

"Food and shelter . . . *that* helps orphans. *That* is practical."

The man's eyes grew sad. Reaching over with his hand he lifted Levi's face up. "An orphan you say?" He pondered for a moment then stood up and paced. "Listen to me. Begging is something you do. It is not who you are. An orphan is something that happened to you, it is not who you are. Alone? Your body may walk alone, but you are never alone." He pursed his lips then added, "Abide by this carefully, you must understand that all men are at one time or another, alone. Orphans."

Levi's ears perked up at that, eyebrows arched on an attentive face.

"When a man loses his parents, he becomes an orphan no matter what his age. When his children go off to marriage and their own future, he becomes an orphan. When a man rejects God, he becomes an orphan."

46

"I will tell you this now."

L EVI NEVER IMAGINED SUCH things. It seemed at least for the moment to help him consider the lesson. Never had he thought of separating himself from what he did or what happened to him. However he remained puzzled by the man's words about his body being alone. So he asked, "You say my body is alone? I do not understand this."

"Each of us are hidden in our own bodies. Our bodies are separate from other bodies. What propels the body is greater than the body. The heart of a man controls him. The heart is not alone. You experienced that today."

"I did?" Levi said.

"Yes, as I explained, God used your eyes on my behalf. If you were truly alone, how would God know where you were? These are matters you must take hold of. Never have you considered such things, have you, boy?"

His face blanched, still processing what had been said. He could only shake his head no. They both remained quiet for a time. Levi gave his attention to petting the dog.

"I tell you this, that when you lose something, your sight for instance, you begin to value all that is left with more appreciation." Folding his arms he continued. "I will tell you this now. You are just a boy yet I believe you can understand what I am going to say to you. Remember it well that my words will remain with you. You are not meant to live through the eyes of others, because then the world will appear to you just as others present it. You will spend your life living in their view of the world rather than what God has created as true." Glancing down he could see the boy pondering. "This means you do not live your life nor identify yourself by other people's opinions, what they believe about you, the stares, the words and attitudes they portray. You see, their perception must not be your truth."

The boy did not respond. But his eyes and ears absorbed it all in.

"You are startled at that, I see," said the man.

Levi replied in a mild stutter. "Other people . . . have always told me . . . what I am. I have always told myself what I am."

"And, both are incorrect," the man pronounced.

Such thoughts had never occurred to the boy, but what the man said rang true.

"You understand now why I said being an orphan is something that happened to you, and begging alms is something you do? These are external to you as a person. Let me ask you, have you ever considered what things you have done to help someone?" The bald man leaned in, "Surely you have made some attempt to help another person!"

Help someone? His life consisted of nothing but self help. Trying to recall something Levi squinted his eyes. After a moment he blurted out, "I helped Metha and . . . and a small dog." His body swayed as though suddenly ashamed at only naming two events to the man, one being a dog.

"Ah, but you have not counted me today in the marketplace, although you do not need to provide a list. It is not how many things you have done; it is the intention of that kindness that matters. Whatever you have done, these are the caring acts that you should dwell on; what comes from your heart and not from the words of others."

"You hold much knowledge," Levi said.

"Wisdom!" said the bald man. "This is the wisdom which comes from heaven. And so it is with you."

Levi sensed another riddle forming. His face conveyed it.

"You do not believe this? Well, then how do you explain the fact that you are so young and have been a beggar in the streets, and yet you are alive and have the ability to care for yourself. Does that not require wisdom?"

Levi shrugged.

"Knowledge applied well . . . that is wisdom. You must have applied certain knowledge well to live on the streets. Do not be confused by the word, wisdom, consider its practicality. Do you see what I am saying?" The man probed.

He did see. The explanation held. He accepted it. "I have never known that. I only thought about surviving."

"And you have, because God gave you these abilities. That which you cannot see is often more real than that which you can see."

At that Levi considered the chalice and how it warmed. Yes, he could accept this and he did. The man's lesson fostered a new expectation. He could not doubt that did happen to him. He would need to think on these things more carefully now.

"I need to go find the new place that the Teacher spoke of. Then I will learn more of these things," said Levi.

"If only my eyes were clear, I might have knowledge of many more people, and could have guided you to this new place. Alas, I am not so young anymore. Yet I feel deeply that you will find it if you do not give up. I wish to help you on your journey." With that the man rose from the table and walked over to his wife, quietly saying something to her. A moment later she came to the table with a cache of bread, fruit and vegetables and a jar of pomegranate juice. She smiled at Levi, brushed her hand across his face with a gentle touch then placed the items on the table. The man had stepped into another room. At length he returned sitting down again. Reaching over he took Levi's hand and turned it over so his palm faced up. The man's hand hovered over it. His thumb and index fingers held two coins that he placed onto Levi's palm.

"A deserved reward," is all he said.

The moment the coins touched his palm, the chalice warmed, more intensely than in the past. He reflexively glanced down to his side where the warmth pulsed then turned back to view his palm, stunned at the sight, recalling him back to when he had made the very same movements with his hands in giving his coins to the old beggar at the first encounter. He did not toss the coins on the beggar's cloth, but instead he placed them into his open palm.

If this had happened a few days ago, he would have clamped his hand shut and ran off before the giver of the alms changed his mind. Today he found himself glancing up at the man saying something he would have never ever thought to utter, "This is a great deal of money. I could not have saved you this much from the shopkeeper with false scales."

Tipping his head the man said, "You are considering only what you saved for me alone. However, your action affects other buyers who trade there today and likely the next few days as well. So actually, you have saved much more than I have given you."

Puzzled, he asked, "How can you know the seller isn't cheating more buyers after we left?"

"Well," said the man, "the shopkeeper does not yet know if I turned him into the synagogue officials or not. Therefore, he will be certain to conduct business honestly, at least for a few days in case the officials visit his booth with other witnesses. Your courage has done well." The man leaned over and stroked his dog's head. "As I said, my dog knows people of good character," he smiled broadly.

47

"Stop my hand when it points to a mountain."

"**I** WONDER HOW MANY PEOPLE that man will cheat after he knows you have not turned him in."

The man chuckled, "That, my boy is a matter for God. Just as he saw fit to see through your eyes today, another person will come, and he will also see. But all these things are matters of heaven, not for simple men as we."

Surely there was a time when Levi would have stuffed his ears with sheep's wool to silence all the talk about God, and fairness and heaven and caring adults from which he had been abandoned. Yet he acknowledged what the man said. Levi began to feel things that were never apparent before, and he realized something unusual and surprising about himself, he was smiling inside.

Levi stood up from the table, collected the food, the jar and walked toward the door. The man walked behind him. Outside the house, he strapped his sandals on. When the boy looked at the man, he saw sadness in his eyes which caused him to be unsure how to act at that moment. He recalled the sadness of the shepherd who carved him the staff when he departed from there. He didn't know how to feel or what to say either.

Sensing this, the man lightened the moment saying, "You would do well to get a dog. You will have good companionship as you travel."

The boy kneeled, vigorously petting the man's dog. He expressed his gratefulness for the lessons and provisions. He turned to step off the porch.

The man said, "You know what I am thinking," the man said. "I am thinking you may find this new place and the teacher you seek in Jerusalem, the great city. There you will find the Temple and you will see The Gate

Beautiful. This you should do. In Jerusalem are many teachers who may help you."

Jerusalem, he thought, *just where I said I would never return.* Regardless of his self-annoyance at this he understood what must be done especially if Jesus' men where there as the man in the purple sash had said. Since he had no idea of his geographic location, he asked, "What is the way there?"

The man pointed with his arm outstretched and slowly swept in a half circle. "Stop my hand when it points to a mountain."

"There," the boy called out, stopping the man's arm.

Holding his arm out in place he said, "Do you see that mountain? Go there. As you go up you will see a clear path leading further up to the mountain. Follow that path until you arrive at a fork in the passage along the way. A very large boulder rests there. You will see a large grove of trees. This is important." The man now spoke in an ominous tone. "You must not continue straight . . . you must turn to the left path and continue. You will have to journey the long way to Jerusalem. Shalom," the man said, and then stepped back into his house.

"Wait," Levi called out.

"Yes?" The man stopped and turned back to face the boy.

"If there is a long way and a shorter way, why would I not take the shorter way?"

The man gestured, "Come sit." They both sat on the steps together.

"I realize you are young and there is much for you to learn. You cannot travel the short journey to Jerusalem because it will take you through Samaria. The Pharisees do not permit us to pass through Samaria so follow the longer route through Peraea."

"Why?" Levi asked, somewhat perplexed at the notion of going the long way. It made no sense.

"You will one day come to know . . . the Jews must avoid contact with Samaritans. You see, they built a rival temple on Mount Gerizim. There is too much to tell in one sitting but remember this saying." The man closed his eyes as though calling up something once memorized. "He who eats the bread of a Samaritan is as he who eats a swine's flesh." His voice became like a knife cutting through air before him. Levi had witnessed grown men fight each violently other over less insulting words than this. His astonishment lay in the perplexity that the man could be so generous and kind to him, and speak of God and justice in the marketplace and yet express so deep a hatred. He stood up and again thanked the man as he departed. *I never thought I would go back to Jerusalem.* He heard an echo of the man's dog barking as he made his way from the house toward the mountain.

48

"Nonetheless, we are both paralyzed, boy."

P ASSING OUT OF THE city walking along the path leading up the mountain, Levi finally arrived at the thick grove of trees and the large boulder where the man said not to continue through Samaria. At the moment the grove of trees offered appealing shade from the sun. Walking over to the largest tree, he sat down with his back against the trunk. He drank from the jar. Then he let his body relax. Just as his eyes began to rest he heard a voice calling.

"Alms! Alms, for the poor!" the voice called out again.

He recognized the voice, turned his head to listen while coming to his knees. He stood, grasped his staff and slowly moved away from the tree, looking toward the sound of the voice. Walking a few steps forward and around a boulder he stopped in his tracks, shocked to see the same old beggar. His vibrant eyes and old body gave him away immediately. There he sat on a pallet as before.

"You! How . . . how can you be here?" he asked stunned.

"Why should I not be here?" The beggar replied, "You are here!"

Levi shook his head, "Why would anyone seek alms all the way up here? When I begged in the busy streets of Jerusalem, there were many people there and hardly did I receive any money. In this place." Levi swung his arms as though presenting the grove of trees. "You will collect nothing. I cannot help you . . . I already gave you the last coins I had."

The old beggar adjusted himself on the pallet. "You ask how a crippled old beggar could be in the same far-off place at the same time as you?"

"This has been a difficult journey for me, and I can walk" Levi said.

"I have a pallet, do I not?" the beggar replied in a confident tone.

Levi stepped closer, "You cannot carry yourself on your own pallet." He said it adamantly.

The beggar replied, "And you cannot carry yourself on yours, either."

Wiggling his legs, almost annoyed, Levi reacted with, "You can see that I have legs."

"Nonetheless, we are both paralyzed, boy."

Levi stepped back, adjusted his head covering and said sternly, "This is wasting my time old man. I have no time for your riddles and disappearing tricks."

"No riddles, boy. I speak truth. You are as crippled as I. Your mind, just as my legs, cannot carry you forward. The distrust, the abandonment prevents you from moving. Oh, indeed, your legs carry you here and there, and yet you go nowhere. Every new place you find is nothing more than the old place in a new place. It is not a man's legs that give him freedom, it is his heart."

"Tell me who . . . or what you really are. I can see that your body is old, wrinkled and worn, but your eyes do not belong in that body. Even I can see that."

"I answered when you first asked, I am but a messenger. Did I not speak to you of the event to take place?"

Levi said, "Yes, and the Teacher has died and yet lives. I do not understand any of this," Levi said, murmuring under his breath and childishly stomping his foot as he started walking away.

"What then has the chalice told you?"

The words immediately stopped Levi causing him to turn back to the old beggar, speechless and clearly shaken.

"Tell me who you are. You hold the trickery of a magician . . . you are no beggar."

"I am a messenger."

"You speak in riddles."

"What has the chalice told you, Levi?" The beggar spoke with a clear insistence.

The question silenced Levi as he sat down on the ground, becoming more submissive. He sensed he was in the presence of something he could not comprehend. So he told the truth. "I have been thinking about the chalice. I feel it become very warm sometimes."

"I did not ask what the chalice does. I asked what it has *told* you!"

Levi had to think about that for a moment. Then he shrugged his shoulders and answered, "I think it becomes very warm . . . when I do something good or when some goodness is done to me. This seems to be so."

"Well then," the old beggar stated with some satisfaction, "perhaps goodness and mercy have always accompanied you. Focusing only on the worst things prevents you from seeing it. Surely you have seen loving parents walking and caring for their children. Surely you have observed in the marketplace, acts of kindness between people. These things you have determined not to see. Then you become blinded from seeing something greater."

"When the Roman soldiers march I do not look up," said Levi, "This way I do not see the Roman soldier's banners of war."

"That may be true however, Caesar and the Roman legions continue to reign and oppress even if you choose not to see their war banners. Hiding your eyes changes nothing."

Still puzzled Levi said, "You speak of goodness and mercy, but there is so much hatred. A man with a dog showed me much kindness. He told me lessons about myself. When I left his house, he told me there were two ways to travel to Jerusalem. He said to go the long way because the shorter path would take me through Samaria, and I should never go that way. He said with hatred, that Samaritans were like swine."

"You see how quickly you recognize hatred, Levi?"

The words pierced him like a pang of deep hunger. No one had ever brought such a question to him. He could only hold his head in his hands.

The old beggar softened his voice, "Levi, hatred and mistrust have been the only friends you have permitted. That is why you recognize them more often and more clearly than anything else."

"That is what I see in the streets, where I survive," he replied in defense.

The old beggar smiled. "And yet you *have* observed goodness and mercy. They too have been near all along. And perhaps they hope to befriend you as well."

"I do not know what is happening to me, old man . . . messenger . . . whatever you are. I only know that I want to find the Teacher, but they say he has died . . . or is alive again . . . I no longer know what to believe about this. That is what you meant when you told me that I would learn of an event that could cause me to stop searching, isn't it?"

"And indeed . . . you have endured. This will be pleasing to the Teacher," said the beggar.

"Somehow you know things about me . . . you know I have the chalice . . . then you must know the truth about the chalice," he stated with trepidation. He didn't expect an answer. His chin fell against his chest.

49

"I already had a message to carry."

"THE TRUTH IS THIS, I am his messenger. I cannot be a messenger for someone who is dead! His message continues on."

The statement came across as logical to Levi. "Tell me the message of the chalice."

"Communion!" The beggar exclaimed it loudly.

"I do not understand this?" the boy replied.

"Communion; to be together, to be in union."

"The chalice is a message of being together with others?" Levi responded.

"More than that, but for now you should think on that as you go," said the beggar.

"I see no communion," Levi responded in matter of fact.

"When a farmer lays a grain of wheat seed into the soil, the sun, the rain and the soil itself function in communion in order to help the seed grow. But unless you remain to see the harvest, then you have seen nothing other than wet dirt," the old beggar taught.

Levi considered the words about remaining to see the harvest, and asked, "You again tell me to continue on even if I cannot know where to go?"

"I ask you boy, have you lacked for food or drink since you have been on this journey to find the new place?"

Levi recalled Jesus reminding his men that they were sent out with no provisions, yet they wanted for nothing. "No," the boy said, "I have not. The Teacher reminded his men of that in the upper room," he said.

"Why do you think the Teacher reminded them?"

Levi shrugged his shoulders.

"A true messenger must focus on hearing and carrying the message above all else. The messenger is in communion with the message. All else shall be supplied."

"I already had a message to carry . . . about the betrayer. But now—"

The old beggar jumped in, "The ancient scriptures have foretold betrayal would come to pass."

"The men with the Teacher . . . they did nothing to stop Judas," the boy persisted.

"How long has that concern been in your heart?" the old beggar asked.

Levi reached into his tunic and removed the chalice. Holding it out he said, "Since the Teacher left this on the table for me in the upper room. And I do not understand why?"

The old beggar's eyes smiled. "But did he not leave you something else?"

Levi was well aware by now that this man already knew the answer. "Yes, he left a coin for me under the cushion of the man named Peter."

"Were you not in the room to find money, your primary concern that day?"

"Yes," he said reluctantly.

"Yet you have held more concern with giving the Teacher a warning than you had with the money."

Levi's eyebrows lifted. Until that moment he hadn't been consciously aware of this shift in his thinking. It was true. He stumbled at a response, "I . . . I had . . . not . . ." Then his words ran silent, barely enough to breathe out a reply.

"You have a good deal of money in your tunic from the man with the dog. Will you continue your journey to the new place, or will the coins hold your thinking in the old place of survival? You must decide what will guide you."

"I have no understanding of what you speak. No one guides me. I am alone."

"Then perhaps it is time to learn of something greater." The old beggar leaned forward, his face tightened. He whispered in order get the boy to lean in and listen. "Learn and enter into the divine energy of the world."

Levi stood befuddled. "The divine energy of the world?" he reiterated.

"It fills the world and remains present to all."

"What is this . . . energy?" the boy asked.

The old beggar swung his arms in large sweeping circles. "The Ancient of Ancients, the vast Creator . . . everywhere present to embrace all who will come out of their loneliness, broken heartedness, abandonment, scars; out from every shackle the world has bound them with. And yet this energy often remains untapped by wounded hearts that need it most."

"Where is this energy?" Levi asked.

"The energy of the world is not in some outside place. It is not in the mountains. You will not find it in the meadows . . . no boy . . . these are not the places at all."

"Then you give me another riddle," Levi replied in frustration.

"No. Not a riddle. In the ancient of texts we are told that in the beginning God formed man and breathed into his nostrils . . . life! Life, Levi. Life is the expression of love! It flows as divine energy through all things that have been created. Love is God's own signature."

"Love does not seem to travel in the streets of Jerusalem where I begged. I have always been alone, surviving," said Levi. His frustration stammered out.

"Are you alone? Are you? Although you allow your wounded heart to hold you separated," the old beggar countered quickly, "has not the chalice been with you? Even when it should have been stolen it remained with you. When you lost your way you found your way. When you were hungry you were fed. When you were thirsty you were satisfied. When you became unsure, someone came into your path. When you encountered danger you were protected. When you had nothing, coins came to you. When you felt abandoned someone invited you in. When you felt unvalued someone valued you. You surely are not slow of mind; does any of this not cause you to think how the very divine energy of the world has brushed itself against you along this journey? Like a thin veil waiting for you to step through."

Levi twisted his torso around to tuck the chalice back into his tunic and asked, "Does the chalice carry this divine energy?" Upon turning back, he heard the words echo from a far of place, "Continue your journey." The old beggar had vanished.

Levi kneeled down touching his hand to the ground feeling the impression the pallet had left. He needed to be sure. Yes, the marks were there. That much he knew. He sat down on the imprints of the pallet, placing his staff down. The old beggar spoke the truth, he had somehow been provided for along the way. As to expressions of love and God's signature, he could not yet completely reconcile to him however; it did suggest some form of practicality to him because he had not journeyed without provisions. But something about the divine energy of the world intrigued him greatly. That could hold power, and that is what he lacked.

"The divine energy of the world," he spoke it aloud. He repeated it in his head. It struck him how all that had taken place along the way must have something to with the power of this divine energy. Removing the chalice from his tunic, he held it up in review and asked, "Where is it? Where do I enter?"

50

Whatever that was, could it be warming the chalice?

NLIKE THE PREVIOUS ENCOUNTER with the old beggar when he resisted what had been spoken. This time he attempted to embrace the words. As he held the chalice he wondered if this divine energy of the world, whatever that was, could be warming it? Power had to come from somewhere. The chalice, just a simple cup, could not warm itself. The old beggar suggested a new reality; that goodness and mercy followed him which presented a contradiction to his life experience. However, he could not dismiss the evidence completely.

In considering he finally admitted that somehow the good things happening to him had to have some connection to the divine energy of the world. If someone told him before setting on this journey that strangers would show him kindness and offer life lessons and give him money and offer opportunity, he would have laughed and spit on the ground.

What other explanation did he have? He recalled overhearing a Pharisee near the Gate Beautiful tell a man that God's presence held all things together and could be found everywhere; that no one . . . nothing could hide from God. He wondered if the Pharisee had been speaking of this divine energy of the world. Thinking back to the Teacher in the upper room, all the promises he made to his men could surely not come to pass without some great source of power. The Teacher, it seemed, possessed power beyond what other men displayed. People had seen the miracles he performed.

These new lessons all the more compelled Levi to increase his efforts to find out for himself whether the Teacher was alive or not, and connect with his disciples. Grasping his staff he walked out of the grove of trees. Standing on the dirt path at the end of the grove of trees he glanced at both paths. With a sweeping motion he dragged the end of his staff across the dirt path. *I will never find the Teacher if I add more time to my travel.* He began the walk toward Samaria.

51

He stood bewildered to see a woman treated with respect

SAMARIA APPEARED FILLED WITH endless hills and valleys. The land looked rich and moist. The boy observed many fields filled with crops. The trees were abundant with fruit. Never had he seen such a rich land, and his eyes were soon consumed with expectation at what might lay ahead. He noticed that he could sense the land presenting a feeling of prosperity to which he was unaccustomed. Even the grass looked proud and thick and lush, with cows eagerly grazing.

The city walls were made of ashlar blocks and as he peered over, viewed great houses that were beautifully decorated. Some of the building facades displayed ornate ivory carved with animal and floral motifs. He observed a large and ornate temple dedicated to one of the Caesars. All pleasantries halted when he stopped suddenly with no small pulse of stabbing fear as he caught sight of several Sebastenaeans ahead, compelling him to quickly duck into an alleyway. These hired men served in the army of Herod, known for their excessive cruelty of which Levi had witnessed in action in Jerusalem. He did not want to be anywhere near those soldiers, yet he couldn't restrain himself from stealing a covert peek around the corner to look at them dressed in their distinctively dark cloaks. Following a good look at them he spit on the ground to detest them with disdain which was followed by the fastest moving feet he could muster. Once he felt a safe distance away he slowed his pace. Closing in on the end of a long, high wall, the sounds of a crowd of people came from just ahead. Moving along the wall he made slow and cautious steps until he reached the end from which bushes continued out few feet. With his back pressed against the bushes he tipped his face out looking through the bush to observe. A small square lay ahead filled with activity and many people. The noise and movement reminded him of a hornet's nest. A number of men and women were crowding in to see something taking place. Levi followed suit. Finally the people stopped moving so he squeezed himself next to a young man seated with his father. Standing in the midst of the group were a woman and two men. The men were getting people to quiet down, saying that the woman brought important news to share with them. Both men proclaimed they knew the woman and attested to the message she was about to share. Then the two men stepped back leaving her in the center. She swayed nervously. One of the men stepped forward again and said something to her. In a moment she lifted her head and began to speak.

"My name is Photini. Many of you have seen me as an unfit woman. But not long ago a Rabbi named Jesus came to me at the well. Powerful, gentle and kind he told me of living water and that I would never again thirst."

Someone yelled out, "What is this living water you speak of?"

"Satisfaction to our souls," Photini replied.

"You believe this?" another person yelled out.

"At the well, he told me all things about my life . . . secret things no one could ever have known. And he spoke to *me*, a Samaritan woman and he is of the Jews."

At this the crowd murmured causing the two men to step forward yelling out, "People do not harden yourselves to the truth. Photini has seen the Christ."

These statements immediately caught the boy's attention. The crowd quieted with some soft murmuring continuing. She started again, "The thirst in my heart for self worth thirsts no more, for today I have seen Jacob's star." At this statement the crowd quietly moved in toward her. They were now asking how to receive the living water. The boy stood there held in bewilderment to see a woman being treated with respect, something he had never witnessed before.

He turned to the young man seated beside him, "Who is this person she speaks of?"

"I will ask my father." The young man turned to ask his father the question. Turning back to the boy he said, "Some are saying he is the Messiah. Others say he is just a Rabbi. My father says he is the one named Jesus who has caused people to rebel against the Pharisees' teachings."

Levi's eyebrows lifted at this and he could feel the chalice warming at his side.

Levi thought the Teacher might again appear at the well the woman mentioned. "Where is this well she speaks of?" Levi asked. But the father now standing up grasped his son's hand lifting him. The young man could only point with his extended hand as they waded into the crowd. Looking in the direction of where the young man pointed, there were only houses. Levi decided the best course of action would be to ask the woman how to find the well. People were crowding around her asking questions. Some people were weeping. Others were praying. A few were arguing about her claim. Turning himself sideways, he held his staff close against his chest while wedging himself through the people. He noticed how the woman's voice although soft carried certain honesty. It reminded him of how the Teacher had spoken in the upper room. He tugged on the woman who looked down at him.

Her eyes intense, her face aglow with joyfulness. "Yes child?" she asked with tenderness.

"Tell me where to find the well . . . I must find the one with living water. Please, I need to find him before he goes. How far is the well . . . please?"

"He is no longer there, child. He departed."

Levi thought he might bite through his lip. Disappointment shown in his face.

A man standing nearby overheard her and asked, "But how can you bring people to the living water if he is gone?"

"His love can be found everywhere," she tapped her hand over her heart.

Levi could not lift his head up. *I am surrounded by people with nothing but riddles.* Then he felt her hand touch under his chin tilting his head up. "Why are you so troubled?"

"I must find him. Again he is gone before I can reach him."

The women kneeled on one knee. "At the right time the unforeseen displays itself. Each day I go up to the well to fetch water. Days ago I went early to the well. It was as if he had been there waiting for me." A smaller group of people were now seated around her and the boy as she continued. Her words were not intended for the boy only, but for all who would listen. "When the Living Water spoke to me, I knew for the first time I was not meant to live for myself alone, and that others can not define my value. I know not how to explain this mystery, yet the living water can reside in our hearts so that we should never again be alone."

"When did you see him?" Levi asked, almost pleading.

The woman thought for a moment. "It was not many days ago."

Levi assumed the Teacher had been there that very day. He rose from his knees and started off greatly disappointed. *What if the Teacher does not want me to find him? Why does he not appear to me?* Levi wondered in dismay as he departed.

The woman, called out, "Wait, child. Stay until we are finished here."

Unsure of what he would do next, he sat back down, waiting.

52

"Where is your family?"

PHOTINI CONCLUDED HER MESSAGE and discussions with people. She and one of the men stepped over to Levi. As they did, Photini said something to the man. Then she looked over, "Child," she said, "come stay with me for a time. This is Jonathan. He serves as one of the guards in our neighborhood." They both bowed slightly in courtesy. "And what is your name?" she asked.

"I am Levi."

They walked a short distance to a modest building with a decorative facade. Once inside they sat at a table. "Child, I am hungry . . . are you?" asked Photini.

"Yes, but I am not a child. I take care of myself."

"Where is your family," Jonathan asked.

"I am on the way to the new place. It is my own journey to make!"

Photini brought a basket of food and a pitcher to the table and tipped the basket toward the boy. "You are my guest, please select what you will."

Levi noticed that the man had glanced at his staff several times. He appeared to be admiring it. Finally the man said, "Your staff is unusual. Do you come from a family of shepherds?"

"The staff is a gift," he said tersely, as though defending some unspoken accusation.

"Do you know the crook of the staff has a lineage to Egypt?"

The boy shook his head, no.

"The great Pharaohs carried similar crooks on staffs to symbolize their rule and leadership over their people. I speak of the shape of the crook not the intricate carvings as on your staff."

"I know nothing of that. This staff was given to me by a shepherd and his son."

Jonathan placed his elbows to his knees and said, "Now I sense *that* must be quite a story," he expressed it with a smile trying to make the boy feel more comfortable.

"Leave the boy alone," Photini said, "Let him eat."

"No . . . I will tell about it." Levi surprised himself with that response. He hadn't ever told anyone about how he received the staff. Finally while placing both his hands securely on the staff, he felt compelled to tell them the story of what had taken place. "One day I heard a crowd of people talking with excitement about a caravan of merchants who were passing through the wilderness area. They said a known prophet would be traveling with them and he could tell people about things yet to come. I thought I might learn something for myself so I followed. The trip turned out longer than I expected, and because I didn't sleep much the night before, I became tired, stopped and sat against a small grouping of rocks off the path. It was going to be just for a moment's rest, but when I woke up the noon sun burnt down on my head. By falling asleep I lost the crowd. Since I had traveled that far I decided to continue. Before long I wandered into an area of pasture land just before the wilderness."

Photini frowned, "Did you find the other people?" she asked hopefully.

"No, they were gone. I walked up a hill where I heard barking, howls and someone yelling so I ran to the top. I saw a shepherd; he didn't look much older than me, fighting off two wild dogs, swinging his staff at them trying to keep himself between his sheep and the dogs." Levi became animated relaying the event. "The dogs looked starved, ribs almost sticking out of their sides. They must have gone mad with hunger. It was scary. I don't know what happened or what I thought, but before I knew it I found myself running down the hill to see if I could do anything. I yelled as loud as I could to catch the attention of the dogs and the boy. Then some of the sheep ran behind the boy and he fell backward, hitting the ground hard, losing his grip on the staff. One of the dogs moved toward him with its teeth bared and growling. Then it bit into his ankle viciously. It then moved toward his face about to bite his neck."

"What happened then?" Photini leaned in.

"I ran over to the boy just in time and picked up his staff. The other dog moved around the back attacking one of the sheep. I turned to the dog about to bite the shepherd again and I slammed the crook hard to grab around the dog's neck, twisted it with all my might and dragged him off the shepherd. The dog fell to its side then started to get up to come after me. His teeth were bare and his eyes wild. It growled at me deep from in his chest looking right into my eyes. Never had I ever been so frightened. So I swung the staff with all my strength, hitting him hard against the side where his ribs showed. I heard a cracking sound. The dog fell over on its side. I had no choice. I had to do it."

Photini gasped as her hand moved to cover her mouth. "Poor child, I'm so sorry you were in that situation."

"The dog whimpered and yelped, it couldn't move. Then I picked up rocks and threw them at the other dog. It backed away from the sheep. The other boy could hardly get to his knees as I helped lift him to his feet. The bites on his ankle were deep and bloody. Still he limped over to where the dog lay on the ground and he picked up a rock. He lifted the rock over his head with both hands. Then he could see the dog lay there already dead so he dropped the rock. More blood came from the bite marks around his ankle. He felt to the ground, yelling to me, 'Look out, behind you.' I swiveled to see the other dog that had backed away now running toward me. 'The goad, the goad,' he yelled. I did not know what that word meant. He pointed. My eyes followed. There on the ground near my feet lay a long stick with a sharply pointed end, and I realized why he said this. The goad would be a good weapon. I reached down for the goad with only enough time to lift up the pointed end on an angle and as the dog ran at me with its mouth open it ran right into the goad and it drove right into its throat, and farther into its body, bringing the dog to the ground. Then the boy fainted."

53

Wild dogs in great hunger are vicious

H E NOTICED PHOTINI GROWING upset. Her lips compressed to a thin line.

"I shouldn't have told you that, I guess," Levi said.

She reached her hand to his face, gentling touching it, "No . . . You helped that shepherd boy. That is good thing. A loving act."

A loving act? He never considered such a thing. His voice became low, "I never told anyone of this . . . I shouldn't . . ."

"You likely saved his life," Jonathan added. "Wild dogs in great hunger are vicious. You are a strong, courageous boy."

The boy's chin dropped to his chest. "I felt sorry for the dogs, too. I know what it feels like to be hungry and alone just like they did. They went mad with hunger."

Jonathan reached out. His hands were large and heavily veined. "Can I look at your staff?"

The boy held the staff with noticeable pride. Reluctantly, he lifted the staff up to the man. Jonathan gently took the staff and studied it, turning it around, feeling the engravings. "This is a fine gift you've been given. The carvings are beautifully detailed." He thought for a moment then added, "I do not believe these are merely art images. I cannot tell you the meaning of these carvings yet I am sure they hold some kind of a message," he said while returning the staff.

As Levi took the staff back he'd never thought of the carvings as a message.

Photini jumped in. "And . . . after the dogs were gone? What happened then?"

"The boy had a knife. I used it to cut a strip off his tunic to wrap the bites tightly. With my arm around his waist, I leaned him against me and his staff. In his other hand he held the goad. I had to move slowly because I could hear his breath coming in gasps. A few times he opened his eyes and pointed the way then fell back to sleep. Along the way I stopped and rested. I carried him all the way back to his father's tent across a pasture and down a hill. When his father saw us, he ran up the hill, lifted his son up and carried him the rest of the way. I followed, carrying his staff, the goad and his knife. As the father cleaned and wrapped his wounds and gave him water to drink, the boy told his father what happened. The father thanked me many times and asked me to stay as their guest. We had something to eat then I fell asleep. I heard the boy's father working on something all through the night. There were scraping and banging and cutting sounds. In the morning I woke up and smelled something good so I stepped outside the tent. The father kneeled by a fire digging in hot coals. Using a metal rod he lifted a pot of Fava beans from the coals. He poured water out of the pot and made breakfast. Very delicious. Then the father asked me to wait. He stepped into another tent returning with his son limping by his side. The father held this staff in his hand. Handing it to me he said, 'My son Avner and I, want you to have this; our gratefulness for helping him.' They wanted me to stay there with them."

Then Levi abruptly stopped talking. What he didn't tell them was that the father, after handing him the staff, dropped on one knee and embraced him. His immediate response was to pull away, but he was too stunned by that kind gesture. The man, his wife and son tried to convince him to remain with them. The father felt a definitive and absolute belief that what happened had been divine providence, and that the boy's appearance meant something significant. Levi recalled vividly the disappointment in the man's eyes after he told him he could not stay with them. Then the father told him, 'Keep the staff with you always. The day may come when you will understand and we shall be here in waiting.' Although he had no idea what the man inferred, the sincerity impacted him deeply. He quickly fought off the memories of not staying with the man and his family, determined to hold back the mounting pressure of tears as he recounted the events. Steadying his mind he quickly moved his thoughts to the fight with the vicious dogs to distract his feelings.

Photini spoke, calling him back to the moment. "You were given a beautiful gift," she said, "crafted by loving hands."

He found the woman easy to talk to which caught him off guard. "I didn't want to take it." He shook his head sorry he'd said it.

"Why?" she asked. Her eyes deep with concern drew him in. "There is no greater gift than love."

"I depend on myself . . . trust myself . . . I was . . . never . . ."

Photini's eyes moistened. "You have never had the chance to just be a boy."

Levi quickly countered her comment, "I am fine. I do not need those things." But in his heart he knew he did, and it radiated in his eyes.

Jonathan gestured to the staff. "I see why this holds such importance for you."

"Levi," Photini said, "I know what it feels like to be alone, to be rejected. This is why I continue to speak about Jesus to all the people."

54

The chalice warmed again

"I MET A MAN WHO told me the way back to Jerusalem. He warned me not travel through Samaria. He did not speak well of your people." Levi said softly, almost not wanting to be heard.

Silence lingered. Jonathan glanced over to Photini, then back at Levi. "The Jews and we Samaritans have held hatred for each other as far back as the times of the patriarchs. Do you not know of Jacob and his twelve sons, and the division of Israel, Levi?"

He didn't know what to say. What came out was, "I have heard people talk of it in the streets where I . . ." Levi's voice trailed off. He didn't want to say anything about his begging. "Where I . . . I . . . spent . . . time."

Photini added, "Israel was divided into two kingdoms. The northern kingdom and . . . well, the history is long and complicated. But there has been enmity between our people. We have our own worship and Jacob's well. So the walls of bitterness were built on both sides, and have remained fortified over the last 500 years."

Breaking the silence Jonathan closed his eyes for a moment, "Levi . . . hatred is . . . the most ancient of human adversaries. This is what makes the visit of Jesus all the more important. First, he spoke to Photini. Jews will not speak to a woman, let alone a Samaritan woman. This was unheard of. It is a sign of communion to us, I believe."

There came that word, *communion* that the old beggar expressed. The Teacher did something out of the ordinary by speaking with the woman. He began to consider how the Teacher did many things that were in opposition to what many people were accustomed to.

Photini noticed Levi's blank stare. She said, "Levi, during these past few days our people have heard the compassion and the kindness of Jesus, a Jew and rabbi who respected them and cared for their souls. This will open a new journey to communion with one another as family. We must begin somewhere, and Jesus has made that first step for us."

Levi responded with, "I met the Teacher in the upper room with his disciples having a meal."

When he said the words, Photini noticed for the first time that his face became softer and she noticed a glimmer of joy in his eyes. Puzzled she asked, "Who is the teacher you speak of?"

"The one you met at the well; Jesus. I have been looking for him. He holds many titles."

The genuine plea in his face touched her heart. She hung her head. All the excitement she had displayed replaced by a filling sadness like an unpleasant dark shadow overcame her. With her head still down, she spoke slowly, as if forcing out every single word. She entreated, "They have," she hesitated, "they have crucified him." Her words were accompanied by tears.

Levi said, "Some say he died and some say he is alive. I do not know what to believe."

"We were told that Jesus taught his disciples in advance that after three days he would be resurrected. We are hearing news that he is appearing to people. You should remain here with me at least to hear what I tell the people today. We must go back now." They stood, preparing to leave for the town square.

Levi read her concern and open hospitality. He glanced at Jonathan who nodded at him with positive eyes. He accepted. At that moment, the chalice warmed again. He smiled to himself, touched the chalice, and followed along with them. Back in the town square Photini again drew a sizable crowd and told of the message of living water.

55

"How often do you need water?"

WHEN THEY ARRIVED BACK at Photini's house, Jonathan departed. Food and drink were set on the table.

"Jonathan thought the carvings on my staff had a message and liked the beauty of it."

"I think for you the staff is much more than just beautiful."

He moved his eyes from her to the staff. "This is my only true friend."

Photini smiled, lifted his head and looked into his eyes. "Child, the staff is much more . . . I cannot say why I know this, yet deep within my heart I know there is something more to this staff."

Levi no longer corrected her when she called him *child*. He came to realize it was her way of being sincere. He decided to receive what she said about the staff, taking it into his heart.

They remained quiet for a time while eating. Then Levi gained the courage to ask her, "Did the Teacher really tell you all these things?"

"He told me many things about my life . . . about need. Not just my needs, but the needs all people hold. For me he spoke to . . ." She quieted her voice and continued so softly he had to perk his ears. "You are too young to understand, but for me, it was . . . my dependence . . . on a man. I thought a man would fulfill what is missing in me. Jesus revived in me what has already been there yet worn down by the life I led." Photini wiped her hand across her forehead sweeping back her hair. "For you Levi, the need is the same; there is something you do not yet know that you already have." Levi held no experience participating in adult conversations and Photini could see that. "Think of it this way, the way Jesus . . . the Teacher . . . told me."

Levi sat up straighter, ears attentive.

"Water", she said, then remained quiet.

"Water?" Levi added.

"How often do you need water?"

"Always," he said.

"So although you drink water, do you thirst again?"

"Yes." He expressed it as an obvious fact.

"Yes it is so, child. You see, the things of this world cannot satisfy; we need them over and over. I now know that Jesus spoke not only of the body's need for water, but the soul's need for living water . . . for the life energy that only divine love can provide."

Levi's face went blank. Then recalling the old beggar's words about divine energy being an expression of love, but it all seemed confusing, like a riddle without an answer.

Just then a knock came to the door. Photini rose and opened it. Jonathan stepped inside. "We should get you back to the square and tell the people more of the message."

Photini looked down on Levi, "Please, join us."

Jonathan touched Photini's arm, "Let us go and we will talk more along the way."

As they walked toward the square, Levi became more comfortable with them. He told them what happened in the upper room. He shared the story about encountering Judas and how he rushed out of the upper room upon Jesus' words about betrayal. He also told them about his run-in with Judas in the marketplace and what he accused Judas of doing, and also the chase with the Roman Guard who hit the camel and the smelling cud all over him.

Hearing the details about Judas, Jonathan leaned his head over to Photini's ear as they walked. "I believe his story to be a young boy's imagination or at the least, a misunderstanding that could damage the reputation of a man, especially if he is going around speaking this man's name out loud for others to hear."

"No, Jonathan," Photini said, "he may be a young boy but he is ahead of his age. I believe he is sincere in what he has shared. He has shared his story with us . . . why would he need to contrive a tale like that?"

Levi walked behind them and could not hear their animated whispers to each other. But he knew something caused disagreement between them. Despite Photini's protest, Jonathan turned to look back at Levi, stopped and raised a finger as to instruct. "You are young. You must be extremely careful in telling such tales about your elders, Levi. Accusations, well, they are very serious. People can be taken to the courts for such things. And the law requires at least two witnesses. Telling tales opposing a man's reputation for instance, can only get you both into serious trouble. You never know who is listening. It would be best if I take you to the officials. You can tell them of this event with the man named Judas."

Levi stopped. Frozen. Cold fear turned to a quickly building rage. He leaned forward and by sheer impulse and anger yelled with no constraint, "You . . . you are just like all the rest. Adults lie all the time . . . and betray, and . . . and . . . they don't believe the truth and . . . they take advantage, and . . . and . . ." he couldn't get the words out fast enough for the burning, stuttering anger. He suddenly stopped talking, turned and found himself running. Running as fast as he could. He could hear Photini calling after him to come back.

56

"Who are you looking for?"

P HOTINI'S VOICE DRIFTED OFF behind him. He ran and ran for the longest time unable to stop. Fear and anger fueled his legs. Finally, with no energy remaining, his body gave him no choice but to stop, heavily winded, coughing, spitting and completely sweated. The long run had depleted his energy and anger, and had taken him to the outskirts of the city. A large wheat field lay just ahead offering the perfect spot where he sat down in between the rows. The events of the last few days played in his mind at high speed. He wanted to believe that the old beggar may have been right. Perhaps goodness did exist in the world. But Jonathan's accusations reopened the old wounds of mistrust. Maybe he should have stayed in Jerusalem after all. What did he think he would be able to do about anything? Who would give a young beggar without a family a second thought? And the new place? Maybe no such place existed. As to the divine energy of the world, such lofty ideas wouldn't put food in his belly. All fables, he thought. Wrapping his arms around his staff he glanced around the area and fell into a deep sleep before he could consider another thought.

The darkened hallway appeared to go on and on with no end in sight. The children were a range of ages, seated on the floor on both sides of a long hallway as though piles of rags. Levi moved between them as each varied group looked up at him asking, no, more like taunting, "Who are you looking for?" they cried out. The voices echoed over and over like jeers poking at him. He covered his ears as he picked up the pace and the faster he moved the longer the hallway seemed to become.

"You will find no one here . . . we have found no one . . . you cannot either." He ran. The children's voices ran along with him. More children in

more groups. More voices calling, "There are no parents here, we are alone
. . . you are alone. Stay with us." Their hands reaching out for him. "Stay with
us. Stay with—"

Levi awoke startled, throwing his head side to side trying to shake off
the images and the voices. The sweat poured down his face. He couldn't
recall the last time he'd had that warped nightmare. The nightmare caused
him to reflect back on his years at the alms house. The Head Master would
speak to all the children while they ate what meager meals were provided.
He spoke constantly about how much harder they needed to work; after all
they were there by the graces of people who were paying for their shelter
and food. The working hours were slowly extended with less and less time
for sleep provided. They were child slaves who the alms house used to profit
from the free labor.

Then he smiled, remembering the night that he and one other boy had
occasion to escape. They parted ways after escaping, vowing never to come
back. They were ten years old and over the following three years he had
survived, never encountering the other boy again. He yawned widely. Hud-
dling back into the stalks of wheat, his eyes closed once again to a welcomed
uneventful sleep.

57

"Boy, you carry a notable staff."

As though it had been timed, sunrise awakened Levi from what turned out to be a needed deep sleep. Standing up he yawned deeply and gaining his bearings once again started back out of the wheat field toward the road. He walked a few miles and as the wind kicked up it blended its own sound through the trees with that of sheep herd sounds accompanied by commands being called out by shepherds.

Stepping back he watched them approach along the roadside. A dominant ram led the broad-tailed sheepfold. Four men walked alongside the sheep herd; three younger men and one older shepherd. As the older shepherd walked to where Levi stood, he glanced at him as he approached. The man made a second glance. Slowing his pace he cast a studied look at Levi and then stopped walking. He shouted out instructions to the other three men. They slowed the herd down turning across the road toward a hillside running on a slight incline just off the way. As the old shepherd approached, Levi stepped back a few paces on guard with uncertainty. The man stepped close to Levi, his eyes trained on the staff.

"Boy, you carry a notable staff," he said. Now standing in front of the boy his eyes widened and so did his smile. "Ah, praise be; you are of the House of Abendan," he said warmly.

Levi hadn't the slightest idea what the man referred to. "I do not know of this."

The shepherd looked incredulous. "You say you are not of Abendan's house?"

The boy braced himself for another judgment or accusation. "I do not know of this place," he said, stepping back.

"This is odd . . . that you do not honor the man yet you carry Abendan's mark on the staff."

He shrugged his shoulders. "This staff was given to me by a boy's father as a gift. I did not steal it. The staff is mine," he stated in a defensive tone.

"Why then do you not acknowledge the man while you carry his mark on the staff?"

"I do not understand what you are saying," said Levi.

The shepherd pointed to the staff, "Abendan's mark. Is your mind dull, boy! There!" He tapped the staff with his forefinger.

"A man gave this to me but I did not ask his name. He carved it for me as a gift." He held the staff to himself tightly. He didn't want to say much more about the event thinking he might be accused of stealing the staff. With that in mind he thought it best to at least share the highlights of what had happened with the wild dogs and what the father did and how the staff came to be his. "I did not steal this staff," he proclaimed as boldly and confidently as he could.

The shepherd laughed in amusement, "Of course you have not stolen the staff, boy."

Levi offered a puzzled face.

With a smile he said, "Here, look here," as he pointed a finger to the staff. "This is your name, Levi, and Abendan carved the mark of his house above your name. You have been most honored. Do you not understand these things?"

"Honored?" Levi said, with eyes frowning.

The old shepherd seemed to be stunned at this naïve reply. He could only assume that the boy could not read or perhaps was slow of mind. Unsure of the boy's situation as to whether or not revealing the fuller meaning of the staff, he held back. Telling him what Abendan had claimed about him might in some way affect his relationship, whatever it was, with his own father, or perhaps create confusion or remorse. With that in mind the shepherd thought being concise would be best. "Yes honored. Honored indeed! These symbols honor you from the House of Abendan."

Levi stood bewildered at the statement, finally breathing air in.

The shepherd tilted his head in surprise. "The staff is much like a signet ring telling of heritage." The man could not figure what had happened to the boy as to who had raised him or from what province he had come. Clearly the boy held no practical understanding of his culture. The one thing he knew, and it was the most important thing, Abendan had greatly honored this boy, and that was all he needed to know. "I suppose then you know nothing of the Glory of the Fields?" he asked throwing up his hands.

"No." Levi said. Unlike adults he held no concern that he might appear ignorant of such events. The important thing to know focused on survival. He had more important things to do than waste time learning of things past. The past would certainly not put food in his stomach. With that he clearly admitted, "I do not know anything of which you speak."

The shepherd offered a wondrous grin, as he dropped to one knee to look straight into the boy's face. He held both of Levi's shoulders in his big hands and said to him, "Those befriended of Abendan are friends to me and my house. You must learn of the magnificent happenings that have taken place in our land. Come across with me and meet my sons."

Levi, although befuddled and somewhat reluctant, followed behind the old shepherd. The sheep were grazing as the shepherd's sons made their way over, having seen their father summoning them. The old shepherd introduced each of his sons by name and added the meaning of their names. "Elazar: meaning, God has helped . . . Alon, Oak tree, and Shimon, to hear." Then he placed his hand on his chest and said, "My name is Yochnan which means God is gracious."

Levi listened noticing the endearment of the father for his sons. He thought of his own name and how it had come to him of his own choosing. But he decided not to say anything.

"Now here is something important," the shepherd began again, catching Levi back to attention. The old shepherd had them all sit in the grass. "Show the boy your staffs," he told his three sons. Each of them held out his staff horizontally. "See the markings," said the old shepherd. Levi nodded studiously.

"Can you see how similar they are to your carved symbols, Levi?" asked the shepherd as he tapped the symbols on one of the staffs. "My sons are of my house . . . the house of Yochnan. Your staff is of the house of Abendan." He turned to his sons, "Our young friend knows nothing of the Glory of the Fields. Shall I enlighten him?" He didn't pause for an answer. "Where shall I begin?" He said with utmost pride.

As the shepherd prepared himself, Levi's thoughts rummaged through what he'd just heard. According to the shepherd, Abendan had given him more than just a nicely carved staff. Levi didn't know that man's name was Abendan nor did he know the name of the man's son whose life he saved. Still he did not grasp the depth of what the old shepherd had proclaimed about his staff. In fact he felt unsure of anything, but because the chalice warmed in his tunic he held attention. Placing his hand on it the thought occurred to him that he never thanked Abendan for the gift of the staff. Until now such thoughts of courtesy were nonexistent to him. He only focused on himself. The shepherd stopped funneling his beard evidently now prepared to begin reciting the story. He raised both hands up like a drummer about to strike a beat. No sooner did he speak a first word when Elazar, his oldest son spoke up. "Forgive me father, but look at Levi's staff again." He held up Levi's staff while turning it horizontally. "It also carries the burn mark of Gideon," he said, with no small amount of wonder on his face.

58

"Lions dug his grave?"

T HE SHEPHERD TOOK LEVI'S staff inspecting it closely. "May heaven be blessed," he proclaimed.

Levi, unable to contain himself jumped up asking, "What does this mean? Who is Gideon?"

Elazar lifted his eyebrows in a frustration at Levi's ignorance, but the old shepherd waved him to sit down and remain quiet.

"I shall tell you," the shepherd said. The man wanted Levi to have some understanding of these important events. He related the story in summary form hoping to give the boy an understanding he would remember. "Gideon was a farm boy. God selected him to lead men into battle to defeat the Midianites. You see, long ago the Midianites came against our people. For seven years the Midianites swept over our land at the time of harvest. They would carry away all the crops of grain, until our people no longer had food for themselves. Their sheep and cattle were also taken. Our people fled from their homes and farms, and hid in the mountain caves. The grain they raised had to be buried in pits covered with earth, or hidden in empty winepresses so the Midianites would not take it from them. One day, a young man named Gideon threshed out wheat, when an angel appeared sitting under a tree. The angel said to him: 'You are a brave man, Gideon, and the Lord is with you. Go out boldly, and save your people from the power of the Midianites.' Gideon told the angel of his family poverty and that he was the least in his father's house. He held no battle training and knew nothing of war. But God said to him: 'Surely I will be with you, and I will help you drive out the Midianites.' Gideon believed God spoke with him through the angel. He brought an offering, and laid it on a rock before the angel. Then the angel touched the offering with his staff. At the exact moment the staff touched the offering, a fire leaped up and burned the offering; and then the angel vanished. Gideon feared greatly when he saw this; but the Lord said to him: 'Peace be unto you, Gideon, do not fear, for I am with you.' Gideon went on to defeat the Midianites with only 300 men."

Levi felt the amazement of the story.

"You see, Levi, this burn mark, all this discoloring stain Abendan added to the staff proclaims you as an overcomer."

Levi drew a deep meaningful breath with confusion and apprehension. He felt as far from being an overcomer as a lamb would feel far from being a wolf. Again, the chalice warmed as though comforting him.

"You must give the meaning of this staff your attention, Levi. Yet there is a greater message in it, which I cannot explain. Only you can find its significance for your life. Do you understand?" he asked.

"Yes," Levi said, yet having no concept of what this might mean to him in any practical way.

"Father," said Alon, "are you going to tell of the fields?"

The old shepherd glanced over at Levi to determine whether or not he held interest. Levi understood what the shepherd's eyes were asking.

"I would like to hear of this glory," Levi said.

The old shepherd looked out as though he could see something in the distance no one else could. His index fingers tented before his lined face. At length he spoke. "Abendan and our members were out in the field keeping watch over our flocks at night in the pasture where our ancestor, King David once tended his own father's sheep. That night held darker than most; the others were asleep in their tents." The shepherd moved his hands and swung his arms as though reliving the event, "Centuries ago, our ancient prophets foretold the Christ child would come to his people in the deep of the night, just as the observance of the Passover in Egypt. And so it came to pass, a star unlike any ever seen, appeared above us sweeping away the darkness." Then the shepherd bowed his head, "The glory of the Lord shone around us . . . the *Shechinah glory.*" The shepherd stopped speaking, staring out into the distance for a long moment. "Then an angel came first to Abendan, a frightening sight, but he told Abendan not to fear, that he had come to bring good tidings of great joy. Then above us in the sky appeared a host of angels . . . a multitude, likened to the expanse of the stars arrayed as no man has ever witnessed before." The shepherd's face filled with adoration. "They sang. Such voices unlike any man . . . unlike any sound ever heard . . . they sang, 'Glory to God in the highest, and on earth good will to men!'" The shepherd looked up as though he could see it all happening again. "The angels were gone. By then all our families had awakened to see it; all falling to our knees having seen the Glory of the Fields."

"When the angels departed to heaven, Abendan decided we must go to Bethlehem, to see what had come to pass, of which the angels proclaimed. We traveled to the place and found a babe lying in a manger. Abendan spoke to the parents of the babe, sharing in detail all that had taken place in the field, and everything the angels told him."

Levi's eyes grew as wide as melons, envisioning every scene being described in detail by the shepherd. Then the shepherd bowed his head slightly and appeared to be weeping. Levi remained still, simply remaining seated and waiting quietly. He glanced over at the shepherd's oldest son with a quizzed look. The son raised an open palm, and Levi understood he should wait. At length the shepherd continued.

"I believe that night was the first time men had to look down, not up to see heaven . . . in the child's face. How my heart holds gratefulness for us lowly shepherds, the first to hear heaven's announcement of the birth of the Christ child. The honor continues to overwhelm me. That the Christ would first reveal himself to lowly shepherds in a field," he stopped to bow his head then added, "rather than to kings and nobles." He glanced at Levi, then his sons, "The angels could have appeared to the kings, the nobles or the high priest of our land . . . yet they appeared to us in the fields . . . what glory!" His eyes moistened.

The oldest son leaned over and spoke to Levi. "Can you see why our father honors Abendan, and also the regard he gives you with your staff?"

"Yes," he replied quietly. Once again the chalice warmed in his tunic. All of this must be important, he thought. He rose and stepped toward the old shepherd. "I am grateful to you for telling me of these great things."

"Many things we tend to dismiss hold great value, even one's name. As we have shared with you this day. However, you must understand that although names hold value, every name is written in sand, it is your soul that endures above all. That is who you truly are. It is also of great value to prize what has been given to you, Levi." The shepherd had early on assumed that Levi had no family. Perhaps he had run away, or his parents may have died or been killed by the Romans. Whatever the situation, he wanted to give the boy something foundational. "Levi, you must promise to make learning your concern. One must know of his heritage . . . to know of those who have prophesied to our nation and fought for it. Those that came before us. Those who have held our people together." Levi nodded. The shepherd then thought that perhaps a unique story of the past might stir the boy's curiosity enough to seed a desire to learn. The shepherd turned his head and made a particular gesture to his oldest son who quickly understood what he must do.

Coming along side Levi, he began, "Levi, the great men among our ancestors were gallant servants of God. I admire Jeroboam who saved an entire village from enemy attack . . ."

His father chimed in, "And, it was Jeroboam alone who defended all the people in an almshouse until reinforcements came. Badly wounded, he made his way back to the wilderness where he died soon after."

"Tell him of the lions, father."

"Yes, lest I forget. May it never be Levi, this great man, Jeroboam, had become so revered in heaven that angels instructed two lions to dig his grave where his body remains buried until this day."

The idea that powerful lions would be instructed to bury the man totally intrigued Levi. Having barely enough breath to get it out he asked, "Lions? Lions dug his grave?"

"Yes, Levi. Two lions. There is much tradition you should know. This is the fiber of who you are . . . who we are! We are not living out today and tomorrow alone, we are woven into the fabric of what our God has done through the ages."

59

"You are welcome to stay among us, Levi."

AN EXCITING SENSE ABOUT the lion story and the idea of being part of something greater than himself formed the seed of some appeal in him. Although he felt deeply about learning more, he held a compelling desire to find the Teacher, and the new place, and then all his experiences would be explained to him. All else would have to wait. He fended off doubts as to why he felt so compelled to follow the Teacher, hoping against hope it would not be yet another disappointment. If that were to be the case he sensed a foreboding that there would then be nothing left for him. No hope. No change. He would end where he started, belonging to nothing or no one.

"The Christ child . . . is he now living in a palace?" Levi asked.

"Palace? No, no, no. He travels the countryside speaking of the coming kingdom, the one long ago promised to our people. They say many have been healed and many follow to hear his teachings."

This description instantly struck a bell for Levi. Could the shepherd be speaking of the Teacher? Levi began to ask then stopped, realizing that if he asked using the title, Teacher, the shepherd, like the others he'd asked along the way, would likely not know.

"Do you know this Christ child's name?" he asked.

The shepherd immediately answered, "Jesus the Nazarene."

Excitedly, Levi pounced on the information. "Is there word of where he can be found?"

"I know only that since his resurrection he has been appearing in the countryside."

"Sir," Levi said, to the old shepherd, "I must leave now, to complete my journey. I must go back to Jerusalem as fast as I can."

"I see," he responded sadly. "Well then, do you need provisions?"

"No, I have a few coins."

"Coins cannot feed you if there are no merchants, and if you are going to Jerusalem from here, there are none along the way. Let us bless you with some food and water to take along." The shepherd placed his hand on Levi's shoulder as they walked toward the donkeys strapped with supplies.

The shepherd gave him a bag with provisions. "You are welcome to stay among us, Levi. Yet I can see this is a journey you must carry out," the shepherd said. "As to your journey to Jerusalem; you continue along this path," the shepherd pointed it out, "it will take you to the edge of the wilderness desert. Keep the sun always on this side of your face and you will eventually come to a place where you can see in the far distance, low lying mountains. That is where Jerusalem is." The shepherd stopped and seemed to be thinking about something. Then he shook his head as though saying yes to himself. "Should your journey there take you into the night and it shall, you may need to continue on your path in the darkness. This is something that will guide you so your direction will be clear. When you stop for the night," the shepherd lifted his head to look up, "you must look up into night sky and scan the stars until you see the one that outshines all the others. You will have no trouble seeing it. That is the ancient star . . . the star of Bethlehem. Once you see it, take your right arm, and lift it so that your finger is pointing directly to it. Hold your arm there steadily while you turn your body to the left. The direction of your nose is the path that will lead you to the direction which you must go. This will keep you from straying and wasting time getting lost."

"I understand. Thank you," said Levi. "I am grateful for your help and what you have taught me."

"But that is only the beginning," added Yochnan. "The way across the desert is a long journey. You will need a mule or camel."

The stress of hearing that soured Levi's face. He looked to the ground.

To encourage the boy, the shepherd then added, "I know this one thing for certain, Levi. Listen carefully now. God will guide your journey!"

Levi wanted to embrace the feeling of remaining there with the man and his sons, but he thwarted it away. The rattling thoughts reentered making him almost feel despair on some level because for the first time in his life he felt terrible pain, a pain of realization as to what it meant to be alone in the world. But this was not pain as it felt in the pangs of hunger or in the pain of mistreatment; but a pain that touched his very soul. The last words the shepherd uttered were, "God's blessing and protection upon you as you discover who you are. Learn of the staff, Levi."

To avoid what he knew were tears forming; Levi quickly thanked them again, profusely and darted off running. He knew how to run. He could run, and he could run fast. And now as he ran back into aloneness, he would try to outrun the tears.

60

Peter spoke directly to the authorities standing in the crowd

A GREAT DEAL WAS HAPPENING in Jerusalem following the death of Jesus, of which Levi had no knowledge whatsoever. In Jerusalem the news spread rapidly that one of the disciples of Jesus stood publically in defiance of the temple officials, speaking boldly of Jesus' message. Despite these warnings some people came to hear out of curiosity and others truly seeking to know more. Slim at first, the crowd swelled to several thousand people. Due to the sheer numbers of people the authorities did not attempt to disperse them. Pacing as he spoke, a man named Peter told the people how the authorities and the religious leaders condemned Jesus to death, an innocent man.

Then Peter spoke directly to the authorities who stood on the outskirts of the crowd. "Hear this truth. Jesus of Nazareth, a man attested to you by God with mighty works and wonders and signs that God did through him in your midst has been delivered up, and you crucified him, in league with Pontius Pilate. But God raised him up, releasing the cords of death, because it was not possible for him to be held by it. Just as the prophetic word has foretold."

Standing at the edge of the crowd the high priest fumed, his face flushed red, his eyes flatted to slits, at hearing these words. Turning to the temple guard he commanded, "Arrest him immediately."

The guard advised against it saying that the large crowd would likely turn on him and a riot would ensue. Knowing he was right, the high priest abruptly turned and departed telling the guard to be alert to arrest him on an opportune day.

Once Peter finished speaking he walked among the huddled groups of people, answering questions, praying with them and instructing them on what to do next. As he walked along, Veronica approached him.

"Peter. I have heard much talk about the authorities attempting to stop you from speaking these messages."

"They may well stop me, but they can never stop the risen Lord," he replied.

Her eyes saddened, "My very soul mourned in grief as they dragged Jesus through the streets carrying the cross. I broke through the crowd to wipe the blood from his face. I could hardly recognize him." She broke down, "I could not help him."

Peter grasped her by the shoulders, gently turned her and walked her over to his wife.

Lydia consoled her. "What darkness has come is now light, for Jesus has indeed risen. The time now is for rejoicing and expectation. If we share tears now, they must flow from joy not sorrow." Lydia invited Veronica to her home.

Section Three

Home

61

"The divine energy of the world has flowed into your path."

HAVING DEPARTED FROM THE shepherd and his sons, Levi could not evaluate how far he'd run and walked, nearly non-stop, but his heavy legs let him know it had been quite a trek. The sun started its phase of melting into the horizon giving way to the night's blanket, offering another testimony to the distance he'd covered. He sought out a place to sleep for the night as it became impossible to continue on. Walking along studiously, a familiar and now unwelcome voice called out, "Alms! Alms!"

Levi's shoulders dropped. He looked everywhere around him unable to see the old beggar. He somehow heard the words clearly yet the old beggar could not be found. He concluded that the voice had in some mysterious way come into his head.

"The divine energy of the world has flowed into your path. Heed this carefully. You must understand that there are only so many times you can burn a bridge down before it can no longer be rebuilt." It was clearly the old beggar's voice and yet he did not appear to him.

Before now the thought hadn't been conscious to Levi. The words were true; he had refused to acknowledge the kindness as anything more than some unexplainable oddity. Yet the truth remained that even when begging in the square he did observe parents caring for their children and other displays of kindness although he gave this no passage into his feelings. He once believed that such events were only handled with care for others to see since they were in public. There were many acts of kindness on display, but he refused to see them. The words pierced sharply.

The observations weighed on Levi. No longer could he think that way and risk missing important messages the Teacher instructed him to embrace.

The beggar's words ceased. He considered the thoughts he held before, his discouraged thoughts, questioning whether to leave Jerusalem, the anger and the doubts. All of it rummaged in his mind. What came of this pondering recalled to mind the old beggar's words of being paralyzed. In a sudden flash of clarity the boy understood that he had been focused only on the physical world. Although his entire life fused with the physical, the chalice and the encounters he experienced along this journey now opened a window. Something beyond the physical world hovered near to him. The veil that the old beggar spoke of, that would give entry to the divine energy of the world. Not knowing exactly how he knew, it became certain that the way would be provided in one of the messages, causing him to reaffirm his alertness.

He continued walking, searching for a place to stay the night. Along the side of the path he found himself near a fence partially standing, and partially bent over and broken. Near the fence stood a large pile of rotting logs and scattered debris. Beyond that lay what had once been some kind of building, now only a remnant of burned char and ash. He couldn't tell much about it because night had fallen. Looking around the log pile turned out to be the only available accommodation. He wondered what this place might have been due to the odd location. Only yards away the desert plains started with nothing else nearby. The draping darkness did not allow him to look to the horizon to see if the mountains the shepherd had told him would lead to Jerusalem were out there or not. He could only hope he had arrived in the right place. In the morning light he would know for sure. Looking into the pile of logs he saw a small open gap, just enough for him to squeeze in and sleep the night out of sight. Levi inspected the pile of logs. He pushed his foot against the area over the gap to determine the sturdiness of the pile. Not a budge. Scanning the area to be certain there were no other people there, he dropped to the ground on all fours, reached his staff into the gap and tapped it on the hardpan which caused the field mice to scatter away. Then he backed out to stand up. He focused himself on the instruction the shepherd gave him about marking his direction. Lifting his head to the night sky he located the ancient star with a sense it had welcomed him. What a wondrous sight it presented. It even caused him to smile. Could that be the star that led the shepherds to the Christ child in the manger? He gazed at it for some time trying to feel its welcome with more reality.

He then lifted his right arm and pointed his finger directly over the star and carefully turned his body to the left just as he had been instructed.

Freezing in place for a moment he then looked to the ground and pushed his sandal into the dirt twisting it so he could find the hollowed out spot in the dark. Following the instructions given by Yochnan, he kneeled down, found a small stick and drew an arrow pointing in the same direction his nose had. Now he would have a marker in the morning to assure he would continue on the right path. Try as he did, he could not see anything in the distant curtain of darkness where the arrow pointed.

Unable to see what lay ahead he would have to wait for the light of day. Learning to wait, he felt, would be applied to the remainder of this journey. He would follow the way that shown clear as not to stumble onto the wrong path. The bald man with the dog came to mind, who told him how heaven had used his eyes when the barley seller attempted to cheat the weights. *If heaven gave me eyes to see, it will have to do it for me to find the way,* he thought confidently. This self agreement held practicality for him.

62

"Has the desert blown sand in your ears, boy?"

TURNING BACK TO THE wood pile he wedged himself into the opening, drank some water and ate a dried fruit. Yawning he laid his head on the dirt and no sooner dozed off. His dreams were like a vivid kaleidoscope, more so than ever before. He saw Judas storming out of the upper room. Partial words that Jesus spoke flitted in and out. The old beggar spoke to him but he could not hear all the words. The stout man's hookahs seemed to melt as smoke released from them. His staff danced in the air as though beckoning him to follow. The old shepherd appeared pointing up to the sky saturated with stars. His body tossed and turned. He saw the bald man's dog running toward him. Metha's face danced about without a body. He glimpsed the Teacher calling his name. Then he was running away from the man, Jonathan. His feet were moving at full speed. He ran and ran and ran, but he seemed to be going nowhere regardless of how hard he tried. Then came the loud bellowing, bleating and moaning sounds haunting after him. The sounds grew louder and louder until he found himself sitting up with a start, completely awakened and sweated. Early morning rays of light were already breaking through the spaces between the logs.

Recollection of the dream dissipated except for the most vivid scene of his staff dancing, beckoning him to follow. The bleating sounds persisted, growing louder. In a handful of moments he connected with the sounds of high pitched bleats and bellowing moans. Camels were nearby. Crawling out into the open area he glanced at the arrow and the stick he had placed there. Walking to it he dropped to a knee and gazed out directly in front of him. Just as the shepherd had said, there were the low lying mountains. They were so far off they looked small and they were a pale gray color as they blended with the gray morning mist. The sounds of the camels were now very close. Turning his head he observed a caravan of camels coming to a halt. Upon seeing the camels he unexpectedly, and with no small surprise started laughing. Deep belly laughs poured out as though escaping a long imprisonment. He couldn't help himself and it made him fall on his backside. The deep laughter felt wonderful. Seeing the camels called him back to when he had run from the Roman Guard after seeing Judas in the marketplace. The Roman ran right into the camel and was completed covered by the camel's inflated vile smelling cud sac fluids. Now for some reason it amused him thoroughly. Finally composing himself, rubbing his sore belly, he studied the caravan just ahead.

The rope on each camel's halter strung back to the saddle of the camel behind it and had fallen slack as they came to a halt. It appeared they were just in preparation to travel out into the desert. The camel driver wore a large white turban and his beard shone as black as he had ever seen. The man dismounted while grumbling. Then he walked back to the second camel to help a woman dismount. Levi watched the man removing and readjusting the load strapped on the camel. Cautiously he walked into view and waited until the camel driver noticed him. Lifting his staff he called out a greeting, asking permission to come forward.

The man called out, "What is it boy, you see I am busy here!" the man snarled.

"Can you tell me the way back to Jerusalem?" He found it difficult to even think it. *I am going back to where I began, where I never wanted to be again*, he thought. He also knew that he would never find the Teacher if he stayed away.

The man turned his torso and stepped away from the camel, pointing toward the low lying mountains far in the distance. He stretched out his arm with a finger pointing south, "Sixty-five miles."

"Sixty-five miles?" He repeated.

"Has the desert blown sand in your ears, boy? Sixty-five miles." He repeated belligerently.

"That is a long way," Levi noted out loud.

"You will need provisions for that journey on foot," he said sarcastically. "Now, take your leave . . . I have work to do." The man turned back to the camel, adjusting the load straps. The rest of the people in the caravan had also dismounted to stretch their legs and make adjustments. It seemed that the camel driver would require some time to strap the cargo back on the camel.

63

"You are able and young. Walk."

L EVI TOOK ANOTHER CHANCE to ask the camel driver, "Sir. Will you allow me to go with you to Jerusalem?"

The man's eyes turned to slits, "I cannot, and I will not. These people
are paying for the journey. I cannot have you travel at no cost when they
have all paid. This is a caravan, boy, not an alms house. You are able and
young. Walk. I can see you are a shepherd boy, you should know how to
travel. Make a plan . . . do something other than annoy me."

"I can pay."

The man shook his head uncaringly and gave a price. What coins Levi
had were not nearly enough. Levi sensed the camel driver gave him a price
much higher than it should be. He understood that merchants realized that
those who were desperate would pay more. This turn of events would add
more passing time, another hindrance to finding the Teacher. He began
walking past each of the camels in the caravan. His head hung in no small
disappointment. Now that he began to understand some of the messages
and lessons he'd been given, he wanted to go forward. His aim had been
to stop feeling so angry and disappointed and commit to go forward. Why
then did he continue to face delays? Why haven't the Teacher appeared to
him yet? *He must know I'm looking for him. Where was this divine energy of
the world now,* he couldn't help wondering with some friction. The chalice
warmed causing him to recall his decision that he would look for clarity as
not to stumble in the wrong path. He realized a deeper meaning; the wrong
path could not only be a physical path but a mental path. With this he lifted
his head and brightened his eyes . . . just as all along his journey he believed
something would take place to guide him.

Passing by the last camel, a tall, lean man noticed him. He assumed the boy to be with the caravan so he called out, "Boy, where are you going? Do not stray far from the caravan. It is easy to get lost, even for a shepherd boy."

Levi turned his head to look over at the man who stood lean and tall. He had the largest mouthful of teeth he had ever seen. "I am not with the caravan." Nor was he a shepherd boy but the staff indicated to people that he was.

"Then what in the world is a young boy doing out here in the wilderness alone?"

"I asked the camel driver to join the caravan. I must get to Jerusalem. But he will not allow me."

"He will not allow you?"

"No, and I offered to pay what little I have," said Levi.

"Come over here, the tall man said waving him forward."

Levi approached the tall man cautiously.

"You have nothing to fear from me," the tall man said, handing him a water flask. "What makes Jerusalem so important to you?"

"I have to find someone before it is too late," Levi answered.

The tall man observed the sincerity in the boy's eyes. "Before it's too late you say?" He folded his arms across his chest. Then he pointed to the flask. "Drink and wait for me here. I will return in a moment. Do not depart."

The tall man didn't have to ask him to wait there, Levi's thirst kept him in place with the flask as he drank deeply. Stepping away from the camel he looked on to see where the tall man went. He watched as the tall man walked to the lead camel where the camel driver worked at finishing up the straps and cargo. The tall man and the driver seemed to be having a disagreement, hands waving around. Finally the driver stomped his foot and threw both his hands up in a symbol of surrender. The tall man removed something from his pocket, giving it to the camel driver.

The tall man walked back and announced, "You shall ride with me. What is your name, boy?"

Stunned at this turn of events, Levi stood speechless. Another adult appeared in his path being kind and helpful. The chalice warmed, and he understood. He had just told himself to stop complaining and now he again found a path forward. The words of Yochnan the shepherd from yesterday rang in his mind, '*I know one thing for certain, God will provide for the journey.*' No longer did he consider those words as mere words, they were coming true in the physical. Although he did not yet understand, it seemed that his idea of God was being challenged. Levi handed the water flask back to the man. "I am Levi, Sir."

"And, I am Joktan. Come, Levi, let us mount up. The caravan is going to move again."

Levi mounted up on the camel seated behind Joktan. At length, Levi finally asked, "Joktan, why have you done this?"

"I must go to Jerusalem for a purpose of course!"

"No, sir, I mean why did you speak with the camel driver and allow me to ride?"

Levi nearly jumped off the saddle blanket when a long, loud belly laugh echoed out of Joktan as his head jerked back. Levi could not figure why the man laughed so heartily.

"Why? You ask me why I allowed you to ride; because I wanted you to ask me why. I want everyone I encounter for the rest of my days to ask me why I try to serve them."

Levi quizzically shook his head.

"You see, Levi, I have learned something astounding . . . something . . . well . . . miraculous." Bellowing another laugh, he lifted himself, twisting his head and shoulders back as far as he could as the camel jockeyed them in an up and down rhythm. "Can you hear my words well from back there, Levi?"

"I can hear."

"Freely I have been given . . . and now . . . freely I shall give. You see, I have become a free man . . . free, free, free!" He yelled it out joyfully as though the happiest man alive.

The boy had never observed such a powerful exclamation of joy. And he actually felt the energy of the man's joy and celebration.

64

Even mentioning
the word sets one to fear

THE MAN'S ACTIONS INTRIGUED the boy so he asked, "Were you freed from the Roman prison?"

"That would have been a much preferred to the prison in which I had been confined . . . oh, indeed, by far . . . much preferred."

"Then what prison were you in, Joktan? The Roman work camp?"

Joktan lifted the sleeve of his tunic up and stretched out his bare arm to display before Levi. As he held it out he asked, "What do you see?"

Levi looked, trying to see something other than a bare arm. "I see only your arm."

Joktan then placed his palms down on the camel saddle and lifted himself enough to be able to swivel his torso and face to Levi. He then pointed to his face, "What do you see here?"

Again, Levi tried to spot something unusual that he might answer the man. It was obvious that he wanted to make a point of some kind. "I am sorry, but I see nothing . . . only your face . . . that is all I see."

"Halleluiah! Halleluiah!" proclaimed Joktan. "If you saw me only a few weeks ago, you would have run from me."

"Why?" asked Levi.

"Leprosy. My walking prison."

Levi instinctively pulled back.

"You see there, even the mention of the word sets one to fear. But I am clean . . . you have seen with your own eyes. No need to fear. The temple priest has declared me clean. I have a sealed certificate from him." Once again the man laughed deeply exuding great joy. "The heinous prison of leprosy brings with it two deaths. The obvious one is what you see on a man's physical body, his decrepit skin, his body parts fall off, he is coming apart piece by piece as he walks to his death. Yet the greater prison is the inner death. The loneliness. Being an outcast. Abandoned. Several of the men I knew imprisoned by leprosy had wives and children. By law they were forced to leave their families. It is a slow, lonesome and painful prison from which there is no escape. And that prison assures you remain alone, abandoned."

"Yes," said Levi, "I have seen one such leprous man walk into the market square in Jerusalem. He called out at the top of his lungs. 'Unclean. Unclean.' I remember how people swarmed away from him saying they were afraid to even breathe the air around him. But I cannot understand this, how is it you no longer have leprosy?" He asked with no small astonishment. "A man does not heal from leprosy."

"Oh, I was not healed alone . . . I and nine other outcast lepers. We walked along across the border of Samaria through a small village for we had heard of the man of miracles would be there."

"The man of miracles?"

"Yes, Levi. And we sought him out and we found him with his disciples entering the village. May our God be praised that he stood there right before us in the road." Joktan smiled so widely, his large white teeth showing with happiness, that Levi thought the man might strain his mouth. "The moment my friend saw him, he cried out loudly, 'Jesus, Master, have pity on us.' And at that very moment—"

Levi stopped him. Lifting himself up off the camel's blanket and with a strained voice asked, "Jesus? The one who healed you was Jesus?" His voice incredulous.

"Yes, Jesus. He healed all ten of us. Do you know of him?"

"I met the Teacher in the upper room, in Jerusalem."

"The Teacher? Who is this person?"

"Jesus. He holds many titles, Rabbi, Master, Lord . . . Teacher"

"I care nothing of titles, I am only grateful that he showed mercy to all ten of us lepers. Each one healed. Each one of us snatched from the prison of walking death. Each of us declared clean by the Chief Priest, and able to return to our families, towns . . . our very lives! We are free men now. Halleluiah! Halleluiah!" he proclaimed again.

"Joktan . . ." Levi hesitated, "they . . . have killed the Teacher and two other men."

The man's face dulled. "That is why I am going to Jerusalem. I will seek out his disciples. They continue to speak his good news to all who will hear.

My brother and his wife live in Jericho. They are all the family I have. I must see them first."

"People are saying the teacher is appearing to many. They claim he is alive again!"

"Yes, I too have heard of this," said Joktan. "This is why it is important for me to have the papers from the high priest declaring me clean. So I will be accepted by his disciples."

"Why did you go to the priest to be declared clean if you were already healed?"

"This is the law. Jesus instructed all of us to go show ourselves to the priest. We were at first, greatly disappointed as we did not feel or even looked healed at all. He did not lay hands on us. He said no healing prayer. He told us to begin walking and go show ourselves to the chief priest. And upon our very first step our disease began falling away from our bodies, as we walked we became cleaner and cleaner, healthier and healthier, liberated and more liberated. After three years of our bodily imprisonment, a miracle of miracles had been granted to us. When we reached the chief priest, we were completely healed. Clean. Clean. Clean. Smooth skin everywhere . . . not one blemish. The Chief Priest inspected each of us, and provided letters that assured we were clean. He placed his seal on each one. I immediately ran back to find Jesus and when I did, I fell to my knees and thanked him with all my heart. But along with my joy I carried great shame also."

"Why, Joktan?"

"I was ashamed for the other nine . . . they did not return to thank him. I came alone. And I was . . ." he lowered his voice, "the only gentile. A foreigner and yet . . . he healed me. This is why I go to Jerusalem. To become his disciple."

"Why did the Teacher need to be thanked?"

Joktan could not withhold another joyful burst of laughter. "Levi, it is not that he needs to be thanked for himself. So many people . . . so many of us . . . live life without a sense of gratitude which is birthed in one's heart for love shown, love that is given selflessly. The love Jesus shares is drawing people together to be as one, no longer isolated from who we are, no more enmity with God. Gratefulness is health to one's soul and being."

After a silent moment Levi said, "I have always been alone. I never knew my mother and father. I live in the street begging alms. Now I no longer want to be alone or to beg because the Teacher told me something in the upper room after his Passover supper."

"Can you tell me what he said to you?"

"First he told me he would soon be alone, but it would only be for a time, and then he would no longer be alone. Then he said it would be the same for me."

"Heaven be praised," Joktan shouted out. "You see then, both truths have come to pass."

"Both?"

"Yes, my boy. When I had the leprosy, I stood alone trapped in my disease. Then when Jesus healed me I walked forward and out of abandonment and into a new family, the family Jesus is bringing together. This I have learned. When you see the world through caring kindness you begin to see God at work within you and in this wounded world. There is place inside," he tapped over his heart, "one cannot see until he opens new eyes."

New eyes? Levi thought of the old man and the dog saying that God had used his eyes with the barley merchant. "I saw a merchant cheat weights on his scale when selling barley to an old man because he could tell the man could not see well. I told him he was cheating. The old man said that God had used my eyes to see for him that day. I cannot understand how God could use my eyes."

"What a marvelous thing you have experienced; to see truth," Joktan said. "Yes, of course God used your eyes; you must understand that nothing is impossible for love to accomplish. I bear witness of this my boy. Trapped in my own prison I could not see beyond myself and my condition. I sought healing from the outside. After meeting Jesus I came to understand this truth, first comes the spiritual, then the physical. When you trust Jesus your mind will be transformed to a new way of seeing within and without his kingdom."

"The Teacher spoke of this to his men in the upper room. He told of his coming kingdom. I thought he and his men were planning a revolution against Caesar. But he had no soldiers . . . only the men in the room. I am seeking to find the new place where his kingdom and his men will be." His chin dropped to his chest.

Joktan pondered something then looked at the boy straight on. "I believe fully he spoke of another kind of kingdom. You see, when I left the chief priest after being declared clean, I walked through the city when I heard one of Jesus' disciples speaking to people, teaching that the kingdom was close to them. I knew of this nearness because my healing took place there."

The kingdom of God near? Levi wondered. "Your healing took place in the new kingdom? Show me where can I find his kingdom . . . where do I go?"

"You are not understanding. The kingdom is not a place out there."

"How can a kingdom be nowhere?" asked Levi.

"There are things that exist beyond what we see and touch. Consider . . . how did Jesus heal me? He did not touch me physically, yet my physical body healed as I walked." Seeing the boy's confusion Joktan added, "Let me ask you this, how often have you heard the wind?"

Levi's eyes squinted as though the question might be a riddle, but he answered. "Many times. All the time."

"Were you able to see the wind itself?"

"No," Levi said quickly.

"So, my boy, you observed something you could see with your eyes that represented something you could not see with your eyes!"

"Uh . . . I . . ."

"Did you see the wind itself is what I ask you?" Joktan asked.

"No. No one can see the wind."

"Then how do you know the wind had blown?"

Levi smiled with an understanding. "I could see the trees and branches move. I could feel the wind in my face."

"Yes, so there are things we cannot see, however, we can see their effects physically. So it is with the kingdom. It has no limits, and cannot be exhausted. This truth is one we should be grateful for. This energy from heaven reaches and touches all people in various ways everywhere in this world, and never hides itself from anyone"

65

A life without hope
is a daily death of despair

"THIS ENERGY OF HEAVEN touches everyone? Then it must touch bad people? They do bad things, why should they be included?"

"That is a serious question. Let me ask, have you ever done anything bad?"

The boy's head dropped, a gesture signifying his guilt. "I . . . have," were his only softly spoken words.

Joktan smiled. "I and every person will give the same answer; you are not the only one who has done so. Now, there is more to it. Although I did bad things in my life, still healing had been gifted to me so that I might understand a truth of the ages. A person who lives his life without God can only live one way . . . all he can do is function in survival. In order to survive one must be willing put himself first and to do whatever is needed including participation in what is bad. The energy of heaven flows to each of us with the power to unshackle us to freedom. In other words every person needs to be freed of their own particular form of survival which is a prison. These matters are complicated . . . I hope this explanation helps?" Joktan asked.

"I never would know such things," Levi said. "Yes, what you say is more clear for me because I have lived this way and I see now how people that I hated were living as I did, in survival as you said."

Joktan added, "Yes, the problem is that we cannot easily see this happening to us because we are so ingrained in survival. Jesus brings the power to transform us from surviving to living. I am not certain of this yet but it seems to me this is the existence of the kingdom which fosters hope. As a leper I always remained hopeful for the chance that somehow I would be released from the walking prison. You see, Levi, this is the power of hope . . . it will keep a man alive in the most hideous of circumstances. Without hope men die."

Joktan's words recalled what the old beggar had said about hope, that even as small embers they could be rekindled.

Joktan continued, "Each of us is free to do what we choose, good or bad."

Now this was something Levi had never heard or thought, yet carried a level of believability to him. "You were exiled and diseased for three years?"

"A life without . . ." Joktan's eyes became deep and moistened. He placed his hand over his eyes and he turned forward to continue speaking. "A life without hope is a daily death of despair. As a leper I walked and walked yet never outwalked my leprosy."

"Why did God take my mother and father away?" Levi said abruptly. The question unintended yet out it flowed in response to the gentle strength of Joktan.

"My boy, God does not take away. God is a giver. I cannot know what took place with your parents, but if it was something bad, and it would likely be the case, then it came from the hand of men not God. You can however, know something of your parents."

"I can? What, how?"

"Well, you have survived in the streets begging, caring for yourself . . . never giving up. There is a spirit of determination, courage and resourceful- ness within you. These things are carried in your very blood. The blood of your parents flows within you. They are alive in you in this way: their cour- age and resourcefulness flows in you. The life . . . is in the blood."

Following these discussions they continued on with neither of them speaking. Finally the caravan stopped and settled for the night.

As Levi laid his head down to sleep, Joktan's words about his parents seeped in. He allowed this to be his truth. And for the first time he sensed deep within him a faint connection affirming that the Teacher had been with him all along the journey. This connection, he wondered, might be the divine energy of the world and yet he still did not understand that if it had been so close, why could he not enter?

Levi reflected back to the old beggar who had summed up his life as doing the very same thing as Joktan; walking and walking and going no- where. This now held more clarity in his mind. In meeting Joktan he held a new confidence that leaving Jerusalem to seek out the Teacher and his men had been the right decision. Levi processed all the people he'd met, all the things he had seen, all the difficulties and kindnesses . . . and . . . he gave some way to think that . . . love had been experienced.

Something else he had not realized came to him almost randomly. The people he'd met did not look at him as a dirty, worthless beggar orphan, they regarded him with value. He also observed the unexplained exuberance of the people who had been with the Teacher. Each of them from what he had heard enjoyed some good result from it. He had no explanation for it, only the living evidence. Levi glanced at Joktan who looked up at the stars while softly singing praises to God. Never had he encountered a man as happy and joyful as Joktan. This man he well liked and held a new and different feeling in him. Gratefulness . . . he had experienced a brush with gratefulness and it felt very good. He told himself that his time would come and then he would know, and would finally be part of a family just as Joktan had mentioned.

The next morning the camels and the travelers all moved about preparing to complete the last leg of the journey. Joktan shared a morning meal with Levi. Very little conversation took place as they worked to check cargo straps.

Once they mounted up and moved on, Levi perked up. "Joktan, do you know the Teacher brought a dead boy back to life? He passed by a funeral procession with his disciples near the gate of Beit Shemesh. He saw the boy's mother weeping and mourning, and walked up to the coffin. He raised him from the dead right in the street, right there in front of many people. There were many, many witnesses."

"Halleluiah! Praise be!" shouted Joktan. "And, he brought me back to life, out of my own walking coffin. You see, he is the man of miracles . . . the man of miracles."

"You say you want to be the Teacher's disciple?"

"This is my pledge," said Joktan. "But what about you Levi . . . what are you seeking?"

"I want to find the Teacher. I want him to appear to me so I can understand what to do. I hope we get to Jerusalem soon," he said.

"The caravan will travel into Jericho first. We can go to Jerusalem from there, it is not far. Is that where you live?" Joktan asked.

"This is the first time I have ever been so far away. I wanted to find the new place. If I find the Teacher in Jerusalem, he will tell me what to do."

Joktan did not fully understand the boy's response. "You understand he has left his work for his disciples to carry on? They can teach you what you need to know."

"I understand, but I must see the Teacher first."

"I am sure you will. The caravan will stop in Jericho which is a beautiful place, you shall see. It is a lush land. The name Jericho means *fragrant*, and indeed it is. Every good land requires two things; water and good soil. Jericho possesses both. Its waters are clear and cold . . . so rich it bubbles from the ground at Elisha's spring. Do you know of the prophet, Elisha?"

"I do not," Levi said.

"Elisha made Jericho's water safe and blessed the soil."

"How?" asked Levi.

"In our ancestor's time, the people of the city came to Elisha. They told him the water turned bad . . . bitter . . . not drinkable and that the soil sat unproductive. The prophet asked the people to bring him a new bowl which he carried to the spring and with a prayer declared that the Lord healed the water and the soil, and it has remained pure to this day. And I cannot wait to be there once again now, as a free man. My brother must believe that I am dead by now. After seeing him I will go to Jerusalem where I shall become a disciple to carry his message through the land," Joktan exclaimed. "As a disciple I shall show gratefulness for the miracle, to tell all the people I see about his mercy and power. I will show my letter from the high priest if they do not believe me."

66

The man's presence had shifted something in his heart

As the caravan entered Jericho, Levi could already see all Joktan's ravings about the city to be true. Lush and green; an oasis in the desert with fruit trees planted everywhere. The caravan came to a halt and passengers dismounted, gathering their belongings. Joktan and Levi followed suit.

"Levi, you should come with me to my brother's house. He will be greatly shocked to see me. I have been gone so long; he may not believe it is me," he said with a brimming smile. "Yes, you should accompany me." He waited for Levi's response.

The boy wrestled inside feeling deeply torn. This man had helped him, and if not for him he had no idea how he would have gotten back. Joktan also made an impression on him with his outgoing happiness and explanations of gratitude and joy and dedication to the Teacher. Levi knew how deeply Joktan had affected him with his great joy and laughter and quiet strength. His presence had shifted something in his heart.

Levi came back to the moment. All the people were removing their bags and items. As they dismounted the camels, Levi's jaw tightened, he did not want to look up into Joktan's eyes. He steeled himself not to allow any tears. Yet he could not deny that sadness overtook him. How badly he wished to stay with Joktan and yet he must continue on.

His heart weighed down and he found it difficult to say. Finally he spoke. "Thank you Joktan, for your help and kindness. And for the lessons you have offered. I am happy to know the Teacher has given you freedom. I must leave for Jerusalem now. I cannot wait." Joktan didn't just talk about the Teacher, but had been personally touched by him. He found great comfort during the time he had traveled with Joktan—the displays of joy and celebration were new experiences.

"I will come to Jerusalem also, but first I must see my brother and celebrate my miracle. You should reconsider . . . go with me."

Levi nodded with a sad smile. His stomach panged with a deeper hollowness.

Joktan placed his hand on Levi's shoulder, "I want to say something to you. Remember this for it is a lesson I learned. Do not doubt what presents itself to you as kindness. If you only live on your guard all you do is hold things away. Hope brings us near. Fear creates distance. Hope is the ladder out of fear. May the Lord keep you and bless you. And, I truly believe we will meet again. I will look for you in Jerusalem. Surely I will." Although he made his large toothy smile he could not disguise the presence of his sadness. Somehow he knew that the boy was attempting to do what he did; out walk his troubles. Levi squeezed Joktan's hand tightly; nearly unable to pull it away, but finally he summoned the will to turn and walk toward the crowd.

"Levi, wait," Joktan shouted. He walked to Levi as he removed the bag strapped over his shoulder. Reaching inside the bag, he removed a small flask and a hand full of dried fruits. "I will not need these. My brother lives only a short distance away. Come to the side with me for a moment. I will look for you in Jerusalem, but if I do not see you again you must heed what I tell you now."

Levi attentively looked up at Joktan.

"Jesus has already placed his presence in you when he told you that you were not alone. This was an invitation just as he had given me and the nine other lepers. When an invitation is given it must be accepted or it holds no value for you. If he said you were no longer alone, then you are to believe you are no longer alone. Remember the lesson about the wind. Just because you cannot see this now, does not mean it is not true. You continue to seek this truth in the physical. You must begin to seek him not merely out there; you must seek him within you. This is where he can be found . . . beyond the physical."

Levi nodded affirmatively.

Joktan continued. "You have been begging alms most of your short life, have you not?"

"Yes," Levi said.

"You had to learn the ways and the tools of begging did you not? And this took many years did it not?"

"It did," Levi said.

"Well before I became a leper, I worked as a stone builder. It requires five years to become a stone builder as with many other skills. So I ask you,

Levi, what is it that makes a man think he can learn God's ways in one moment or in a matter of days?"

Levi offered no response.

"To know of God who is not physical, but spirit, you must first observe
God working in others and then see him yourself. You will then begin to feel
God. Above all, remember this. Love is more than a feeling. It is an action."

Levi thanked him again, and without reluctance, hugged Joktan for a
long while. Levi strapped the items over his shoulder, turned and melded
into the crowd. The stout man, the old man with the dog, Photini, the shepherd, all those he encountered had helped him, shown kindness and offered
lessons of help. He thought fondly of each one, but Joktan displayed such
an overwhelming joy, and a confidence he had never observed before. To
Joktan the power of the Teacher seemingly held no limits in his ability to
cause good things to take place. As he walked through the crowd he wanted
to look back to catch another glimpse of Joktan then thought it best not to
do so. Something deep within, a breaking of some kind distressed him. He
wished it would depart, but in the moment he experienced what he had
until now only heard some adults speak about . . . what it meant to have a
heart soaked with sadness and that made it weigh more heavily. The chalice
warmed at the thought. He picked up his pace, his staff moving by his side
in cadence. They became the most arduous steps forward he'd ever taken to
this moment, and he knew full well he could not outrun what he felt.

Suddenly something caused him to stop in his tracks. How could he
have forgotten to ask such an important question of Joktan? His heart raced
as he turned, running back through the oncoming crowd weaving in between people hoping Joktan would not be far ahead. What if he had already
reached his brother's house? On the thought of it he ran all the faster. He
had to try. How on earth would he find him in the massive sea of people
and animals? He reached the place where they had departed so he began to
call out Joktan's name. He tried to jump high enough to see over the crowd
to no avail. He called out again and again. No response. People and faces
all a blur. He nearly knocked over a young man carrying a lamb across his
shoulders. Then he thought he heard it; "Halleluiah! Halleluiah!" There was
no mistaking that shout of pure joy. Joktan's voice just ahead . . . somewhere.

Joktan turned his head back thinking his name had been called, but
saw no one, just a flood of faces. He continued along, singing praises aloud.
Levi could hear him. He was close. Then without warning, a fold sheep cut
across his path as well as the others walking near him. They were followed
by two men yelling out as they tried to gather the sheep that ran off frightened by something. With the delay Levi no longer heard Joktan. Covering
a few more paces he finally saw Joktan who had captured one of the sheep,

holding it in his arms calling out to the shepherd as he walked on. Jumping up and down, waving his hands Levi called out Joktan's name. He saw Levi and stopped. Placing the sheep down between his ankles he called out, "Levi, are you all right?"

Levi approached, out of breath, waving his hand indicating he was fine. Catching his breath he said, "Joktan, I am so glad I found you."

"What has happened?"

"I forgot to ask you something. Something . . ." he paused to breathe, "Something very important."

"What is it? How can I help?"

One of the shepherds came to Joktan, thanking him for capturing the sheep as he grasped it and walked off. Joktan and Levi stepped over near a small corral of camels to move out of the crowd's activity.

"You held urgency to return to Jerusalem. What's happened?" said Joktan.

"I need to know the secret."

"The secret? What secret?" Joktan said confused.

"I know now that I have been very near the divine energy of the world all along my journey. I can see that you have entered into it. You said it is not out there anywhere. Will you tell me how you were able to enter into it? When did you?"

"I will tell you what took place and perhaps this will be a way for you consider it." Joktan said with that bright toothy smile of his. "It began when I and the other lepers were seeking to find Jesus. Each of us, as far as I know, believed he held power which could heal us. This is the key of entry; *trust*. Accepting what has been said to the degree you do not falter from doing what must be done."

Levi looked on mesmerized.

"Trust . . . one must feel sure of its reality. Unless one trusts in the person who makes the promise, there can be no entry into it. I know this to be true because I experienced it as I told you. I did not receive any healing of my leprosy until I began to walk as Jesus instructed. It required trust first, then the healing. There is a teaching in the ancient writings that tells us, 'The secret things belong to God, and it is the glory of men to search it out.' Therein you must walk."

For the first time since starting his journey Levi clearly sensed the existence of a world not visible and yet he did not fully comprehend just how to actually enter, despite Joktan's attempt to clarify. One thing did make practical sense to him; he should remain alert to locate the gate that provided entry.

"You must depart for Jerusalem, Levi. Place your trust in what you heard in the upper room, and nothing else. Search out the secret, just as the ancient text instructs. I shall hope to see you again when I find the disciples of Jesus."

Levi started walking away, and in doing it occurred to him that he had given Metha a secret about the upper room. Now Joktan spoke of a secret. How everything seemed to connect and how odd it seemed to him.

67

"Wait, you were a
beggar and blind too?"

THE FARTHER AWAY FROM Jericho his steps carried the boy the closer his heart drew back to Joktan. He did not push that warm feeling off as he would have in the past. No longer did he hold doubts about the divine energy of the world. He began to look at it differently than before.

Many people were walking past him heading in the opposite direction back toward Jericho. On the one hand he wanted to turn and go with Joktan to meet his brother and be part of the celebration, on the other he knew the importance of finding the Teacher while he could still do so, having no idea if the Teacher would continue to appear.

At this point he placed every bit of his embers of hope into holding tight to the promise that the Teacher made in the upper room. The combination of nervousness, and the heat of the day caused him to reach back to adjust his tunic, and wipe his forehead with the back of his arm. In so doing he slammed into someone and found himself knocked to the ground. Quickly gaining his knees he held his forearms over his face protectively, expecting to be slapped.

"I did not see you," he said quickly to the man standing over him.

Observing that the boy's arm covered his face, he realized that he expected to be hit and quickly said, "It is I who did not see you, take my hand," said the man, as he reached down.

Although stunned by the man's words and gesture Levi grasped his hand. The man pulled him up on his feet. "You seem to be fine, boy."

"I did not see you sir."

The man bellowed a laugh. "Oh, how I love to hear those words." He laughed once again.

Levi's curiosity at this behavior got the best of him so he asked, "What words?"

"See . . . you . . ." the man emphasized each word. "These words are precious. Come to the side here. I shall tell you of a great and mighty deed my boy." Crisscrossing through the crowd to the side, they sat on a small knoll together.

"Some time ago I sat on the side of the road in Jericho begging . . . as I have most of my life." The words immediately absorbed Levi. The man removed a flask from his strap and they shared the drink. He went on. "I heard much about him, the one to come. I never knew in my greatest dreams that he would walk by my road."

"Who is this one to come?" asked Levi.

"I shall tell this to you now my boy. Listen and learn." He adjusted himself, replacing the flask. Becoming very animated he swung his hands around as though drawing out the scenes in the air, "There I sat begging alms as on any other day. As you may have noticed already, many people meet in Jericho before traveling to Jerusalem, so the road leaving Jericho is always abundant with beggars. I being among the many. Then the commotion started. People began yelling and shouting. I sensed much movement, and could feel people moving by me quickly. Then the moment came . . . when I heard people crying out that Jesus of Nazareth was there. The one of whom everyone had been speaking about."

Levi's heart leaped at hearing the name of Jesus.

"I knew of the ancient prophecy that he would come. And when I realized he walked close by me I stood up shouting as loud as I could with every breath my chest could push out. Son of David, have mercy on me. If a man's heart could speak," he patted his chest lightly, "mine did so in that moment."

Son of David? Jesus of Nazareth? Jesus had been called by many titles. Perhaps these were simply more of the same.

The man placed his hand on Levi's shoulder. "Yes, I called out so loud that all of Jericho must have heard my plea. And yet the men walking with Jesus pushed me back. They warned me to stay quiet and keep my place." The man relived the event, mesmerizing Levi.

"I would not relent," he continued, "I cried out all the more, all the louder, Son of David have mercy on me. My cries, it seemed, silenced the crowd and then I heard him. He told a man named Peter to bring me to him. Me! A poor, blind beggar and the one to come stopped to show me mercy, boy."

"Wait, you were a beggar and blind too?" Levi asked incredulous.

"Yes. And that is why I said to you, I love to hear those two words you spoke after falling; see . . . *you*. To hear the words of seeing, of sight, to have my sight, a merciful gift he gave to me, a lowly man, Bartimaeus, the son of Timaeus."

"The Teacher healed you?" Levi asked.

"The teacher?"

Levi said, "Jesus, it is Jesus, he has many titles. I am here to find him."

"I encountered him in Jericho, where he healed me," said Bartimaeus, "So I went to follow along with Jesus. He explained it would be best for me to go my way and share my good news with others. How fortuitous you bumped into me. I have not yet been able to share this love with a young person until now. You have many years ahead of you. So you too can share this love with others. As a blind beggar I remained alone, set aside on my own. I forged what I could in my own strength, and in doing I did not realize I had remained limited to my own strength and no more."

68

"Is that the divine energy of the world?"

FOLLOWING A LONG, PENSIVE thought Levi said, "Being blind must have made you even more alone than being a beggar."

"I shall tell it in this way," Bartimaeus emphasized with an animated gesture. "Have you ever reached for cluster of grapes and when you tugged, not only the grapes, but the branch ripped off from the vine?"

"Yes, many times."

"What becomes of that broken branch?"

Levi thought a moment. "It dries up."

"It dries up and it dies does it not?"

"It does."

"I was very much like that cluster of grapes and branch. On my own, alone, I no longer had anything outside myself feeding me nutrients. Separated from the vine I died spiritually . . . until Jesus grafted me into the vine once again. Can you make sense of what I have said?"

Levi thought a moment then responded, "I think I am a broken off branch as you were?"

"It would seem that Jesus is already working at restoring you to the vines."

"He is?"

"Of course. This must be so, if he began a work in you. Why else would you seek him if he has not? On that day as I sat begging, something deep in me told me that I must remain alert. And that is exactly what took place."

Bartimaeus thought for a moment and said, "If you have been on a journey to find him, what has kept you going? Have you thought about that?

192

You have not yet found him and you continue to seek. Something is compelling you just as it did me."

"Is that the divine energy of the world?" Levi asked.

"I am not familiar with these words," Bartimaeus nodded his head, "but this is a good description. God's love is indeed energy . . . it pierced me for healing. Although it cannot be seen it is more real than the physical. Somehow he caused some form of divine energy into my eyes bringing them back to origination."

He looked up at Bartimaeus with a blank stare. "Such powers are hard to believe."

"Then I will ask you this. Can it be any harder than believing your sight will be given back to you? You must become determined," he said with his arms in motion. "Listen carefully, the more they pushed me back away from Jesus the more I called out to him. The more they said I should keep my place the more I jumped up and down. You can believe whatever you wish about yourself, and that is what you will be. The world said I was a useless, poor and blind beggar worthy of a few pitiful alms. Yet the Son of David thought otherwise . . . he valued me. Not only did he return my sight to see the outside world—he gave sight to my heart to see that love is the greatest force of the world. When I heard his presence I immediately threw off my cloak, let my begging bowl fall to the ground. No longer would I need to be identified as a blind man. That is the power of absolute trust."

Trust, Levi thought. This man, like Joktan experienced trust with the Teacher.

"Why do you call the Teacher the Son of David?"

"In our ancient writings we are told that King David received a promise that one of his offspring would rule forever. Jesus is the fulfillment of the prophecy of the seed of David—the promised Messiah—which means he had to be of the lineage of David. This is why I called out to him as Son of David, to show my respect for him and the kingly power he possesses."

"I am trying to understand all these happenings," Levi admitted to Bartimaeus.

"There are many things we cannot understand. But I have come to know that it is sometimes better to receive and apply gratefully that which is given rather than struggle with trying to understanding it. When you eat a pomegranate you do not spend time trying to understand how it grew from a seed. No! You enjoy the flavors and the juices."

Levi nodded his head.

"Here, you see," Bartimaeus pointed to his eyes to emphasize the point, "these eyes were in darkness and now light enters and they see. I know not how the Son of David accomplished this—a miracle of course—yet I waste no time in trying to understand how this has come to be. I celebrate it, I hold gratitude for it, and I tell everyone who will hear me."

Levi knew he must no longer harbor doubt because he did not want to move back to his previous way of thinking and fall into doubt and mistrust. He looked at Bartimaeus. "I need to find him. I missed him everywhere I have been."

"And still you seek," Bartimaeus said.

Levi squinted, processing the comment.

"I told you that people tried to stop me from reaching the Son of David . . . that the more they pushed me back, the more I called out?"

"Yes?"

"Determination calls not for understanding it calls for trust. It demands action! Your mind shows you what your eyes see and your ears believe. Whatever you are dealing with will either be nurtured, overcome or removed by what you think. Your heart actually sees much better than your eyes. I perceive there is something wonderfully mysterious happening between you and the Son of David?"

"Yes . . . something," said Levi, knowing this to be true.

69

"Your inner fence may be closed to that which needs to enter."

B ARTIMAEUS RECOGNIZED THE LOOK in the boy's eyes. "I will tell you this from my experience, and I pray it will be of help to you."

Levi pushed his shoulders back at attention and looked up at Bartimaeus.

"If you define everything through the ways of this world you will always be limited by its boundaries. However, if you have faith in . . . what did you call it . . . ah yes, the divine energy of the world, you will see and hear what the world will not tell you. You see, your heart is a fence. And what do fences do?" Bartimaeus swung his left hand in and out away from his body and back, "Fences keep things in, and they keep things out." Bartimaeus gently tapped his finger over the boy's heart. "Your inner fence may be closed to that which needs entry."

Levi felt relieved that someone had spoken to him clearly. "This I understand . . . the fence . . ." he stood pondering the words.

"This is a good thing. So remember as powerful as the divine energy of the world can be, the smallest fence will keep you from entering."

"Thank you Bartimaeus. I will think about your lesson."

"Praises to God. Now you must continue on your journey, and I on mine. If the Lord wills we shall meet again." He patted the boy on the shoulders, smiled confidently, turned and departed. Levi watched him depart and no sooner had Bartimaeus taken a few steps when he again laughed loudly as he stopped a man and began telling his story. Levi appreciated what he learned. It seemed a practical thing he understood and reflected back on the times he risked opening his heart to others on this journey. He now became more aware of it. He would need to remain more alert to this as he went on. He turned and walked out into the crowd facing toward Jerusalem. His circular journey now began closing in. Ahead, scattered groups of people walked in the opposite direction toward Jericho. As they passed by him, he occasionally asked if any of them has seen Jesus.

An older boy walking with his parents spoke up excitedly having heard Levi ask about Jesus, "He fed many people. We had so much fish and bread, all we wanted. He fed all the people on the hillside."

"You say Jesus did this?" Levi probed.

"Yes, and he told us of many things of God."

"Is this hillside far from here?" He asked with exasperation.

"No, but we were there many days past." The boy pointed in a direction, then another with uncertainty.

Levi launched off running forward; this time undeterred. Not being focused as he moved, a large tall man stepped into his path so he quickly swerved to go around him. Not far behind the man a girl walked, head in her hands, sobbing loudly. At first he paid no attention, nor did anyone else. Something within made him look again. Startled, he stopped in his tracks. He thought he recognized her, and called out. She continued walking.

"Metha! Metha," he called out louder as he stepped next to her. "What are you doing here . . . what's wrong?"

She didn't respond. Levi gently grasped her shoulder to stop her. As though waking from some inner trace, she looked at him in with vacant eyes. Her wide oval face covered in dust and dirt with a small scratch across her cheek. Her long black hair matted and tossed. Her general appearance didn't startle him, she looked much the same all the time, like all the beggars did, but her large almond eyes were different. It wasn't hunger, or sadness, they reflected emptiness. Levi reached for her hand leading her off to the side of the road. They sat against a tree, remaining quiet for a moment.

"Why are you here? What is happening?" asked Levi.

"I come here sometimes," Metha said. "I come to find out." Her head dropped down and her speech drone-like. "Now I know . . . but I wish I did not know."

"Know what?"

"About my parents . . . from my aunt."

Levi stated, "If you have an aunt, why are you living in the street, begging?"

"Her husband is a tax gatherer. He doesn't want children that are not his. My aunt finally told me that my parents . . . died in a Roman work camp. I have been hoping they would return to me . . . now . . . she finally told me the truth and I am sorry she did." She ran her hands through her matted hair pushing it from her face smudging it more.

With no point of reference for such matters Levi had no idea how to respond, he remained silent. Her sadness invaded him as he placed his hand over hers. For Levi this act was intimate, significant and unexpected. The chalice warmed. "Metha," he said as he took her hand and placed in into the tunic pocket. "Do you feel that warmth?"

Metha looked at him puzzled, "That is the chalice I saw in the alley when you were . . ."

"The Teacher gave this chalice to me in the upper room."

"What Teacher? You do not go to school?"

"No. I don't mean that." He held a loss for words to explain. "Metha, come with me." Although he did not know what caused him to have such confidence, he continued, "The Teacher has risen, we will ask him to help you. He holds great power. "

Metha abruptly stood to her feet speaking angrily. "A Teacher? A teacher cannot bring my parents back to me. What has happened to you Levi? You are acting strange. We are orphans. Beggars! No one will ever help us." She stomped her foot down.

Levi stood up. "Listen to me," he insisted. "The Teacher will help. Come with me and see." He looked into her face waiting, trying to will her to agree.

70

"You just felt the warmth from the chalice, he insisted."

ETHA TURNED HER GAZE away, wiped the remaining tears from her face. "You know we cannot trust anyone, especially adults. Their titles don't change anything. You know that."

Levi shook his head. He raised his hands almost in a gesture of surrender. "You just felt the warmth from the chalice," he insisted.

"The cup is warm from being in your tunic. The day is hot, that's all. You are acting foolish."

"You will not go with me then?"

Metha stared at him for a long moment, then turned to walk away.

"Wait," Levi called. "Come and see what I say is true." Metha did not respond. "Then at least take this with you." He ran to her side and handed her the flask and the food that Joktan gave him. Warmth flooded the chalice.

Metha reached for the items. Concluding he would not be able to convince her he stopped. Walking away he heard Metha call out to him, "Thank you for remembering me, Levi."

What did she mean by that? She said the same thing to him in the alley when he shared the secret of the upper room. What an odd thing to say, he thought, glancing back over his shoulder as she disappeared into the crowd. Sadness overshadowed him. He could do no more for her. Reminding himself, he pondered that going forward would lose him nothing since had nothing, even if Metha was right, but he refused to accept that. He had come too far to go back to his old ways. Bartimaeus captured his thoughts; a beggar like him and on top of that he had been blind. Then ruminations flowed as he recalled that Joktan had been a leper, and Photini had lived dependent on others, the stout man had no one to take his business over. The old man with the dog could hardly see yet he shared a lesson on how he should view himself as a person. The shepherd revealed details about his staff. The insight captured him completely as he concluded how near he'd been to the divine energy of the world all along his journey, and Joktan provided him with a key to it secret entry. These people and events he accepted as messages. *There are only so many times you can burn down your bridge before it can no longer be rebuilt.* The old beggar's words echoed. He could only hope he hadn't learned this too late. Metha came to mind over and over as he walked. Did he do enough to convince her? He didn't know what else to do other than what he did. That fact did not make him feel any better. Breathing in deeply, softening his countenance, he had to be concerned now with picking up his pace toward his committed goal. The chalice warmed and he garnered a new confidence in going on.

71

He tried to focus
on the men not his hunger

H AVING COVERED A FAIR distance he came to a hill. Once at its crest he saw four men standing in the distance. Levi skidded down the hill. When he came closer he recognized one of the men from the upper room. He did not see the man they called, Peter. Could the Teacher be there, making an appearance? Were they waiting for him? A wave of uncertainty overtook him like a splash of cold rain. Just walking over to them, for some unclear reason, suddenly seemed a foolish thing to do. For now he would keep his distance and observe. Once his nerves settled he experienced hunger pangs, his mouth dry of thirst. Coins sat in his tunic and no merchants anywhere to purchase anything. All the provisions from Joktan he had given to Metha. He didn't regret the gesture, but found himself surprised at the idea that he liked having helped her twice. He wondered if he had acted in the loving kindness the Teacher had spoken about.

Keeping his distance he tried to focus on the men not his hunger. The men slowed down as they approached a woman by the wayside seated on the ground. Her face held buried in a small blanket she held in her hands, weeping, deeply distraught. He watched as they spoke with her for a time, then departed leaving the woman. He held his place trying to figure out what to do next. Watching the woman, she suddenly stood up very quickly, turned and greeted someone. He could not see anyone there yet the woman carried on a conversation as though someone stood before her. Finally she kneeled and bowed her head. Maybe she had gone mad and spoke to nothing but her imagination. The boy had seen mad men running through the town square screaming and talking to no one. This woman however, appeared very settled except for her whaling tears. The whole thing came across very strange. He made the assumption she had been talking to herself or perhaps she'd had too much wine. After a time she arose looking as though in some fog as she walked away unsteadily, leaving her belongings on the ground.

Levi walked to where the woman had been sitting, finding a few dried pieces of fruit and a flask in a basket. He picked up the fruit and ate, washing it down with juice. His thirst and hunger overrode any guilt about taking the woman's provisions. Glancing up the road the woman continued walking along. She appeared to be following the group of men. Why she would leave perfectly good food seemed puzzling. A small yellow ochre colored blanket rested in the basket which he lifted off. The blanket material felt soft in his hands and had a tiny blue tassel hanging from each corner. He recalled the prayer shawl with tassels worn by the seller of jars as he prayed in his shop. This blanket's size and tassels were much smaller. He rolled it up and carried it under his arm not sure what use he might put it to.

The woman grew smaller as the distance between them increased. Walking briskly again; his energy heightened with thirst satisfied along with the fruit having been just enough to perk him up. Levi kept the woman in sight while maintaining his distance. He couldn't help wondering what had happened to the woman. She couldn't have been robbed since her belongings remained on the blanket. She didn't appear to be hurt. The surprising thought had him wondering if something about the woman had to do with fences. Thinking back to Metha he experienced his own inner fence in opening up to let her in both the first time, in telling her the secret about the upper room, and in giving her the provisions that Joktan had given him. The sky began closing to darkening shades.

72

They were orphans
like him, he believed

THE OUTSKIRTS OF THE wilderness area grew cold in the evening, and the added sounds of animals, and clicking insects in an unfamiliar place, all made for an unsettling feeling. By the time Levi made it up the next rolling hill, the view revealed a campfire glowing amongst a large grouping of boulders. Approaching cautiously he could see that the reflecting light of the camp fire didn't show the woman, just the small group of men that had talked to her.

Having studied the scene for a few minutes he decided to move in closer where the reflecting light relieved some of the darkness. As he progressed he threw the small blanket over his shoulders for the little warmth it could offer. Levi walked cautiously as not to step on any dried sticks or kick small rocks. He didn't want to make any noise that might give his presence away. He assumed the men would know more about where the Teacher might be. He wondered what the men were going to do now that the Teacher had left them. After all, they were orphans like him, he still believed. He had questions to ask them, but found himself not yet ready. Besides, a chance remained that the Teacher would appear to him.

Seeing his way by watching the dancing reflections of the campfire's light against the boulders and trees he came to a large single boulder close enough to see the comfort of the campfire flames and chose this to make his place for the night. Sitting against the boulder he tucked the small blanket up behind his neck and leaned his head back, his staff across his thighs ready for action. After he relaxed he heard sounds. Hoping this was not the old beggar again he listened. The sound did not come from an animal, but a human sound and it came from the opposite side of the boulder. Quickly grasping his staff he came to his knees, stood and with very deliberate movements cautiously made his way around the boulder holding his back against it as he moved. There sat the woman, her back against the boulder, arms wrapped around her knees. The sounds came out of her shivering and chattering from the cooling night air. Slowly, he slinked back to his side of the boulder. *Why do adults do such careless things? She left the blanket and the fruit.* And he continued arguing the point with himself until he thought of Joktan's refrain, '*I want the people I serve to ask me why.*'

Whether caused by respect for Joktan or his own new way of thinking, he did not know. In the next moment he removed the blanket from around his shoulders and walked it back to the opposite side of the boulder. The woman seemed too cold to be startled by his approach. Finally she looked at Levi. Her eyes were soft and her face lovely. Raven hair thick, disheveled around her face and onto her shoulders. Her eyes were swollen from weeping. He didn't say a word as he carefully tucked the blanket over her shoulders. Levi started moving back toward the opposite side of the boulder when she spoke.

"You are going to be cold now," she said without looking at him.

"The blanket belongs to you . . . I picked it up where you left it on the ground." He now began shivering.

"Well then, at least be wise . . . come . . . sit next to me, we will be warmer that way," she said, lifting a small corner of the blanket up in a gesture. He wasn't sure he should take her invitation. Her voice tender and honest finally drew him to sit down. No sooner did he sit when he stopped shivering. A welcoming warmth traveled to the woman as well. The chalice continued to wonderfully increase in warm flowing right down to their sandaled feet.

The woman said, "Strange, my blanket is not large enough to give off such warmth." She turned to look at him. Levi said nothing. He placed his hand over the chalice, and tipped his head back. After he gave Metha his provisions on the road from Jericho the pleasant sense of having done a good thing touched him uniquely, and now the feeling became present once again. Over the next few moments they were both fast asleep.

73

"I am fine.
I need no one to watch for me."

LEVI AWOKE, TENSING IN place until seeing the woman and regaining his bearings. He picked up the distinct smell of cooked fish leading him to walk the short way down to the camp. Several fried fish had been carefully placed over a wine flask at the makeshift camp where the men had been. They were gone, the small fire pit barely smoking. He stepped down reaching for some of the fish then ate and drank from the flask. His scuffling around woke the woman.

"There's fish and drink," he called out. "They must have left it for us."

When she walked to the camp he had his first look good at the woman. It seemed as though someone had pulled back a curtain to reveal two bright green gems for eyes that would have diminished the value of any emerald. A slight outline of red remained under her eyes.

"I have to catch up to them," said Levi.

"You could have talked with them last night," she said puzzled. "And why are you so far out here alone? Where is your family?"

"I am fine. I need no one to watch for me."

"I see . . . well, then, what is your name?"

"Levi."

"I am Veronica." Levi stamped out the remaining embers then started off without a word. He walked along and Veronica paced just behind him. In a few moments she said, "If you have no family . . . how did you get your name?" She felt unsure that the boy had told her the truth and she held concern for him being alone.

Levi swallowed the last bit of fish and wiped the back of his hand across his mouth. "I named myself," he answered with a bit of a prideful tone.

"Well this is quite amazing, Levi."

"What is?"

"You have selected a wondrous name, a strong name," she said. "Have you any idea what your name means?"

"It is a name just a name!"

"No, names have meanings and in many ways mark the course of our destiny."

Levi almost laughed. He wanted to tell her that beggars have no destiny. But he caught himself and didn't. Instead he refocused on his commitment to alter his old way of thinking. He now understood this would not be such simple task. The old way had been the only way he ever knew. Again he recalled the man who spoke to his friend about leaving Jerusalem and his decision not to stay but venture out to something new. Deep in his thoughts he could hear Veronica speaking to him so he turned to her, "I did not hear you."

Veronica stated with some authority, "Do not down play the value of a name, Levi."

The idea lifted his curiosity recalling how the old shepherd had introduced his sons by their names and meanings.

Veronica noticed his thoughts churning in his eyes. "Shall I tell you what your name means?" They both walked down the short incline heading toward Jerusalem together.

"I gave myself this name, so the meaning cannot be about me," he said.

"I see," she said, quietly. "Your parents . . . they must be worried over you. Where are they?" Her question showed genuine concern.

"Nowhere!"

"*Nowhere!* How can they be nowhere?" Veronica prodded.

An unrealized frustration released, causing him to respond tersely, in a way he didn't intend. "Don't you know what this is?" he stated as he lifted his hair from over the side of his face. He placed his thumb and forefinger to his left ear lobe, stretching it out from the side of his face to offer a better presentation of the small triangular wedge cut out of his earlobe. In a moment she realized it was the mark given to orphans. She felt a flush of sorrow now for pushing the boy to answer questions about his family.

"I am so very—"

"I have to find the Teacher. That is the only important thing," he said with a clear tone indicating that the point about his parents didn't matter to him. But she knew it did, and in his heart he knew as well.

"Who is the one you call, Teacher?"

"The one called, Jesus. He holds many titles."

"Yes," she smiled with the same joy Levi had witnessed in Joktan.

He walked faster now. Veronica trailed behind.

"Levi . . . it is important to know the meaning of your name," she called out. He slowed his pace as she came alongside him.

"I cannot understand how a name I gave myself means anything about me?"

"Because it may well be divine intervention by which you have chosen this particular name among all the names you might have selected for yourself."

Because so many unexplainable things had already crossed his path, and due to something he liked about her, he decided to at least hear her out. After all, what could it hurt? So he asked, "What is the meaning?"

74

"Oh, I assure you . . . indeed, Jesus appeared to me."

ALTHOUGH THE BOY DIDN'T think he cared at all about the meaning of his name the notion caused his curiosity to still, so he listened.

"Your name means *to be attached*. This indicates that you belong."

Those last few words penetrated Levi and made him almost stop in his tracks for a brief moment. His face betrayed his puzzlement.

"Something has pierced you. Do not be afraid to tell it."

Following many steps he decided to reply. "I saw Jesus in the upper room. He said I was no longer alone. Then several others on my journey said such things also. And now you say my name means belonging."

She smiled broadly and lovingly replied. "I assure you if Jesus spoke over you then it cannot be chance that you selected this name among all others you could have chosen." She hoped to reassure the boy. "You said Jesus spoke those words to you?"

"He did."

"I would then be most careful to heed his words. He has performed many miracles in the entire countryside, and in the temple itself."

Levi continued walking. Her mention of the miracles was something he neglected to include in his thinking about his own situation, and wondered if what had been happening to him were miracles.

"I saw you last night," Levi said, "you were taking to someone, but no one was there."

"Oh my boy I assure you . . . indeed, Jesus appeared to me."

This stopped Levi in his tracks.

"How could he be there? I could see no one but you talking to yourself."

207

"I am not the only one he has given visitation. First some of his disciples spoke to me. They could not comfort me. Jesus appeared and he did so. He gave me comfort and I trust that."

Levi did not reply. They continued walking.

"This is your blanket," Veronica said. He glanced back to see her arms outstretched holding the blanket, as she quickened her pace toward him.

"Why are you saying this?" *Adults are confusing*, he thought.

Veronica's voice carried a pleading to it. "Please, Levi, it would bring me much joy if you would receive this blanket as your own." They now walked in tandem, no one speaking.

Levi stopped, turned to Veronica who remained with her arms outstretched presenting the blanket. Her emerald eyes now longing. *What can it hurt to take it?* He thought. It would be a simple gesture. Levi reached over lifting the blanket out of her hands. Her warmth lingered in the blanket as he grasped it. He worked at making the slightest of smiles for her, then turned and walked again.

"I too have lost something," she said to Levi.

Odd how Levi already knew she had lost something. Her face painted the same look of loss always underling the landlord's face. The only difference showed in her softness whereas the landlord had become a hardened and bitter soul. Everyone he'd ever encountered, adult or child who had been beleaguered in some way with tragedy held some sense of loss. He recognized it because the same thing worked in his own heart.

The words escaped his mouth, forced out disregarding his own inner protest, "What have you lost?" he asked. Amazed he would ask such a thing, he didn't want to hear anymore about loss.

Too late, Veronica stopped. Her head tilted down and following a silent moment, tears burst from her eyes like an unobstructed waterfall through the rocks. The tears unrelenting, and weakened by emotion she dropped to her knees, hands covering her face. She cried out, "My baby, my boy! I lost him!"

Without warning her words repeated in Levi's head. How strange and disquieting. The words rang clearly, '*my baby, my boy, I lost him.*' The words spoken were not being spoken in Veronica's voice.

75

"What does this blanket mean?"

A SHADOW HAD CROSSED OVER his eyes as the words echoed in his mind. The words he heard were being spoken in genuine grief, but not by Veronica. The words were being spoken in another woman's voice. Words from a voice he knew, somehow deeply familiar. The woman's voice . . . strangely he knew it, and yet he didn't. The shadow projected a blurred image in his mind like trying to see something clearly in a torrent of rain. At that moment it came to him, an inner knowing—deep in his very essence he knew it—he was hearing the words being spoken by his own mother. A prickling traveled up from his spine, his nose clogged.

A force summoned itself behind his eyes as tears made their way to the outside world to claim their pain. He lost all control. Veronica's grief overwhelmed him, and now blended with his own sorrow. As though in the moment they had held a mirror to one another's loss. The full force of missing the parents he never knew, and of being alone, struck him, touching a sorrow deep in his heart, one he never expected; buried for so long. His hardness collapsed and he fell to his knees in front of Veronica. She folded him in her arms as they rocked back and forth. Levi didn't want to retreat as he experienced something totally new, the feeling of a caring embrace. He wanted to stay right there with the pain that had melded between them. The woman felt his heart beating against hers as they wept. They embraced for a long while. Finally, she reached her hand under his chin to lift his face.

"It will be well, it will, child . . . it will. Jesus will help us."

Levi remained silent. Once they finally separated, they sat down. Veronica's hair wet with the melded tears through which her pain had been carried. Her hair clung to her face. She pushed it back over her ears. Levi wiped his tears with his dirty hands, leaving dark streaks. He reached over to pick up the blanket. "I am sorry for you," he said.

Veronica smiled at him. He absorbed the kindness it offered.

"What does this blanket mean?" he asked, tugging at the tassels.

Veronica lifted the blanket from his hand. "Mothers make two kinds of blankets for their babies. First, swaddling clothes. If you know of the birth of the Christ child the story is told that after the shepherds in the fields saw the angels and the star announcing the child's birth, they traveled to Bethlehem to witness the event. They told everyone upon their return what they experienced. They reported that the Christ child's mother had wrapped him in swaddling clothes. And this is a very important detail in what the shepherds reported."

"What is . . . swoadd—" Levi tried to pronounce it back to her.

"Swad—dling. It means to wrap. The shepherds mentioned that about the Christ child and it is very important."

"Why?" Levi asked.

"Because it is a ritual performed for all legitimate babies. A mother would anoint her baby with fine powered salt and olive oil and then place him on the swaddle cloth she herself had made in advance of the child's birth."

"Did you do this for your baby?" asked Levi.

Veronica paused, composing herself. "Yes, and although you cannot remember that event, your mother did the very same for you Levi."

He wanted it to be true so badly. "How can you know that?"

"Because, she would follow the customs of our people. Once the mother has anointed the baby, the corners of the swaddle cloth are pulled up and over the baby's arms, legs, and body. Then pulled up like a hood over the baby's head. The swaddled baby is then held in place securely. Then there is a second blanket." She held it up. "This blanket holds four tassels at the corners," she gestured to them, "and indicates throughout its life the child will always be in God's presence, whatever direction he travels and whatever he does, for God is everywhere."

"This blanket is important to you. I see it in your eyes, why have you given it to me? I do not understand." Levi asked.

Veronica's chin fell to her chest, her hand moved to her face. "My boy only lived a few days after being born. He is with God. The blanket cannot bless him now. You are here, and I wish to pass a mother's blessing to you. I would pray this for my son . . . now I will also pray this for you."

Levi nodded respectfully, remembering the prayer shawl on the seller of jars with the four tassels signifying the same thing.

"You will now remember that every step you take in any direction," Veronica touched the four tassels, "you will be in God's eyes which are everywhere present."

Could she mean the divine energy of the world? Levi wondered. *God is everywhere? If God is everywhere why then . . . why am I still . . .* he thought better of allowing his doubts to invade him, and simply rolled the blanket up and thanked her.

Levi stood up, brushed himself off and lifted his staff off the ground. He helped Veronica to get up. She used the water in the flask to wash her face, adjusted herself then wiped Levi's face just as a mother would do. Levi did not object.

"Levi, it seems we have both been brought together, and we both have loss and we seek after the comfort of Jesus. Shall we journey together then?" She posed it more as a logical statement than a question.

He admitted to himself that he liked her, and sensed a true honesty about her. Something about Veronica's motherly presence draped over his sense of aloneness. He nodded yes, and then said in an uncertain voice, "I heard something when you were crying."

"My tears were painful. I believe they also brought some portion of healing. I hope this for you too, Levi."

76

"I've wanted to ask you a question."

LEVI QUICKLY CLARIFIED. "No . . . that is not what I mean. I heard the words you cried out . . . but . . ." he hesitated.

"What? Please tell me," Veronica encouraged. He struggled to find the words. His face intense. "It will come to you," she placed a hand on his shoulder and brought her smile out. Both her demeanor and voice calmed him.

"Another voice spoke the same words you spoke," he said. "I could hear it as you were crying. And . . . I do not understand how . . . but I knew that voice . . . it was not your voice, Veronica . . . but I knew the voice."

"And this voice repeated my words about my baby?" Veronica asked sincerely.

"Yes, but they were not your words when I heard them." He stopped to think. Veronica remained silent, waiting.

"I think . . . I heard my mother's voice speaking . . . the words, but I am not sure now. How could I know her voice? How can such a thing be?" The chalice warmed him, and then he knew, absolutely. "Yes, I did. I heard her voice. I do not understand."

Veronica looked into his eyes while placing her hands lovingly over her heart then moving them over Levi's heart. Her lips quivered, her eyes moistened, no tears left in her heart to shed. "Levi, dear boy, listen to me," she said, touching his chest, "your mother . . . will always be right here."

Levi wavered between crying and running. Neither would cooperate so he stood in place. "How could I have heard her and how could such a thing happen? I do not even remember her," he spoke softly to himself.

Veronica smiled. "The heart remembers all things, unlike the mind which can hinder our memories. I know this is true. That is where her voice has been stored in you all along. Part of your mother's heart and spirit are in you, her son. You will always be her son. She will always be your mother. I can say such a thing to you only because I am mother. These are mysteries only mothers can know."

Levi accepted this explanation. She hugged him, crushing her hair in his face with her arms. "I've wanted to ask you a question."

"What question?" he asked.

"Why are you seeking after Jesus?"

Levi gave this some thought. He trusted Veronica, but he was unsure how to express everything. "I need to find the new place," is all he said.

"What is this new place?" Veronica asked.

Unsure how to explain it completely, since he didn't fully understand it, he said, "That is where the Teacher will bring a new kingdom, and care for his disciples who are orphans . . . like me."

None of that made any sense to her. After a few moments she ventured a thought. "Have you considered that this new place may be more than merely a physical location? Perhaps you must also seek within yourself for this new place. A path that can take you out of what you have believed and have understood until now."

Her comment held a certain sense of practicality since having serious shifts in how he thought, and reacted to his circumstances.

"An old beggar told me it is called the divine energy of the world. Another man said it was a kingdom that is everywhere for all people. But I still think there is a place . . . a real place to find. How can all the Teacher's disciples fit into someone's mind?"

Veronica smiled at his youthful naivety. "You say this is the divine energy of the world. Consider this. If this energy is divine, its power cannot be restrained. And, if the energy is in the world, then it is too vast to be in one single location. The world is a large place. That is why my baby's blanket holds the four tassels. They point to all directions in the world."

Levi concluded her description to be correct. He believed the divine energy of the world had flowed near him, wherever he went, whoever he encountered.

Veronica easily observed his pondering and added, "Levi, can you think of something you have done in the past? Or a place you enjoyed being?"

Thinking it over he said, "Yes, the candle maker's tent. I liked to visit there sometimes. I felt good there . . . the flames and the smells of the candles. How he shaped the wax into whatever design he wanted."

"Did you see the candle maker's shop in your mind as you just spoke of it?"

He had to think about that for a moment and substantiated that he did somehow in his mind see the candles and could even smell the aromas. "Yes I did," he said with surprise.

"Can you picture yourself talking with the Teacher as he spoke his words over you?"

"Yes," he replied with some exuberance.

"So are you here with me or are you at the candle maker's tent, or with the Teacher?" she asked.

Levi's eyes squinted, trying to figure this out.

"You are in all these places, Levi. Then it must be true that the divine energy of the world can also be present wherever you are. Peter, one of Jesus' disciples told of a time when Jesus said that he would be with us always, even to the end of the age."

"You know this man Peter?"

"Yes, I have met him with his wife when he spoke to people about Jesus. It was after I wiped Jesus' face along the way to Golgotha. I became distraught and his wife Lydia consoled me."

"Have they seen the Teacher too?"

"They have not said. At least not to me," she replied.

The revelation conquered any remaining doubt he had about finding the Teacher. Now he wondered about Veronica and asked, "Why are *you* seeking the Teacher?"

Veronica shook her head and shrugged her shoulders. "Being near Jesus brought me comfort when he appeared to me, comforting my pain . . . my loss. I do not want to lose that comfort, so I will follow him. Like you, I thought I had no one else. Now I know that is no longer true."

"You speak as though you know the Teacher," Levi said.

"Yes, I was among the women who followed him for a time. I went to him when he carried the cross to Golgotha. I wiped his face, but then a Roman soldier threw me back into the crowd where I fell and they nearly trampled me."

Uncomfortable as to how to respond, Levi asked, "Then you know where Peter lives?"

"Yes, but he is going around the area speaking of the Good News and the teachings of Jesus. We will likely see him as we go on."

Levi suggested they continue on. So they started off together in silence. Veronica tossed a thought around over and over as they walked. Her uncertainty cautioned her as to whether or not to say what she had in mind. She felt strongly it would help although the subject seemed a fragile one with the boy. *No,* she concluded, *it would be wrong of me to hold this back.* "Levi?"

"Yes?" he answered while continuing to walk.

"I need to tell you something very important. I believe it will be of help to you," she said tentatively.

77

"I know for one very important reason."

HE STOPPED WALKING AT the tone of her seriousness. "What is it?"
"Your parents," she stopped to gather the thought, "your parents, like most, sometimes find themselves in circumstances where, and I know this will seem odd to you, that they must take an action that will save their child from some greater harm by giving him up."

"It cannot be better than staying with them," he insisted.

"Please, hear me out. Many parents have been taken into custody for the work camps, and they had children . . . some with babies. They could not, as parents, want their children to be placed in a camp of slavery or worse, so they give them to the almshouse unless they have family. As a mother, I cannot even imagine having to make such a choice, yet I would have done the same in hopes of keeping my son alive."

Levi's feelings were already rushing in contradiction.

"I believe with all my heart this is what happened between you and your parents. I do not believe they abandoned you; they did what they had to do to protect you. Even on your own you would have a better chance at life than being a baby in the work camp, you could have become a sacrifice to some strange religious group." Veronica recognized his inner turbulence at what she said.

"How can you know any of this to be true," Levi asked in a voice growing faint.

"I know for one very important reason."

Levi tilted his head anticipating her reply.

"I believe with all my heart the answer comes in the fact that you heard your mother's voice. This could not have happened if she had abandoned you because she would hold great shame which would not have allowed her to have deposited words into your spirit. It is of significance that she repeated my words. We have both lost our sons, we did not abandon them. There is a vast difference."

Levi seemed to be staring at something no one else could see. He then slowly nodded his head in affirmation of Veronica's words. She smiled her gentle smile.

"How could she be in my thoughts?"

"To that I say, Jesus! You have heard of the miracles. He possesses a divine power not comprehended by us. Yet the important thing is we can see the evidence of it."

Levi wholeheartedly assimilated her explanation. To his view of things it held a practicality. What stunned him was the fact that it was not some authority in robes, or king's scribe or even or a prophet that provided the heartfelt lesson, it had come from a common woman, a mother. The fact that she was a mother held a certain weight of authority with him.

78

"You understand how difficult this is to believe?"

Levi and Veronica walked for several miles until just ahead stood a grove of trees buzzing with activity. As they drew closer they observed many people gathered together. Mothers and fathers with children, some children with mothers only, all mingling together. The people stood in a semi circle around a large flat rock. A woman sat upon the rock.

She had just begun to speak when a man called out to her, "We cannot hear what you are saying."

The woman then stood, turned and climbed up on the rock and began again.

"Many of you know me. For those who do not, I am Mary Magdalene. I followed Jesus with his disciples. He loved people, healed them and comforted them. And for all his good . . . they killed him. Darkness . . . that is all I could see, and as to hope . . . all lost as I stood at the foot of the cross. Yet as I arrived here today many of you heard me singing a joyful song—me—the same woman who stood at the cross. I am not hardened of heart as some have said."

Levi grasped Veronica's hand and moved closer to the front of the crowd.

"Yes, many want to know how you can sing after such a tragedy you yourself have witnessed," a man in the crowd shouted out.

"First, it is true I did see death . . . then," she lifted her hands and her face up to the sky, "then I witnessed life. I have seen Jesus. He appeared to me . . . I spoke with him."

Veronica squeezed Levi's hand as she heard these words. She knew Mary's testimony to be true for she too had seen Jesus.

"You understand how difficult this is to believe," the same man called out.

"As I look out . . . many of you have known me all my life. I have no reason to be untrue with you. I face the risk of being arrested more than any gain I would have by reporting this to you."

"Do you think you saw his spirit?" Someone called out.

Mary placed her hands to her forehead as if pondering. "I do not know. If a spirit can speak, then yes. But what does it matter if his presence came in body or spirit. In either one he spoke, he cared, he lives. I am not alone. Others have seen him, and many of those people you know also."

She lifted her head scanning the crowd and then she saw him. "Peter," she called out, "many of you know Peter well. See how he has changed to great boldness for the truth. He speaks in public even against the threat of our authorities placing himself in danger of arrest."

"There is Peter, Veronica whispered to Levi," as she pointed.

Immediately people turned to look at Peter. He stood straight up. "If Jesus has not risen I would not spread the good news in the face of such overwhelming opposition, nor would I hold back that Jesus has kept the promise he made to us, his disciples."

A man not far behind Peter who was dressed in the robes of an authority responded to Peter. "This Jesus has been crucified on a Roman cross and sealed in a guarded tomb. No man can escape the end it assuredly brings." The man swung his arm around and sternly stated, "All of you followers are seeing things. You are merely in your dreams. Dreamers . . . each and every one of you."

"Yes, but is it not always the dreamers who have changed the world?" Mary called out.

At this, the man departed, making his way forcefully through the crowd. Then others began leaving and the crowd thinned. Peter and his wife Lydia stopped to answer questions with small groupings of people as they made their way to where Mary sat on the rock.

"You see," Veronica said to Levi. He has not really left his disciples or us.

Levi walked along with her with no reply. As they drew closer to the small group of people standing around Mary and Peter at the rock, Levi thought his name had been called out. It wasn't audible. It seemed more like a soft bell tolling far in the distance. He stopped walking, letting go of Veronica's hand.

"What's wrong?" she asked.

"I hear my name being spoken."

"I hear nothing" she said. Then she backed away saying with great jubilation, "Pay attention, for I too heard my name spoken when Jesus appeared to me."

She stepped back a few yards as Levi stepped closer to a grove of trees. A muscle twitched in his cheeks right there and then as he gazed upon Jesus standing before him. "Teacher, it is true . . . you are alive."

Jesus said, "Yes, it is so. But what about you, Levi? Is your trust alive?"

"Teacher, I am looking for your kingdom to come. How can I find it? How can—"

A broad smile from Jesus immediately calmed the boy down from the rattle of questions. "My kingdom needs not be found. It is already formed, and I am already there."

Levi had no response. His face drew blank.

"You have come so far and now so close. Go with Peter. Stay with him and Veronica. I will send you a message. You do remember the words I spoke to you in the upper room, do you not?"

Levi nodded.

"Listen carefully. In the upper room I told you that I would be alone for a time, and then I would no longer be alone. And after saying that what words did I speak to you?"

Levi looked into his eyes, almost pleading. "You said it would be the same with me."

With eyes that penetrated the boy in a realm of comfort and believability, he said, "Just as I remained alone for a time and then no longer, so it will be with you. My words over you are words of life . . . of a destiny, one you must experience for yourself and if you trust you shall." He reached down and touched the carved symbols of Levi's staff as he spoke. Levi observed the Teacher's fingers deliberately trace over the intricate images. "Have you begun to see messages anew as you have traveled along?"

"I do not understand all that is happening. I have felt you near me . . . I think in the chalice."

"You see then its effect, now you must realize its presence. Will you trust me?"

"Yes, yes," Levi replied immediately.

"Allow yourself to continue being guided along the way, and trust in what is taking place. Truly, truly I say you will understand when you arrive . . . you shall know with certainty. Will you do this?"

"I will. But the chalice you left for me?" Levi reached into his tunic to retrieve it when Jesus stopped him.

"The chalice is mine to give, and I have given it to you. Continue to seek the message; begin to see it with your heart."

"Yes. But where are you going?"

"You cannot know these matters now. All will become clear through my disciples."

Jesus then placed his hands on Levi's head and prayed a blessing. A warm, soft and gentile feeling coursed through him—the most wonderful feeling—but it was the most unique smile on Jesus' face that gave Levi assurance, and softened his eyes.

79

Veronica held the
boy's shoulders tightly

"LEVI!" CAME THE CALL from behind causing him to turn away only to see Veronica running up to him. Her smile so bright it seemed as if the sun had found its way through and out of her. "I saw you speaking to him."

At that, Levi spun on his heels turning back to find the Teacher gone. "He is gone again."

Veronica held the boy's shoulders tightly. "Yes, he is gone. He must see others as well. Be not disappointed, but joyful!"

"But—"

Before he could say it, Veronica continued. "Do you not understand how much he loves you? Of all the people he must see, he came to you Levi . . . *to you!*"

He hadn't considered such a thought. The words she spoke were breathed into his mind deeply and filled his heart with a feeling just like he had with the Teacher in the upper room.

"Let us go join Peter and Lydia. They are waiting for us."

Walking out of the trees, Veronica and Levi noticed that Mary remained seated on the rock. Peter stood next to her. Parents were coming up to speak with them. In some cases they laid hands on the children's heads, saying a blessing over each one and then spoke something to the parents.

Levi noticed that all the mothers who carried infants had them wrapped in the same blanket Veronica gave him. Each blanket fashioned in the same color, the same tassels, and texture. He now better understood the value Veronica held for the blanket. Something told him to give Veronica the blanket and have her bring it to Mary. But he found such a thought unsettling. What right did he have to instruct her? Nonetheless the sensation grew stronger, and the chalice warmed vibrantly in his tunic. With that he removed the blanket from his shoulder.

"Veronica . . . I believe you are to take this blanket to Mary."

Veronica stared at him with incredulity. "The others . . . they have blankets wrapped around babies. My blanket is empty," she said in a near whisper.

Levi looked at her deeply and said, "But Veronica, you told me that my mother is in my heart. Is not your son . . . in *your* heart?"

A long moment passed with Veronica speechless. Tears formed along with a smile appearing as a statement of comfort without words as only a mother could express. Her own belief had been spoken back to her by a mere boy. And she knew he was right.

Placing the blanket in her hands Levi stepped back.

"I will wait here." He continued to step backwards until she stopped looking at him, and glanced down at the blanket.

Just as she turned to walk toward the line of people she stopped. "Come with me."

Regardless of his reluctance, Veronica wrapped her arm around his shoulder and pulled him in. They were the last in the line. Veronica stepped up to the rock. Mary greeted her first, then Peter. Veronica then placed the blanket on Mary's lap and grasped her hands.

"Your child remains vibrant in your very spirit," Mary said. "You seek Jesus as a comfort to your heart. I have felt this desire as well. But now our comfort must learn to rest in faith and trust in the peace that he has left us."

"This is something no one can explain to you," Peter added, as he stepped closer, "you must experience it, and you will. You will soon come to understand if you trust him."

Veronica kneeled as her head fell into Mary's lap. But she didn't cry. Mary kissed the blanket returning it to her. Peter quickly moved to the back of the small group as Mary spoke to the last few people. Veronica and Levi also walked around the back of the crowd. Peter stood with one arm around his wife and the other touching the shoulder of his little son. Levi's breakdown with Veronica had released something he held in check for so long. He no longer blamed the world and everyone in it for the loss of his parents. He did feel a painful loss for being alone, but overriding that, for the first time, he held a deeper pain for his parents. Until he met Veronica he had never considered that something grave must have taken them away, and they would have also experienced the striking pain of losing him just as he had witnessed in Veronica's pain for her son. He experienced a growing sense of release. And he could not deny the experience.

Levi replayed the Teacher's words allowing it to bathe him, and that would be the direction he dedicated himself to follow. He walked closer behind the group of people standing along an incline. As he stood observing he noticed Peter's son stepping back on one foot as though trying to steady himself from falling over, but he stumbled over himself unable to keep balance. The boy began falling backwards. A sharp rock sat jutting out of the ground. The boy would directly strike the back of his head against the pointed edge of the rock which would surely cause severe damage. Peter heard his son scream as he turned to see him falling backward, but missed grabbing hold of him.

Levi threw himself forward extending his staff pushing the boy to the side. Instead he landed on the rock. The wind knocked out of him and he blacked out.

80

"I am aware you were in the upper room."

"ARE YOU HURT? LEVI, are you hurt?" Veronica's voice called. She kneeled next to him with Peter.

"Wake up boy," Peter added, lightly tapping his cheek. Levi opened his eyes and in a few minutes focused and breathed normally.

"My son is safe. Thank you," said Peter, placing his massive hand under Levi to lift him up. Levi steadied himself and glanced around for his staff.

Veronica held it up. "I have it." She placed it in his hands.

Lydia immediately hugged Levi. Peter made the introductions to his son Benjamin. They both thanked Levi. Lydia offered him water. Levi drank quite a bit. Peter invited Levi and Veronica to go to his home. Levi requested to talk with Peter. He obliged the boy.

"The Teacher told me to learn from you and the other disciples."

"The teacher?"

"Yes, Jesus, our Teacher."

"This we shall do, Levi."

"I wanted to tell the Teacher about Judas' betrayal. I was in the upper room when—"

"I am aware you were in the upper room. The Lord told us."

"I do not understand why this has happened to the Teacher. I have been living in the streets on my own and I have seen hatred and bad people and dishonesty and . . ."

"Levi. None of us can change what resides in people's hearts. And you must understand that we cannot change the course of prophecies. I admit to you that I thought I could do so, and stood before the Lord trying to hinder his entry back into to Jerusalem. There is much we still must learn, but this is sure . . . what must come to pass . . . *will* come to pass."

"What happened to Judas?"

"We did confront him, but he is in league with the temple authorities. I am certain that he will have to deal with himself for what he has done. We have heard he remains in Jerusalem, preparing to leave."

Levi shrugged his shoulders, head toward the ground.

Veronica walked over to them. "Is everything all right, Peter?"

"Yes, I am trying to answer his questions."

"Then I will go back . . ."

"No, remain with us," Peter said. "There are no secrets, Veronica."

She looked at Levi.

"Stay," Levi said.

"Let me assure you Levi, what is taking place and some of the teachings are also hard for us as disciples to fully understand right now. And we were the closest to him."

Levi pondered the words for a few moments. Then he reached into his tunic, removing the chalice. "I have something I thought should be returned to the Teacher." His voice rang as he held up the chalice, gesturing it toward to Peter.

"A chalice? Why would anyone be carrying a chalice?" Peter spoke it as a statement rather than a question.

"The Teacher gave me the chalice in the upper room, after all of you left."

"Did he tell you its purpose?"

"He only said that I was no longer alone, and gave it to me and I've carried it with me until now. But an old crippled beggar sitting on a pallet has appeared to me, and asked what the chalice told me?"

"What do mean he appeared to you?" Peter asked.

"He was just there, and he knew that I wanted to warn the Teacher about Judas. He spoke to me of my anger and . . . and . . . he even knew my name. He asked me what I was learning from the chalice, and he knew it warmed when good things happened. He told me he was a messenger of the Teacher. And then he was . . . gone."

Peter put his hand up to stop him. "Your excitement is making you speak so fast I'm not hearing it all—slow down. You said the chalice warmed?"

"Whenever I did something good or when someone did something to help me, the chalice warmed up. And the beggar . . . he knew many things about me."

Peter lifted the chalice from Levi's outstretched hands. He placed his hands around it firmly to see if he felt any heat. Levi realized what he was doing.

He looked up at Peter, "You do not believe me, do you?"

Veronica reached for the chalice. "I think Peter is trying to understand what has happened, to be able to explain it . . . perhaps?"

Peter said, "I cannot explain it. If the chalice was given by the Lord then it is his business to deal with it; which means I cannot take the chalice and you must not give it away."

"And the crippled beggar, you never saw him before?"

"Never," Levi stated.

"You say the beggar appeared and then he was gone?"

"Yes, several times he appeared and then disappeared completely, and there was nowhere he could have gone . . . he sat on a cripple's pallet so he could not move himself that quickly."

"What do you make of this Peter?" asked Veronica.

Peter rubbed his forehead, and sat down on the ground, and so did Veronica.

Levi continued, "I was afraid when he told me all these things he knew about me, and when he was gone from sight."

"Did he give you any warnings?" Peter asked.

"No, he told me the Teacher did not need to be warned about betrayal, that he knew everything that would take place. He said to pay attention to what the chalice tells me. But I don't hear it speak . . . it just warms up in the way I said."

"Messages do not always come in words." Peter rose off the ground and reached into his tunic. He removed some coins. "Here Veronica, would you be kind enough to go into the marketplace with the boy and purchase some honey? My wife needs it for the meal tonight and I need to go look into another matter. Meet me at the center of the marketplace where the large well is." Peter smiled and jostled Levi's hair, "Everything will be all right, boy."

Levi and Veronica departed for the marketplace.

81

"Where has the seller of doves gone?"

L EVI AND VERONICA WALKED through the Jerusalem market. Levi decided to visit the candle maker's tent where he had often gone before.
They agreed to meet back at the well. Upon arriving at the tent, the candle
maker stood busily shaping wax sticks. In a moment it dawned on Levi that
the seller of doves no longer stood across the way.

Just then a man came by looking all around for something. Finally he
waved at the candle maker and asked, "Where has the seller of doves gone?
Has he moved to another place in the market?"

"Many others have been asking me this same question. An incident
occurred . . . very strange. All his cages were knocked over which allowed
the doves to fly off." The candle maker looked around and leaned in toward
the man. "Some say that the moment those three men were crucified on
Golgotha, the dove cages throughout the marketplace were all knocked over
and hundreds of doves were seen flying away. Some claim it had to do with
that self-proclaimed young rabbi from Nazareth, Jesus. But I hold no such
superstitious beliefs."

"Where then can I find doves for an offering," the man asked.

"That is a good question to which I have no answer," said the candle
maker.

Hearing this Levi smiled with a joy believing this somehow did have to
do with the Teacher. As the moment passed he discerned a growing connection to the presence of the Teacher. He could tell he had drawn nearer. With
that he began to make his way to meet Veronica and Peter.

Just then Judas Iscariot walked through the marketplace purchasing
goods to take on his departure from Jerusalem. Making his way out of a

shop keeper's tent, he caught a movement across the aisle. Although not certain, he stretched his neck for a better view to confirm his suspicion "It's that confounded boy," he muttered under his breath as he watched Levi walk along, occasionally stopping to inspect an item. Judas needed to know who had sent the boy to follow him originally and who had sent him now. Were the other disciples planning to do something to him for the betrayal? Cautiously, he followed Levi at a distance, past the tents and into the town area.

As he walked, Levi felt a sudden uneasiness which caused him to pick up his pace and grip his staff tightly then cut into a crossway toward the other side of the market. He caught the movement of a long shadow overcome him, but too late to run. In a second, a hand grasped his shoulder and pulled him back. Levi twisted to release himself from the grip unsuccessfully. His right hand and the staff were locked in a tight grip against his chest. Stunned, he caught a glimpse of Judas' face, sending terror through his entire body. Levi opened his mouth to yell when Judas' hand blanketed his mouth. Just ahead a large pile of barrels were stacked which allowed Judas to tuck in behind. He stripped the staff out of Levi's hand throwing it to the ground.

"Betrayer." Levi yelled as loud as his frightened dry throat allowed.

With his palm pushing over Levi's mouth, "Shut up, little spy. Now you *will* tell me who sent you? Was it Peter? John? Jesus? Who?" Judas stretched his body upright to its full height, still holding on to the boy. "Did one of the other disciples send you to spy on me, boy?"

"Let me go!"

Judas grappled the boy, changing his grip when he felt something inside his tunic. "What have we here?"

Levi protested which only encouraged Judas.

"What's so important boy?" He reached in, grasping and pulling out the chalice. "So, you are a thief *and a* spy. From what family's table have you stolen this? The authorities will want this for evidence once I'm done with you." He dropped the chalice to the ground. "Listen boy, I know the chief priest, and with a word can have you sent to the work camp." He shook Levi, "Do you understand what I can do to you?" He lifted him up higher into a bear hug and squeezed. "Tell me what I want to know . . . tell me who sent you to keep following me!"

Levi struggled against the pressure as being between two boulders pushing together, not allowing him to expand his chest to breathe.

"Don't make me hurt you boy . . . tell me who sent you to follow me!"

"I . . . can't . . . breathe."

"Then tell me."

Judas could not see Levi turning blue from lack of air as his eyes began to roll back—his lungs about to burst. Suddenly Levi found himself released as he slipped to the ground gasping for breath and coughing. He heard Peter's gravelly voice. As Levi rose to his knees, Judas lay on the ground; Peter stood over him with the crook of Levi's staff pushed against his neck.

"You've already betrayed the Lord, are you now going add more stain to your soul? You could have killed the boy," said Peter harshly.

Judas remained still, not responding. "Here, Levi, take your staff." Peter then bent over to whisper the rest to Levi. "Go to the well with Veronica and wait for me. Go!"

Levi picked up the chalice and ran off.

Judas glared up at Peter, "I acted against his pending rebellion . . . a new kingdom to usher in? You know as well as I that the twelve of us cannot overcome Caesar!" Judas replied indignantly.

Peter loosened his grip letting Judas fall back on the ground. Both men stared at one another intently.

Peter shook his head saying, "How could you have done this thing. The Lord . . . loved you . . . he loved you Judas," the emphasis heartfelt more than judgmental.

With a sudden jerk, Judas clasped both hands over his eyes as he began to weep with a force Peter had never before witnessed. He stood back.

"What have . . . I done . . . what . . ." Judas seemed to be convulsing on his own words as his face flooded over; his body writhing in turmoil.

Peter turned and walked away. When he looked back, Judas hobbled away as a broken man departing the passageway. About to step out, Peter froze in place, recalling the cock crowing at the moment he denied Jesus a third time while standing among a group of accusers. He didn't tell Judas how he had denied knowing the Lord. He knew he had also betrayed Jesus in his own way. The sudden weight of it dropped him to his knees and he wept. After a time, Peter composed himself and made his way to the well.

82

"Those men do not see you . . ."

LEVI WALKED OUT INTO the crowd moving toward the marketplace and the central well. He walked close to the side walls and booths trying to stay in the shadows.

"Alms for the poor!"

The words stopped Levi in his tracks. He knew that voice without doubt. Looking into a narrow side passage where garbage had been piled up, the same old beggar called "Alms!"

"You are following me!" Levi walked up to him bluntly asking.

"Has it occurred to you that whatever follows you is what you have attracted?"

"Riddles again! I told Peter what you said to me, and I showed him the chalice. I wanted him to return it to the Teacher."

"Did the Teacher tell you to return it?"

"No, but it's—"

"Levi, stop trying to remove the good things attempting to come into your life."

"What do you mean?" asked Levi. Just then two men walked through the alleyway. One of them looked down at Levi with a quizzical stare and said to his companion, "Jerusalem is filling up with people who are mad . . . this one speaks to a wall."

The man's words jarred Levi. He glanced at the men and then back at the beggar with a startled look. "Those men do not see you . . ." he said stunned.

Disregarding Levi's comment he continued, "Levi . . . you must no longer give things away that are intended to help you. Hear now, and follow my message."

Levi gazed into the beggar's eyes which conveyed a serious focus.

"Not long from now a feeling will grow within you. Be alert as it will urge you to go, but you *must* stay. This is important. Concern yourself only with staying no matter how much you wish to go. This will be your only way to complete the message and discover the truth. Hear me well."

"Stay? I do not under . . ."

In a flash the beggar disappeared! He stood there holding the thought about staying and not going. Recalling that Jesus' own disciples did not understand all that was taking place, he determined to remain alert. He turned and continued on toward the well.

"Levi, over here!" Veronica called out and waved as he neared the well. She stood on the far side. People were moving in and out of the area. Others were in huddles busily talking. As he walked by he heard a man speaking about Jesus having appeared to him as one who had risen.

Levi ran over to Veronica.

"Are you all right?" she asked. "Peter has been concerned about you."

"He helped me get away from Judas."

"Get away? What happened? Are you all right?"

"I am fine now," Levi assured her, "do not worry."

Veronica spoke up, "Where is Judas?"

From behind, Peter answered, "He has gone . . . for now. Both of you go to my house and wait until I return. Please do as I say," Peter asked as a directive.

"I want to go with you," Levi demanded.

Peter's lips became thin and he spoke softly but with overwhelming authority, "I know, but for now stay with my family until I return, and it is very important that *you do not leave*," adding the emphasis to his words.

Levi instantly heard the old beggar's words echoed in his head as Peter spoke the same words, causing his mouth to drop open in surprise as the words again reverberated in his mind, '*You will want to go, but you must stay.*'

Veronica placed her hand on Levi's shoulder and gently tugged. He reluctantly turned and walked off with her. When he looked back at the well, Peter had already started off. Upon arriving at Peter's home, Lydia arranged a small cot and a place to stay where he instantly fell fast asleep although he valiantly tried not to. His mind and body were completely drained from the events and stress of the past days. Once he had fallen into a deep sleep, Veronica excused herself saying she was going into the barn to be alone and pray. Lydia accommodated her.

83

"Where is Peter? Where is Veronica?"

LEVI OPENED HIS EYES to see Peter's son Benjamin standing at the end of his mat. "Levi, are you feeling better? Mother said you were so sleepy and . . ."

Levi bounded to his feet and walked into the large open room where Lydia stood preparing a meal.

Incredulous, he asked, "How long did I sleep?"

"You collapsed from exhaustion. I'm surprised you didn't sleep longer," Lydia said.

"Where is Peter? Where is Veronica? Did Peter see the Teacher again?"

Lydia dropped the pot she was holding. Her head fell into her hands and she sobbed.

"Momma," Benjamin called as he ran to her side. She embraced him. Levi knew the response held nothing good.

"Has Peter been hurt?"

"Not physically, but his heart is broken. All our hearts are broken. He is with some of the other disciples trying to understand what all these happenings might mean. They now carry a heavy burden and responsibility."

"I should go see them."

"They are determined to be alone for a time. Then we will know more."

"What has happened?" he asked.

She stopped to assure her little boy that she was all right and sent him to do some chores, then walked over to Levi. "After Jesus died, there was so much sorrow and the authorities were trying to silence all of us who followed him. There was no time to truly mourn, to try and understand what he expects from us now. It is all catching up like a moving storm."

Levi gritted his teeth. "I should have tried to stop Judas." He stomped his staff to the floor.

"You could not stop anything. These are powerful men. Rome is invincible. You are brave, but you are still just a boy." He knew this to be true but didn't like the feeling of being helpless.

"Where has Veronica gone?"

"She needed to be alone . . . in the barn." Levi walked out to the barn.

Veronica sat on the floor of the barn in the midst of the animals. A small towel rolled up next to her. Her face red and swollen from despair and her green eyes had lost all sparkle. Her body rocked gently. She appeared to have aged overnight.

"Jesus gave so much love and help to people, and still they . . ." her voice trailed off, her eyes glazed over.

Levi couldn't reply. There could be no reply.

"I used this towel to wipe the blood and sweat from his face as he carried the cross."

Levi glanced at the small towel, stained with dried blood. He kneeled down next to her and reached over for the towel.

"That is not the towel you gave me," he said.

"No, this is an ordinary towel I carried with me . . . I could do nothing more, but wipe his face, the soldier pulled me away. I had to leave him. I could not help him," she cried out.

Levi waited a moment then said, "You were there. At least you tried to help him. I tried to warn him of the betrayer, but I failed." He took the towel off the ground and unrolled it. What he saw caused him to jump. Veronica immediately looked over and tried to stop Levi so she could prepare him, but she unthinkingly had already unrolled the towel. His eyes bulged as he viewed a partial image of Jesus' face emblazoned on it. A long time passed without either of them saying a word. Even the animals remained silent.

84

"He needs to be alone for a time."

AFTER SOME TIME VERONICA said, "When I first opened it I . . . I have never . . . seen such a thing as this," as she carefully rolled it back up. "I must give this to Peter when he returns. Perhaps he will know what it means."

"I will go find him and bring him back," Levi said.

Before Veronica could object, Levi ran to the barn door. Stepping out he ran into a man about to enter, causing him to fall to the ground.

"Are you all right, boy?" asked the man as he reached down to help him get up.

"I have to go find Peter," he said as he arose.

"I am Peter's brother, Andrew. You will not find him right now."

Levi glared up at him, "Why can't I find him?" he demanded.

"He needs to be alone for a time. We must all respect that."

Levi looked past the man as though contemplating a run. Then he glanced up at the man again. "You are his brother?"

"Yes. I am Andrew. Peter is dealing with an inner turmoil and must work it out on his own," Andrew said. "All of us disciples must face this as well. Who are you, boy?" he asked. Just then Veronica walked out the door after hearing their voices. She stepped over to Andrew to briefly explain about the boy.

"I see then, you are one of us," Andrew said.

"I'm worried about Peter," Levi said.

Veronica whispered to Andrew. He understood. "Come over here Levi and sit down." Veronica followed along.

After a few moments Andrew slightly bowed his head and spoke. "Before Jesus was taken; we were with him in the garden. The night melted dark and the sound of the brown owls swept across the garden. Jesus walked across the way to pray. After he faded into the shadows of the olive trees I suddenly became uncomfortable so I walked to look out over the valley. I could just about make out the wall of the Temple standing high when I noticed lights moving toward our location. Jesus then moved all of us to the lower area of the garden. There my brother Peter and John fell fast asleep on the ground. Jesus walked over and woke them. The sound of a group of men became clearer as the torches appeared in a procession. They proceeded across where the Kedron Brook flowed. The flickering glare of the torches revealed their faces as they came to us. An officer of the Temple led the group."

He stopped for a moment, cleared his throat then continued, "We were all shocked when Judas appeared right behind him. Judas did not acknowledge any of us, but walked past and over to Jesus and embraced him. In the next moment the men came forward to take hold of Jesus, and led him away."

Levi stood up. "Why didn't you stop them?" he yelled.

"There is more to what has happened than you understand," Andrew said directly. "More than any of us understands at this moment. Peter drew a sword trying to stop the men, but Jesus demanded he halt," Andrew said, his face sullen.

"Everything I have heard since I followed the Teacher has been confusing. Why did the Teacher stop Peter from helping?"

Andrew shook his head, "I know things can be confusing, and no doubt what I'm going to tell you will be more of the same. The truth is that Jesus did not need our help. He came to help all of us. What he has done is sacrifice himself for all people. This is why it could not be stopped."

"I do not want to hear anymore." Levi felt the pain in what Andrew spoke so he jumped up and started running.

Veronica started after him but Andrew said, "Let him go. He must work all this out for himself now."

As he ran, Levi knew now that he could not outrun the hurt and disappointment. The only place to run was the future. He stopped running, gathered himself and refocused on finding Peter.

85

"You are skilled in tricks . . . like Simon the magician."

L EVI MOVED AT A quick pace although with no new bearings on where he might find Peter. He headed back toward the marketplace area toward the central well. As he walked along the pebbled streets, he peered down every passage way and alley, keeping his eye out for taller large men. No sign of Peter. Then he thought it best to make his way down below the city aqueduct areas where things were quiet and undisturbed.

Once below the aqueduct he heard a familiar voice, "Levi. Who do you seek?"

"I need to find Peter." Levi pointed his staff at the beggar's pallet. "You sit on a pallet, but you are not lame."

"Is my pallet what is important or can it be the things I have spoken each time we met . . . have they not come to pass?" the beggar asked.

"Now that Caesar has killed the Teacher . . ." his voice dropped for a moment, and then unexpectedly he began to weep.

"Ah, yes you see now . . . you weep for someone other than yourself. Consider how far you have come. You are close now."

"I have met good people, I know that now," Levi said.

"The divine energy of the world is so very close," emphasized the beggar.

"How do I enter in?"

"You must experience this for yourself. I cannot provide that message to you. And this is no riddle I share with you now." The beggar's eyes glowed differently than Levi had ever seen them. Something came across with these last words the beggar spoke. Something Levi sensed was not a riddle at all. The chalice warmed deeply.

"Did you not realize the teacher has been with you all along? Did he not appear to you? Take confidence from that. Veronica spoke well in telling you he could have appeared to anyone he wanted to, and appeared to you. His words to you are soon coming to pass. That is the message to receive . . . *trust in it!*"

As the old beggar's words echoed off, a vibration ran across the ground traveling up from the bottom of Levi's feet and up through his body. The air erupted with a whirlwind of motion and pressure. The old beggar's face began to change, becoming almost transparent. Levi instinctively stepped away. A stab of fear raced across the back of his neck, but he could not move. The beggar began glowing in a blinding white radiance.

Levi thought that the sun had fallen from the sky and consumed the beggar. His eyes grew so wide they hurt. He shaded them with the back of his hands, his throat dried. He was terribly afraid. The rays emitting from the beggar caused the wind to blow so forcefully he barely stood against it. The beggar became unrecognizable as a new form began to take shape and elongated upward, taller and taller until it stood nine feet tall, looming over the boy. The form pulsed, with scattering light radiating out, and then retracting. The features of the beggar stretched like clay.

Levi trembled.

"Give heed to the chalice, and follow the staff," the voice thundered with unquestionable authority, "do not run from who you are."

One powerful gust of air knocked Levi down to a seated position, and then the form vanished. Levi remained seated on the ground for a long while. Both the staff and the chalice rested on his lap. Wherever this might lead him, he knew he must follow as what he just witnessed went beyond anything in this world he had ever experienced.

Indeed he knew now that an angel had been in his presence. The only two people he felt to be trustworthy were Veronica and Peter. He would go back. In an effort to gain some confidence he placed his hand on the chalice. For the first time the chalice warmed after he touched it, not before. In a moment its warmth encompassed him. Wisdom beyond his age engulfed him. The old beggar had indeed spoken to him on each visitation with words that required him to open himself, to stretch his thinking and beliefs. In order to understand the messages he would need to allow himself to think in a new way. That is exactly what he did when he decided to leave Jerusalem. He told himself he would do this once again as he recalled the man who told his friend that if he stayed in Jerusalem, he would find only what he had already found. He reasoned this, carefully concluding that although he had left Jerusalem physically; his thinking remained in the same place. The old beggar had given him that very lesson about being paralyzed. Everything that had happened to him, every person he'd met, every challenge, all of it, he understood to be flowing together in a great current that he now believed beyond a doubt had been the divine energy of the world. He now determined not to fight the current, but to allow himself to be carried by it.

86

The chalice and my staff are messages

PETER PACED, ANXIOUSLY AWAITING the boy when he finally returned to the house. He explained to Levi the events that occurred in great detail. He tried to console himself and the boy.

"Peter," Levi said, "the beggar . . . revealed himself to me today as I searched for you. He no longer sat on a pallet, he became so bright I could not look at him and he grew very tall. The wind whipped all around—" he stopped abruptly and asked Peter, "You do not believe this, do you?"

"Oh, I believe you. John and I were present on the mountain when Jesus himself transfigured into such white light that we fell to the ground. Did he speak more riddles?"

"No. He said the chalice and my staff are messages of who I am. What does it mean?" Levi asked, and for the first time he asked in anticipation.

Peter rubbed his forehead looking out toward something distant. "Perhaps this will help." He paused, and then continued, "In the homes of our people each family keeps the Cup of Blessing for the Passover supper. The head of the house recites Kiddush over the chalice of wine and then it is passed around so all will share from one cup. This is done also in the synagogue where the rabbi recites the blessing and then the cantor will drink from the chalice also."

"Then the message of the chalice is about family?" Levi's head dropped. "Can that be for me as I have no family?"

"From all you have told me and Veronica of your journey, it would seem that you do. The message is larger than a family in a house, and more than a family of relatives. This deals with a union between people, and between people and God—communion!" Peter lifted his hands to the sky. "It would not be unwise to consider that Jesus gave you the chalice to symbolize that we must all drink from one cup; the cup of God's love. This is the greatest of commandments."

"What do you mean?" asked Levi.

"The greatest commandment in our ancient writings, to love God with all your heart, soul and mind and the second greatest is, love your neighbor as yourself."

Levi listened and finally said as though confessing, "I have seen love as I traveled here. But I did not want to see it then. People who did not know me helped me, showed me kindness, gave me value, and I could not believe," he paused to gather a thought. "They did not treat me as a beggar." Levi then relayed to Peter about the stout man, the nearly blind man, Metha, Photini, Joktan and the Shepherd and his sons and Bartimaeus.

He recounted the lessons he had been given by the old beggar and how he missed the importance of it along the way. Peter placed his hand on Levi's shoulder. "We can believe one thing with certainty, God's love is everywhere. This is the purpose of communion. One great love for God and love for one another—one cup."

Levi smiled and nodded his head. "The chalice is not the only message I have been given. The Teacher said my staff carries a message also."

Peter lifted the staff from Levi's hand to look it over. "Well, I am a fisherman. I know the things of the sea, but little of a shepherd's staff such as yours." Then Peter stood abruptly, a finger tapping his forehead, "Wait, I think my brother Andrew may be able to help us; he met many different people when he followed John the Baptizer."

"I met Andrew before I went to look for you."

Peter patted Levi's back saying, "I think it will help to have something to eat. A full stomach makes for a full mind."

After they ate and the table had been cleared, Peter spoke. "Levi, I want you to know. Jesus also made a promise to us and although we are mourning, we hold on to see this promise fulfilled."

"What promise?"

"He said he would not leave us as orphans. That he would be with us even to the end of the age, and not leave us as orphans. Everything he told us has come true so we have no reason to doubt that. I am convinced his risen appearances are also signs to show he is true to his word."

Levi jumped in. "I remember the Teacher saying that when I hid in the upper room. I thought all of you were orphans. I wanted to join you because that is what I am too. Now I see there is another meaning."

"I once sought answers just as you do. Jesus told us that one cannot see the wind, but only its effects. I believe Jesus has something in mind for each of us. I realize you have been seeking him on your journey. But I must say that I hold a deep sense that you wish to leave now that he is no longer present physically."

Peter's suspicion held correct; the boy did feel that way. Peter added, "Levi, I feel very strongly you should stay with us . . . see what comes to pass. Many unexplainable things are happening. It may well be that if you depart now you may miss what he intended for you."

Pondering for a long moment, Peter's words made sense so Levi said, "I will stay. Even the old beggar told me to stay when I felt as if I should leave. But I wonder about something."

87

"What makes you say such a thing?"

A DOG BARKED IN THE distance, some of the sheep outside in the pen bleated.

Peter tilted his head in query, "What is your question?"

"The Teacher . . . he knew all about Judas and his plan?"

"Yes. And yet, he loved him as he loves all people even to his own hurt."

"I have seen so many people hurt each other. Especially as orphans . . . we are thought of as dogs with no value."

Peter stood up and paced around the table for a moment. "Jesus, when he died on the cross, was also abandoned, separated and alone. So you see, Levi, in some way he too experienced being an orphan."

Levi's face flushed white at Peter's words. "The Teacher? With the power to heal and to speak wisdom . . . he . . . became an orphan? Like me?" The thought pierced him.

"Yes, like you."

"There is something else I am wondering," Levi stated. "Why have all of you been helping me? Is it only because your Law of Moses forces you to?"

"What makes you say such a thing?" Peter responded. "If we only care for others out of an obligation to the Law, we are not genuine and we cannot bring God's love to others. The Law does teach us to care for others, but the intention the Law is to transform us to the law of the heart. You see we are all like stones being formed and fitted together to become a house for the presence of heaven on earth."

"Everyone is going to be in this house of stone?" Levi questioned incredulously. "Even those people who do not have any care for anyone else?"

"But don't you see? They are the ones who need God . . . in order to become one of his children so their wounds can be bound and healed; they are grafted into his family. Do you recall in the upper room when Jesus broke the bread?"

"Yes, he broke it in pieces to pass to all of you."

"True," Peter said, "but there is greater significance than breaking the bits to pass around. Jesus signified how he himself would be broken to mend the brokenness of others. Every life is broken somehow—every single life. In dying for all of us he took on the brokenness of everyone, so they would be healed of it. So they would become one in God's family, no longer broken or alone. Can you see that?"

"Yes," Levi said. But in fact it bothered him that bad people could come to union with the Teacher.

"This is not fair . . . that bad people can come to the Teacher who is good," Levi exclaimed.

"Yes, it is not fair—at all!" Peter replied. He stated this to make the boy think.

"Peter," the boy said in the most sincere tone, "I am more confused. The Teacher is not fair?"

"If he were to be fair, in the truest sense, no one would be able to have union with him because the hearts of men have become cold and selfish. Therefore he draws us near not with fairness, he draws us near through his grace."

Levi's eyes squinted.

"You have lived your life as a beggar, an orphan alone on your own, surviving. In many ways the streets became your parents, but streets do not make very good parents. Now, you are being drawn into a family where there is unity and caring. Oneness! In a family, what one person does will affect all the others. These are matters for you to ponder. I will return in a moment and we shall go to Andrew."

Levi's thoughts ran through the lesson about family and unity. He recalled catching a glimpse of this at Peter's table. He had never sat at a table for a meal with a family. His first thought was to reach over and take as much food as he could before anyone else took it away. But Lydia at that moment placed a bowl of food in front of him before serving anyone else. The gesture shook him—he wasn't sitting at a table with desperate beggars all out to serve themselves. They served him first as the guest of the house.

Then what came to his mind so vividly was the man and his family on the way to Beit Shemesh and how he guarded his wife and daughter. Even when they departed down the slope into the city, as Levi remained at the top of the hill, he could see the tender care the man gave to his family, watching them as they carefully stepped down the hill. He recalled the man's concern for him regarding being out at night as being dangerous.

Peter returned. "Let us go to the barn to see if Andrew is there. He was the Teacher's first disciple you know."

"The first?" Levi echoed in wonderment.

"Come along." Walking into the barn they found Andrew at work mending nets.

"Andrew, what in the world are you doing mending nets?" asked Peter.

"Well, I suppose . . . I . . . I am being sensible . . . we will need to get back to our fishing business now that," he hesitated to find words, "now that . . . we are unsure of what will take place."

"You should have joined us at the table."

"I feel no hunger," Andrew said, "at least not the physical kind." He lifted a bulk of the nets to locate another area needing repair. "And how are you, Levi?"

"Peter is helping me."

Peter tapped against Levi's staff. "Levi received this staff as a gift."

Levi handed his staff to Andrew.

"The staff holds some message that the Lord wants to convey to the boy," Peter said. "I told him we are fishermen not shepherds, but you know a shepherd that may be able to help."

"Indeed. Joachim! He and his family come from generations of goat and sheep herders. If anyone can tell about the staff, he can. I know not if he is willing however. I will take you there when I am finished with the nets."

"If you are willing . . . I would like to go alone," Levi said, half asking and half stating. At that Andrew glanced up at Peter who nodded his head.

"Joachim is a short distance from us. You will not be able to walk into his house unannounced so I will write a letter for you. Joachim will know my name and that will go well for you." Andrew then moved the nets off his lap, and walked to a far corner where he sat at a table to write the letter. Levi offered his thank you after Andrew gave him the letter and the directions to Joachim's house. He went back to the main house.

"The boy reminds me of you, brother," said Andrew, "always looking for some adventure."

Peter invited Andrew into the house for something to eat. They walked side by side back to the main house. With their experiences walking with Jesus they had become more than natural brothers.

88

"Can this be so?"

JOACHIM'S HOME SAT ON a corner and had been built around a small courtyard, a stone structure covered in whitewashed stucco. The flat roof held a section tilted back to catch rainwater which emptied into a large catch basin. Levi removed the letter from his tunic, stepped to the door and knocked. A child opened the door.

Levi moved back one step. "Please give this letter to Joachim." The child closed the door. Levi sat down. At length the door opened causing Levi to jump.

"Come in," said the child. Levi followed him in.

"I am Joachim, come . . . sit," the man's voice shallow. "Andrew is a good man; this is why I will do what I can to help you." The man wore a long stringy beard, mostly white intertwined with gray steaks around the corners of his mouth, dry as hay. His face, wrinkle-worn. As Levi walked across the tamped down dirt floor the smell and sounds of animals in the neighboring room were strong.

"Let me see the staff." Levi handed it to the man.

As he stepped back the man asked him to bring the oil lamp over from the stand. "Hold it up for me," he said to Levi. The man brought the staff very close to his eyes. He rotated the staff slowly, inspecting and rubbing his index finger over the carved images. Up and down he studied the staff handling it as though a priceless gem. His eyes widened with wonder. Levi noticed a moistening of the man's eyes as he observed the carved images.

"Can this be so?" the man exclaimed with no small excitement.

Feeling unsettled, Levi remained still without reacting, holding the lamp. Over the days since his journey started he had become more accustomed to expect the unusual to take place.

"Praise God. Yes . . . indeed it is the house of Abendan." Then he spoke briefly of the Glory of the Fields. Following a long pause, he said, "Tell me boy, how did you come to receive the staff?"

Levi recounted the event of saving the shepherd's son in the pasture and how the staff had been fashioned and given to him.

"Andrew's letter states that you are an orphan. Is that true boy?" Joachim's words snapped Levi back.

"Yes." He didn't say it in any shame, he simply agreed.

Joachim looked at the staff again, and then glanced at Levi. "And you believe that, do you?" he said softly under his breath as he handed the staff back to Levi.

He had no idea what the man intended to convey with that repeated question, and he decided not to ask.

Joachim raised his hand with index finger pointed up. His hand shook. "Tomorrow I will come to the house where you are staying with Andrew your guardian. You are blessed boy . . . blessed. Now you must depart that I may ponder this further."

Levi could not imagine why the man seemed insistent on going to see Andrew, nor did he understand why he called Andrew his guardian, or what he meant about being blessed. For a moment he feared more riddles coming. *Why doesn't he tell me more about the staff?* He was about to say something in frustration to Joachim when the chalice warmed. Holding his hand to it he sensed he should be obedient.

"You will wait at the house with your guardian until I arrive in the morning," Joachim said.

"Yes sir, I will wait." He knew there would be no sense in asking more questions nor did he want to correct the old man about having a guardian. The episode once again rang a notion of the old beggar warning him about staying and not leaving. He offered many thanks to Joachim and departed.

He walked slowly trying to grasp the few comments Joachim offered. He wanted to hear more. The man knew more about the staff than he revealed, Levi clearly observed that as the man had looked the staff over.

Before frustration took hold he spoke to himself out loud. "I cannot do this on my own anymore, Teacher. There are too many codes and messages and I cannot understand them. All along my journey I have made nothing happen on my own . . . all things came to me. I know you hear me." He placed his hand on the chalice and raised over his heart thinking it would assure his being heard. "You asked me if I would trust you. I said yes, but I have not . . . until now. Right now I stop and trust in you for the message . . . for everything."

Upon these words his body tingled, growing in comforting warmth. His eyes were opened and yet what he observed was not in front of him. Caught in a vision he saw the Teacher's body glow as he stepped out of the tomb and walked away. He stopped, sat down almost exhausted from the vision. *I will be alone for a time, and then I will no longer be alone. So it shall be for you.*

Levi quickly turned to look about at hearing the words of the Teacher. No one in sight. He stood up and as he made his first step it felt distinctly as though he had entered into another realm he could feel, but could not see. Something had shifted inside him. A deep sense of trust saturated him. He knew the Teacher would bring all things about. His smile beamed, and he felt sure he had smiled as wide and big and bright as Joktan did.

89

There! She finally said it.

U PON ARRIVING BACK AT Peter's house, Levi found Peter, Andrew, Veronica and another man he did not recognize in a heated discussion.

Seeing Levi, Veronica asked with no small anticipation, "Did you learn anything from Joachim?"

"He knows something about my staff. He spoke about being in fields with his sheep when the great star appeared in the sky leading to the birth of the Christ child. He was one of the shepherds who traveled to see the him."

"The Christ child . . . Levi . . . that child is Jesus," Veronica said with exuberance.

"That is what Joachim told me. And an old shepherd I met along the way also spoke to me of the Glory of the Fields. I know the Christ child is the Teacher."

"You will come to learn that he is far more than a teacher, Levi," the unknown man stated. Then Veronica introduced John as one of Jesus' disciples.

"I have followed Jesus from the very beginning along with my brother James. We are the sons of Zebedee and Salome," said John. He turned to Peter then back to Levi. "It was Peter and I who came to Jerusalem to find the upper room for the Passover, where I am told you were successful at in hiding beneath the service cabinet. And none of us had any idea . . . except the Lord of course," he said wryly.

Levi smiled with a tinge of embarrassment, and admittedly some pride of accomplishment.

"I want to talk with you about something," John said.

"What?" Levi asked.

"There are times when the best solution is one that helps more than just one person."

Levi's puzzlement telegraphed.

"Can you sit with us?" John invited Veronica. She complied, looking as confused as Levi.

John thought for a moment. "The day that Jesus died, I stood at the foot of the cross." John glanced away for a moment to compose himself. Following a few deep breaths he continued. "His mother Mary stood next to me. Jesus looked down at me saying, 'Behold your mother.' Then he looked at his mother saying, 'Behold your son.'"

"What did he mean by these words," Veronica asked John.

"These words I did not at first understand. Then I thought back to a day when he was speaking to a crowd in a house. Someone interrupted him and said that his mother and brothers were outside wanting to talk with him. He responded in a way I found upsetting. He said, 'Who is my mother, and who are my brothers?'" John stared out for a long moment. "I did not care for the words he spoke about his mother and brothers that day as I thought his response had been disrespectful. At the foot of the cross, hearing his words to me and his mother, I finally understood what I had misinterpreted. There at that very moment Jesus extended his family beyond his mother and brothers. His family now reached out to all who would trust in him. No one need be alone . . . no one outcast and undervalued. We . . . each of us . . . now are part of a family that extends everywhere at all times."

John spoke carefully now to Veronica, "You . . . have lost a son." Turning to Levi, "You have lost parents."

Levi said to John, "I do not understand. You are our father now?"

"No," Veronica said, "John is thinking about our well-being as Jesus spoke to him from the cross." She placed her arm around the boy. "John is saying you and I are family . . . that you can live with me." There! She said it. Something she wanted to express before this moment. Silence hung for a time. Then she quickly qualified, "Only if you wish."

Levi bowed his head. The last thing he wanted to do was hurt Veronica's feelings in any way. "Veronica is a good person and she has helped me. I do not know what the Teacher wants me to do yet. I have been told to wait for the message." He turned to John and asked, "Do you believe what you are saying is the message of my chalice and staff?"

"I cannot say such a thing for certain," John said.

Veronica observed the boy's concern as he bowed his head, but glanced at her a few times. "Levi, I will always be here for you, but as you were instructed, the time now is to wait for Joachim. Then perhaps you will know what to do." Her smile relaxed him.

"John," Veronica said, "Thank you for the words of loving kindness to us. What you have shared is beautiful and kind."

Levi looked at Veronica, his eyes clouded, "Veronica . . . I . . . I . . ."

She stopped him and said, "I understand what you must do. Jesus is working plans for each of us that will take us into a new tomorrow. I am not hurt by what you have said."

Levi's heart warmed. He smiled softly as he touched her hand. Veronica had removed the guilt he felt for his response to her. "I will take a walk and think on all these things." He lifted his staff and walked to the door when he heard the words, "Thank you for remembering me, Levi."

Stopping he turned and asked, "What did you say?" he asked Veronica because it was a female voice.

"I said nothing!"

"But I heard words spoken to me."

Veronica responded with a shrug of her shoulders.

Levi turned toward the door, and again, "Thank you for remembering me, Levi." Realizing the words were in his head, he stopped. Without thought he spoke out Metha's name recalling the encounter with her along the way to Jerusalem. Metha had spoken those very words to him as he left her after telling her the secret about the inn, and again when she departed along the road to Jerusalem. The chalice warmed deeply. He quickly walked back into the room, his hand on the chalice. "You . . ." He became unsure about continuing. Then he did. "Veronica, you can help Metha. I think the Teacher would have you take Metha as family."

"Who is Metha? I do not understand," Veronica asked.

"She is an orphan. Alone like me. She could have stolen my loaf of bread when I fell asleep sick in the place of the broken arches, and not even a bite did she take from it. She also found me and cleaned my wounds when I had been beaten and robbed."

90

Levi gave them details of the two locations

L EVI SUMMARIZED THE TWO events detailing his encounters with Metha. Afterward, Levi mentioned that they had seen each other in various places as they begged alms. He explained how her aunt and her husband the tax gatherer did not want her, and that she finally learned that her parents were not coming back, but they had died in a Roman work camp.

"Oh, the poor child," Veronica said.

"The Roman occupation has hardened the hearts of our people," said John in dismay.

"When I just spoke out Metha's name the chalice warmed. That is why I am telling you about her," he said to Veronica. "She is alone. You can give her communion with you?" He spoke with uncertainty.

Veronica looked at John seeking some response. "What do you feel this means?"

"Does your heart say you should go to the girl?" asked John.

Veronica's eye flitted back and forth in thought. She nodded as she smiled. "Yes," she expressed vibrantly. "But I am concerned about you, Levi."

Standing nearby, Andrew said, "Joachim will come here in the morning. Let us hear him out. What he knows may give the boy direction. He is a man of great wisdom."

Peter then added, "We must remember. The Lord gave the boy that chalice and instructed him to heed its message. He encountered several people along the journey who in one way or another supported that as well. Then he also received lessons from an old beggar—which appears to have been an angel visitation. The Lord would not place all this in his path only to allow it to lead nowhere."

"Yes, Peter . . . I trust the Teacher," Levi added.

"I and the other disciples held trust in the Lord as we left all we had to follow him. And we shall continue to follow him."

Over the past few days Levi had been considering what he would do next. He thought a great deal about the stout man's offer to become an apprentice and design hookahs. The beauty of the art appealed to Levi. He considered going back. But now, he knew not to be too quick to leave or make a decision until a clear message was given to him; one he understood.

"Veronica, I will wait to hear Joachim in the morning. He knows many things about my staff. He can speak of more details that can help me."

Andrew leaned over and said, "Joachim believes in the ways of our ancestors. A child should have a guardian to guide decisions. That is his way."

"I understand," Levi assured him.

"It is settled then," Veronica stated, feeling more confident for Levi. "I will seek Metha out tomorrow. Can you tell me details of how to find her and what she looks like?"

"Yes," Levi said.

"I will send our cousin Elior to accompany you to find the girl. No one knows the streets of Jerusalem as well as he does," Andrew said.

Levi then gave a detailed description of the two locations he knew where Metha would typically be found. He provided her physical description in detail as well. He mentioned the old broken down wagon across from the inn and that she might well be hiding under it. He also described the place of the arches.

"Will you tell Metha that I did remember her?" Levi felt a confident joy that Metha would no longer be alone now that Veronica agreed to go find her. The chalice had provided that confidence to him.

"Of course I will tell her," said Veronica.

"I will go back to my nets now. Tomorrow we shall see," said Andrew.

"Andrew," Levi called out, "Why are you mending nets?"

"I prepare to return to the sea now that Jesus entered another realm, just as I said yesterday to Peter."

"But, then you do not trust the Teacher?" Levi asked.

"Of course I trust him," Andrew responded sternly.

Levi noticed the terseness on Andrew's face and quickly added, "I am only trying to understand . . . to learn. If you go back to the sea and not go where the Teacher has said . . . does that show your trust in him?"

Andrew bit his lip and his face blanched white almost fending off a sense of embarrassment and a stab of anger, all engendered by a small boy.

He quelled any brewing anger as he knew the boy had asked this question in his innocence, but his words were true.

His shoulders drooped. "What you have said is true, Levi. I too must reconsider my own journey." He tapped Levi's shoulders in a gesture of friendship and departed. Peter, Veronica and Lydia remained in the house but said nothing of the encounter. Yet they smiled and nodded to one another. Veronica decided something should be said, "Levi, what you expressed shows growth in your thinking . . . it goes beyond your years in wisdom and gives all of us pause to reconsider our journeys."

"I worried after the words came out of my mouth that Andrew would be angry as I am a boy and he is an adult."

"I can see that, Levi. Yet truth is always a risk."

"I know how important it is for me to trust in what the Teacher spoke over me. When he appeared to me he asked if I would trust him. I said I would."

"Each of us is now realizing this reality as well," Peter said. "For some years we walked with Jesus physically. Now we must learn to walk with him in trust."

"When I met a man named Joktan who was healed of leprosy by the Teacher . . . I—" Levi was cut short.

Veronica's eyes bulged, "Leprosy?" She gulped.

"Yes, along with nine others. Joktan was the happiest man I have ever seen."

"I should think so with such a miracle," said Veronica.

"All he wanted to do was help people and tell of the great thing the Teacher had done for him. He will be coming to Jerusalem to find you Peter."

"I am certain if this is to be, it will come to pass," Pater said.

"Veronica?" Levi asked.

"Yes?"

"Do you trust the Teacher?"

A joyful smile enhanced her face. "I truly do. And, as Peter said, we must learn to live in his presence in a new way."

Levi quietly asked Veronica, "Did you show Peter the towel?"

"I think I am to keep this to myself. I will pray and wait to understand what to do with it."

Levi agreed.

91

"Remember when I gave you the meaning of your name?"

L EVI AWOKE EARLY AFTER tossing around restlessly most of the night. He walked into the front room of the house where he heard grinding noises. Lydia and Veronica were already at work removing grain from the soaking pot. They dried it and with pestle and mortar ground the grain into flour to bake bread. Levi washed his face in the water pot. Peter and the others were outside tending to the animals while the bread baked. The men were summoned when the table had been prepared. They all gathered around the table. The women brought fish and pomegranate juice. Peter prayed a blessing then took the bread, broke it and passed it around.

Levi stared into space not giving attention to those at the table.

Veronica noticed, "Levi, why are you not eating?"

Pursing his lips, eyes squinted he said, "I am wondering what I will learn about the staff." Levi manufactured a bit of a smile.

Before anyone responded, a knock sounded on the door. Andrew went to the door and opened it. Joachim stood there, a young man at his side steadying him. Introductions were made. Fruits and drink were offered. Once Joachim rested, Peter suggested to Veronica that she and Elior should to depart to find Metha. They politely excused themselves preparing to depart. Veronica stopped, glanced at Levi giving him a confident smile, and then waved him over to her.

"I hope you know in your heart that we will find Metha and invite her to into our family," she said in a quiet voice.

Elior proudly said, "I know every twist and turn in Jerusalem, and I will find the girl if she is still there."

"You must promise me, Levi, that if you leave before we return, you will tell Peter where you go so we know where to find you. I must never lose you." Levi heartily agreed and promised.

Veronica stepped closer to Levi and whispered in his ear, "Remember when I gave you the meaning of your name? I said that you would grow into your name. Heed that because you may well be about to walk into that future. God has given us secret eyes and yours may be opening." She kissed his forehead, and her face gleamed with some inner satisfaction. Levi smiled at her as he nodded humbly. He hugged her knowing already how deeply he would miss her.

"Levi, come, come," Andrew called out impatiently, waving him over. Joachim gestured for the staff.

Levi glanced back at Veronica as she and Elior walked out. He didn't have a moment to let her words sink in. He brought the staff over. The group quieted down as Joachim began pointing out the images carved into it. Levi sat entranced.

"Now," Joachim said, with a stark voice inflection, "I felt it important and proper to explain something very necessary with the boy's guardian present in order for him to make an important decision."

Andrew looked around at the others, then to Levi. No one spoke so he did. "The boy is not under our guardianship. He has been instructed by Jesus."

"Instructed by Jesus you say?"

"Jesus gave him a chalice which carries some unique properties and a message that has guided him to us and now to you. The staff was given to him by a shepherd, as he explained to you. Both seem to hold hidden messages."

"I can share nothing of the chalice, but this staff . . . well that is another matter," Joachim said. "The staff carries no mystery. No hidden message at all! What it conveys is quite clear. You see here, it is carved in plain sight."

Then after a moment he added, "In these days most people would be unable to interpret the carved words because they come from the language of Canaan. And not many understand it any longer."

Thinking back, Levi wondered why the shepherd and his sons did not tell him everything the staff conveyed, since they understood the writing.

Joachim handed the staff back to Levi without releasing it. "You must give heed to the message here, Levi. You must understand the significance of what Abendan has fashioned for you. It is a solemn message."

Levi recognized the name Abendan.

Joachim reached for Levi's hand pulling it to the upper portion of the staff and placing his finger over a specific carving.

92

"You saved his son from wild dogs, did you not?"

"I WAS ONE OF THE shepherds with Abendan on the night of the Glory in the Fields where we were tending our sheep. What a night of splendor that was. How greatly we were blessed—mere shepherds to be the first to know—when you consider shepherds were thought of as outcasts by the religious rulers because we were unable to keep the Mosaic Law of ritual cleanliness." Joachim looked out as though envisioning the scene again. He momentarily bowed his head.

"How odd it is that anyone would consider shepherds in that way when many of our greatest heroes were shepherds, Moses, Abraham, Isaac, Jacob, and King David?" pronounced Andrew.

Joachim came back to himself and continued. "What you need to know is that this is no ordinary herder's staff. No, not at all," he emphasized. His index finger wiggled. "Yesterday I asked if you believed you are an orphan. Well then. Listen carefully. The staff carries the burn mark of Gideon, but more, this is a staff a father gives his son who is favored."

Levi's eyes widened as he processed what had been spoken. "A son who is favored? How is it he would give such a thing to me?" Levi spoke out with no small surprise, some disbelief and a good deal of shock. "I do not understand."

"You saved his son from the wild dogs, did you not? Abendan received that as a sign from heaven, a divine sign. You see, only a year before he lost his eldest son to a terrible illness. You came along . . . and perhaps he is correct . . . as a sign from God," Joachim explained hoping to convey a confidence to the boy.

257

"Do you understand what is being said, Levi?" Peter asked.

"Abendan has given me a place of honor?"

"More than that. In his eyes you are his son," emphasized Joachim.

"I am his son?" He marveled at the words. His lips quivered. Often in his life he wondered what it would feel like to hear those words flow over him. He lost his breath while a moistening of tears framed his eyes. Emotions mixed. Joy and confusion fought for prominence. His eyes then smiled. The truest and most genuine smile he ever experienced formed as the chalice warmed in his tunic.

"The Teacher spoke this all along. It is . . . true . . . I am not alone. I have," his eyes squinted in a sense of wonderment, "I have a family." The words seemed to have released, along with his breath, all the experience of being alone as he spoke them out.

Levi looked at Joachim. "I remember . . . hearing the name of Abendan along my journey. I met a shepherd named Yochnan and his three sons. He looked at my staff and told me I was of the house of Abendan, but I did not understand. He was the first to say anything about the staff, and he spoke of the Glory of the Fields also, and many other things. He too gave me food for my journey, and showed me how to read the great star so I would find my way back to Jerusalem."

Joachim immediately brightened. "I have not seen Yochnan in many years. It is good to hear he is well. You have blessed me with this news, Levi."

The comment gave Levi great satisfaction. He thought although it was such a small thing, he was able to give at least something of value back to the man. He very much liked this feeling of giving something.

Peter said, "The message appears clear, Levi! What will you do now?"

Levi looked each man in the eye, "You, and others along my journey have shown me that what I did not believe has become something I cannot help but believe." The entire group came to a long pause as they observed the boy in a deep contemplation of thought. It held clear that the boy had been overwhelmed with the information of the staff. For Levi much more held his reflective thoughts than that alone.

A burst of amazement overtook Levi as he assimilated the peace of the Teacher flowing over him. Everything in his life had been physical and tangible. Now the greatest event of his life had come through something he could not see or touch: trust! Love and light had come to him through darkness on a cross. Care from others and caring for others brought a new joy in him. He recalled the amazing joy Joktan had expressed, and the freedom that Bartimaeus shared with him. He reflected on Photini's release from dependence. The old man and the dog. The stout man. Even the landlord. *All of them were messengers!*

"Thank you for helping me." He smiled as he stepped back slowly toward the door.

"Whatever your plan, there is something you must understand," Peter said, his voice soft and serious.

Levi looked up at him, "Tell me."

"Do you recall your desire to find what you called the *new place*?"

"Yes?"

He lowered to one knee and held the boy's shoulders. "I believe you have finally come to understand where to find that new place." Peter tapped the back of his hand against Levi's heart, "The new place is here. This is where the Lord has ushered in his kingdom. All things grow out from here . . . the heart. Within that you share in communion with the family of God. Here you have the message of the chalice and the staff and above all what a great gift of love Jesus has given you. Now it should be clear to you where the staff desires to lead you," Peter's smile broad.

Levi matched Peter's big smile and now understood why Joktan had smiled so widely while in the caravan crossing. He understood the depth of Joktan's amazing joy at being released from his prison because now, at this moment, he too had been released from a prison of paralysis by the Teacher. For the first time he accepted that he was not a beggar. He understood what the man with the dog proclaimed to him, that begging was something he did. As to an orphan? That was something that happened to him, it did not define him. No, he was none of these things . . . he was a son!

Above all, the Teacher gifted him with this journey to find these truths and to remove the chains of abandonment. He belonged. A sense of something greater than himself arrayed his thoughts. He could actually feel a current, a force beyond his own. He could almost hear the click of his yoke being opened and removed. The weight he had carried so long released. He had entered communion with the divine energy of the world. For the first time he felt its reality. His entire body tingled.

Straightening his tunic and head piece then squaring his shoulders firmly, he said, "The Teacher's message, his chalice . . . has led me to all of you . . . to all that has happened to me. I am grateful to you." He then hugged Peter for a long moment and whispered, "I will miss you most, Peter. You are brave and strong and have helped greatly." Levi held on to him for moment longer as his eyes welled up and Peter's did as well.

They separated. "I will follow the staff now; I know where it will lead me." Each of the other men hugged the boy tightly and he absorbed it open heartedly. Lydia kissed the top of his head.

"I miss all of you already," said Levi, his heart weighing down and sadness in his eyes.

"You sound as though we will never see you again, and of course we will," Andrew said in upbeat tone. "After all, Veronica will want to share what has happened in her search for Metha. And Metha will surely want to see you. Joachim knows the way to where you will go. Do not forget we are all part of your family now."

"This is very good," Levi said, his eyes smiling and countenance uplifted. With that he stepped out the door. Levi turned to look back at the house many times until he had moved too far into the distance to make it out. He knew that he had left something of himself back there, and something of them had been left in him. Something very good.

93

He spoke into the wind

L EVI KNEW IT WOULD require a half day to make the trip. Making his way he thought how right the Teacher had been. His original search to find the new place would have taken the rest of his life and he still would not have found it. The new place had been in his heart from the moment he met the Teacher in the upper room, not out there somewhere.

Now he sensed a tangible closeness to the Teacher in some unexplainable way. His entire being seemed to transform. Only at this point did he begin to comprehend the depth of the divine energy of the world as being the very essence of God's love, which the Teacher spoke to his men about in the upper room. Levi smiled recalling when the Teacher mentioned his father to his men saying he had conferred a kingdom upon them, and how he considered him to be some far-off nobleman or general. That early notion now seemed silly to him.

How amazing he thought, that without communion everyone would remain an orphan in the world. He shuttered at the idea of almost not having left Jerusalem, and what a loss that would have been. Of course he understood that he could not know of this when it all began. The entire journey was required to bring him to this moment.

Anticipation ran high as he finally arrived at the base of the hill over which the pasture lay. There he paused a long while. Anticipation brought along an unexpected traveling partner: apprehension. He wondered if they would remember him. Would he be welcomed? Was Joachim correct about the meaning of the staff? Or was he imagining everything?

"No," he said, "all of it is real and true." He spoke the words into the wind hoping it would carry to heaven itself with his gratitude.

There he stood in a cooling wind, and he regarded it as a fresh new change in his life. Holding still until it calmed, he again flashed back on the landlord, the stout man, Veronica, Peter, the old beggar, Joktan and the others in his encounters along the journey. How terribly he missed Joktan because he knew something changed in him when they rode the caravan together. Veronica came to mind as the one who provided the lesson about his mother. Then Peter crossed his mind, and he realized the list of people would be very long in appreciation. In such a short time so much had changed, and the thought placed him to his knees. First bowing his head, then lifting it he offered thanks to God for the first time. And for the first time in his life he saturated in a freedom he had never imagined. Everything the Teacher shared had come to pass. Remembering Bartimaeus, and how his sight had been returned by the Teacher, he too was now learning see the truth, and would be ever grateful.

After a time he composed himself realizing all these thoughts, although comforting, catered to his trepidation to go up the hill. But the moment had come to take the first step up, and up he moved. Drawing near to the peak he breathed in the sweet aroma of pasture grass. The view from the top of the hill displayed a panoramic scene of many sheep grazing alongside a fence near the place where he had fended off the dogs. There amidst the flocks walked that young shepherd boy. A few feet behind him walked his father Abendan. Levi started downhill.

He didn't get far when Abendan caught sight of him. He froze in place for a moment. Then excitedly he called over to his son, pointing exuberantly up the hill. Both men immediately started running, scattering the sheep as though an unobstructed aisle had opened up for them. Levi increased his downhill pace, but his heart already out ran him. The chalice became warmer than it had ever felt before. As he ran, he reached in to touch it. The chalice had vanished, yet its radiated warmth saturated him. He knew now, that the message had been completed.

Abendan cupped his mouth with both hands, and shouted out as loudly as he could, "Son, you've come home!"

~ *The End* ~